T0149259

A Chuck, Yu, and Farley Book

Invasion: Eris

Penny L. Samms

iUniverse®

INVASION: ERIS
A CHUCK, YU, AND FARLEY BOOK

iUniverse books may be ordered through booksellers or by contacting:

iUniverse
1663 Liberty Drive
Bloomington, IN 47403
www.iuniverse.com
1-800-Authors (1-800-288-4677)

ISBN: 978-1-5320-1642-4 (sc)
ISBN: 978-1-5320-1643-1 (e)

Library of Congress Control Number: 2017903125

Print information available on the last page.

iUniverse rev. date: 03/15/2017

For everyone who bought Invasion: Earth

A Chuck, Yu, and Farley Book

Acknowledgements

Thank you to my mother, Elaine Shears, and my brother, Boom Samms, who continue to buy everything I put out into the world—even at the risk of it being garbage. Thank you also to the rest of my family and friends for their continued support. It's always nice to get an email or a message on Facebook telling me that they bought and maybe even liked *Invasion: Earth A Chuck, Yu, and Farley Book*. I also appreciate all the feedback from everyone who read it. I feel as though my writing has improved because of your input and ideas, but you can be the judge.

Jeff LaFerney also deserves credit for editing my manuscript. He took time and care to ensure that it is perfect. His comments were invaluable and I look forward to working with him again. Check out his website at jefflaferney.blogspot.ca!

I watched my author page on Facebook grow in number of "likes" over the past year (I'm over 7000 now). Most of those people are strangers who have responded to my advertising or who have seen my page through my friends sharing it. It means a lot to me, and if you've bought the book, it means even more. My Twitter and Instagram followings have also grown exponentially, including other authors, actors and actresses from the

Young and the Restless, a bunch of awesome rappers in Los Angeles, and even pilots for the North Atlantic Treaty Organization.

I've since published other books, branching out into children's books. You can buy *Roy the Boy Makes a Spaceship* and *Roy the Boy Builds a Tree House*, with illustrations by Kritsana Naowakhun, and *Missy Zoe Waterfall*, with illustrations by Lucia Monaco, online from Amazon. com. Not stopping there, I was successful in obtaining permission from Wolf Blass Wineries in Australia to do a playful wine-pairing book based on their wines. *Wolf Blass, Anyone?* is available via Amazon.com. In yet another completely different genre, you can escape from reality in a book that applauds the ridiculous in my release for adults, *Talking $hit*. That book was so much fun to write that I dare say it will be a series!

Keep reading, everyone!

Invasion: Eris

A Chuck, Yu, and Farley Book

Penny L. Samms

Chapter 1

"I have a belief in mankind. A belief that extends beyond predicted events, such as the Earth's Ego Implosion, Froggy Turpin's updated interpretation of the alignment of the galaxies and their supposed future collision, and the centuries-old theory that we will be wiped out by aliens. When I was a kid, I used to wish for aliens to come. I thought that it would unite man and obliterate racism and hatred based on religions and other differences as man would have to join forces against a common enemy. We aren't perfect, but we're getting better. There were twenty-one years between World War I and World War II. Then 167 years had elapsed before the third world war, which ended in less than a week. That is the last time any nation has fought against another. We are getting better. We have become more tolerant and accepting.

"We have accomplished space travel for the common person and built homes on Eris. We have done this with all nations working together in peace with a unified view to explore our galaxy and extend man's reach and just to learn in general. It is pride I feel in mankind, my family, my friends, and in myself for choosing Nathan Castle to be my friend. I have faith in mankind, but toward individuals, I don't trust easily. Nathan was one of those people I knew I could trust instantly. He was a genuine, kind, generous young man coming into his own, as I am, and did not deserve to be taken from us the way he was or as young as he was.

"All I can imagine is what our lives could have been like with our new purpose. Things were just getting started for us. Nathan was beginning his training and, as a team—a close-knit team—we were going to do our small part to preserve the tolerance and acceptance that mankind embraces. We were going to stand up to those who mistreat and devalue others. We were going to fight off those aliens and prevent further loss of human life. We had big hopes and dreams and plans, and now, for Nathan, none of that exists anymore. Nathan's death will be avenged, let me assure you. Those aliens I had always wished for took one of my best friends from me. From us. I wish I could wish away every single thought I've had about aliens coming here. I wish I could send them away and make them never come back. I wish I could bring Nathan back.

"In Nathan's memory, we will do everything we can to ensure no one else has to die like he did. I miss him so…"

Chuck's words caught in his throat. He could no longer maintain control. Tears blurred his vision, and sobs wracked his body. He could not continue reading his eulogy. He felt the comfort of two sets of arms wrap around him and opened his eyes long enough to see it was Farley and Yu. Chuck hugged them back, seeing how emotionally drained they also were. The grief had hit the three young men like a meteor once they could let it in. In the week since Nathan had been slashed from life, Chuck, Yu, and Farley, along with Chuck's mother, Sheila, and Grammy and her friends, had worked tirelessly with Yu's associate, Sparks, turning Yu's dojo into their new headquarters. It had seemed like a lifetime ago to Chuck that he and his friends, Nathan, Farley, and Yu, had been back on Earth fighting the aliens on Gros Morne Mountain. Chuck was still in shock over Nathan being killed in front of him. Chuck knew he would never forget the feel of Nathan's hot blood splashing across his face.

A little more than a month had passed since aliens first began attacking humans on Earth. People were reportedly disappearing with red, skeletal beings, never to be seen again. At first, that's all it had

2

been—disappearances—but that had provided hope for friends and family that their missing loved one(s) would one day return. However, the aliens became more and more violent, attacking humans and eating them. Witness accounts claimed that the aliens had been slashing people in half with long, snake-like tongues and sucking up the killed people through those same tongues—skin, bones, organs, and all.

Chuck and his friends had found themselves in the middle of a huge battle against the aliens when they had flown to Newfoundland in search of Chuck's missing grandmother, who everyone lovingly called "Grammy." They found her, but they also found out she had been keeping lifelong secrets from her family. Grammy worked for the Planetary Space Agency and was high up in the ranks to the point where she had once known the aliens and had worked with them. Chuck, a young man who had turned seventeen only weeks before, found himself having to grow up fast and fighting for his life. Chuck's life hadn't been easy before the aliens. He had grown up without a father and had been bullied for years by Mike and Gaz. Chuck also had come to the realization that to hurt him, Lexi, the girl he had had a crush on for years, had tricked him into thinking she liked him back. She was forever Mike's girl and did whatever he wanted her to.

Just when Chuck, at the encouragement of his best friend, Farley, had joined a dojo and was in the process of training with Yu, the owner and master of the dojo, and began to gain confidence in himself, the aliens began to attack. Chuck had been thrust right into the fight against them.

As Chuck stood there with his whole life flashing through his mind, the feel of Nathan's blood splattering across his face brought him back to where he was. He opened his eyes and looked at the rows of people gathered for Nathan's funeral. He saw Nathan's father, known to all as Mr. Castle, sitting stone-faced in his seat, staring at a memory of his son. A single tear coursed slowly down his right cheek before landing on his red, silk shirt. Chuck knew red had been Nathan's favorite color, and Mr. Castle had worn it in honor of his son. The front of his shirt adorned a picture of Nathan standing in front of his space ship, which was also lost on that devastating day. Mr. Castle's face was blank. His short, brown hair was still wet from his shower. Josh had told Chuck moments before Chuck began his eulogy that Mr. Castle had been in the bathroom for over an hour. Josh had found him just standing in the shower, staring at nothing. He had guided him out, dried him off, and gotten him dressed. Josh said that when people had spoken to Mr. Castle to offer condolences, he hadn't responded; he acknowledged in no way that he had even been spoken to. Although people understood, they moved away from the distraught man uncomfortably, unsure how to communicate with him. Josh would step in, expressing thanks and appreciation on behalf of his grieving friend.

Chuck watched while Josh turned to Mr. Castle and offered him a tissue as another tear made its way down his best friend's face. Josh had opened up to Chuck earlier that morning. He had admitted that aside from being there if and when Mr. Castle needed him, Josh didn't know what to do to ease his pain. He said that for his own pain, he would simply cry himself to sleep each night until one day he would cry a little bit less and then further down the road, lesser still. Even though Josh was not family and his last name was not Castle, he had been best friends with Mr. Castle since long before Nathan was born, and to him, the loss was as crushing as though Nathan were of his own flesh and blood. Chuck and Josh had cried together over their loss and recalled how Josh had been hired by Mr. Castle to watch over and protect Nathan at school. Josh had worked at the school as the janitor and had been disguised so well that even Nathan hadn't recognized him. They had laughed at the nickname, "Disease," the students had given him, but Chuck now choked up at the pain evident on Josh's face.

Chuck continued looking around the room. Sheila, his mother, sat on the other side of Josh and cried softly but freely. He sympathized with her because he knew she was deeply saddened by Nathan's brutal death and also for him, who now had to live the rest of his life with just a memory of Nathan and thoughts of everything Nathan would never experience. Chuck winked a sad wink at her that she returned, acknowledging their shared grief. Chuck thought that knowing her, she wanted to throw her arms around the huddled group at the front of the room in a fruitless attempt to wipe away their hurt and pain, but she remained seated; they were cementing their bond, a bond that would last a lifetime—however long that may be.

Chuck saw Grammy seated in the row behind her daughter, Sheila, looking up reflectively toward the numerous holographic images of Nathan that floated above their heads as a tribute to their lost son and friend. While Grammy had never been the cookie-baking type, she was a sensitive and caring woman, and Chuck knew that she was thinking about how it could have been he who had died that day. She was grateful to still have him. She had lost five friends in the battle that had taken Nathan's life and was allowing herself just that one day to mourn. She had expressed to Chuck and Sheila that morning that one day was all she felt she could or should sacrifice until they could put an end to the alien invasion. She steadily dried her eyes with one hand while her life-long friend, Brody, held her other hand in support. Grammy and Brody had helped each other escape the mountain on that fateful day and shared the five friends who did not make it. Brody and Ronnie had reconnected, and Ronnie had nursed Brody's injuries from the alien's well-aimed explosion. Ronnie was Brody's partner and lover, and he hadn't left his side since they were together again. Grammy also cried tears for her friend, Calliope, who had been taken by the aliens on that same day.

Dagny stared ahead. Every time Chuck saw her face, it surprised him. Dagny had been best friends with Lexi and had been Gaz's girlfriend, but somehow she had switched sides and was interested in Farley. Chuck had been wary at first, but Dagny had saved Chuck and Farley from Mike and Gaz; Chuck no longer felt as though she was tricking them like Lexi had done. Dagny had been a good support for Farley while suffering her own torment—she had not located her parents. She had last spoken to them when they told her that they had captured her now ex-boyfriend, Gaz, but when she returned home that day, the house was empty and there was a small pool of blood on the floor. They were supposed to be home waiting for her, and they were going to decide, together, what to do with Gaz. Chuck and Farley had figured that Mike and Lexi had to have gotten there first and rescued Gaz, but they had no idea where her parents could possibly be or whose blood had been spilled. Chuck felt bad for her, but they had decided they were going to help Dagny find the answers. It had been a week with no news. Though Dagny desperately wanted to return home and search for them, it wasn't safe. Plain and simple, Farley would not let her leave Eris. Yu had taken a sample of the blood, but with everything going on (conversion of the dojo to their new headquarters, planning of Nathan's funeral, and trying to find Dagny's parents remotely), there had been no time for him to analyze it. Nor had he had time to analyze any of the tissue samples taken from the aliens they had killed back on Earth during their battle at Gros Morne Mountain. Calls to friends, neighbors, and family turned up no clues whatsoever. Chuck knew Dagny was half out of her mind with fear and worry, and he hoped she wouldn't do something to jeopardize their safety—like contacting Lexi—as that would lead the enemy right to them.

Chuck then made eye contact with Karona, who sat with Dagny, holding a box of tissues in her lap. He watched her pass them out where needed. He had noticed that the two young women were becoming close and thought it was because they were both new to the group. He had sensed in the last week that Karona liked Farley but respectfully kept her distance as she saw something growing between Dagny and Farley. Meanwhile, Chuck was seeing a hidden strength in Karona that in a way reminded him of his grandmother, and he found himself admiring Karona. He realized that he hoped she would stay with them, and he wanted to know more about her. All he really knew was that she had run away from home because her parents were abusive. It wasn't his place to pry, but he felt bad for her just the same. Karona had saved his mother that fateful day when they fought the aliens. Miraculously, Karona had been in the woods and had attacked an alien who was about to kill his mother. He would be forever grateful to Karona and wanted to find a way to properly express that to her. He respected that Karona seemed to want to be like Dagny but thought she was pretty great just being herself.

Karona, like Dagny, had borrowed clothes from Sparks, and he noted how nice she looked in the black skirt and black button-up blouse. She also had her hair tied back in a red ribbon and thought it was considerate of her to wear Nathan's favorite color.

The main room at Yu's dojo held approximately thirty people for Nathan's funeral—the risk of bringing friends and relatives from Earth to Eris was too great. They had to assume that the aliens were waiting and watching for them. The only people in attendance were those who survived the battle: Dagny, Sparks, and anyone who happened to be in training at the dojo that day. At some point in the future, they would have a memorial for Nathan where anyone could attend.

"Ladies and gentlemen, Nathan's favorite band, Grimy Toes." A holograph of the four-member heavy-metal band materialized. All of them, in their ripped jeans and dirty t-shirts, jumped around as they loudly played their guitars and drums. Chuck, Yu, and Farley stepped to the side to watch. Everyone hoped to give Mr. Castle the time he needed to mourn, but their work wasn't done. Dagny's parents needed to be located, and they needed to ensure the alien threat was wiped out for good. Even though there had been no attacks reported in the past week, it meant nothing.

The team consisting of Chuck, Yu, Farley, Grammy, Brody, Josh, Karona, and Mr. Castle had agreed that finding Dagny's parents was top priority. Yu had many well-to-do clients, and in the interest of anonymity, he had arranged to rent a ship from one of them for their missions back to Earth. They couldn't risk Mr. Castle's ship being recognized, and taking the shuttle across with no transportation at the other end was inconvenient and almost ensured they were sitting ducks. While Yu couldn't promise any ship he rented would be returned unscathed, he did promise that the owner would be bought a new ship of equal or greater value. His clients had lined up to help the cause. On the Earth end of things, Mr. Castle's security team would continue working with local police to do their part in the fight.

They had planned for their first trip to Earth to depart the next day. They didn't want Dagny to go with them but realized that only she would notice anything amiss in her home or if any clues had been left behind from her parents. After she had reiterated these points vehemently, the rest of the group had to accept the merit in what she was saying, and they relented. They also agreed that not everyone would go on every trip; they had to ensure if they were attacked, they didn't lose everyone. The first trip would be manned by Chuck, Farley, Dagny, and Josh. As much as Josh wanted to stay behind with Mr. Castle, they needed Yu at the dojo to begin analysis of all the blood and tissue samples he had collected. They had to find the aliens' weaknesses and hope for a solution to obliterate them en masse. Josh and Yu were the only experienced pilots they had until they were able to train others, so they would take turns flying to Earth. The same clients who had offered up their ships were also lining up for advanced training to learn how to fight the aliens. Grammy and Brody were leading the training because they knew more about the aliens than anyone else. In the meantime, Josh would be training Chuck and Farley on how to pilot the ship.

Grimy Toes was just finishing their song in Nathan's memory when Mr. Castle unexpectedly rose from his seat and walked to the front of the room. No one took a breath while they waited anxiously for him to speak. Mr. Castle stood behind the podium, looking at each person for at least five seconds before moving on to the next, as though memorizing each face. He had never had a more captive, more intimate audience in his life. When his gaze moved to Karona, she stood in acknowledgement of his appreciation for her being there, her face as beet red as always. When those he had already looked at realized what was happening, they also stood, as did each person thereafter. Finally, Mr. Castle looked to his right at Chuck, Farley, and Yu. He looked at them each in turn and then beckoned them to join him.

Moving as though in slow motion, the three young men approached Mr. Castle. None could hold back their sobs.

"Mr. Castle, I am so sorry. I'm so, so sorry. I should have been paying better attention. I should have saved Nathan. This is my entire fault," Chuck wailed.

Farley piped in. "It's my fault too, Mr. Castle. I was right there and could've jumped in front of Nathan or pushed him out of the way or something."

Mr. Castle looked at Yu, who grabbed his own nose before looking up. Mr. Castle responded in kind.

Chuck and Farley looked at each other completely stunned. "What does that mean?"

"It is a symbol of our solidarity. We are all in this together. We are a team, and we are made stronger with the addition of you both...and others of course," Yu said, motioning to Dagny and Karona. "It is a sign of acceptance toward whoever stands with us. Chuck and Farley, you are no more to blame than I am, and I am accepting no blame in this. Our own detection devices did not pick up on that alien, so how could anyone predict that we were in such close proximity to danger? We certainly could not, and your apology is unnecessary and therefore rejected."

Chuck and Farley began to sob even harder now that they had been exonerated of their guilt. For a week, they had been beating themselves up, feeling responsible for their friend's brutal demise. They had also been terrified of facing Mr. Castle as they were convinced he, too, would blame them. The relief they both felt meant that they could now move on and mourn the loss of their friend without the weight of guilt added to the grief.

Mr. Castle pulled Chuck and Farley into his arms for a few moments before turning to the rest of the attendees. "I'd like to thank you all for being here. It means a lot to me to see the loving and caring faces and to know that Nathan touched other lives. Nathan was my only child, and I never imagined my life without him. His poor mother gave her life to save his during his birth, and while I have missed her greatly all these years, I am also thankful that she is not with us to experience his horrifying death. It is almost too much to bear.

9

"But alas, we have much work to do and avenging my son is at the top of the list. We will avenge the lives of Alfie, Clara, Slim, Stitch, and Flinch, all of whom fought with us that dreadful day on the mountain. We will avenge the life of Calliope Fillion, another dear friend taken violently from us. We will avenge the lives of everyone taken from our worlds. We may not have known them but they also had family and friends and lives that were cut short. We will find Dagny's parents," he said pointedly, looking at Dagny with eyes filled with conviction. "We will show those monsters that they cannot come to our worlds and take what they want. We will show them that we are *the* force to be reckoned with. We will show them what it feels like to hurt and have their hearts ripped out, assuming they have hearts."

Mr. Castle paused to blow his nose. He held a picture of Nathan in his hand and kissed it.

"In the next few days, as I understand it, we are sending a team back to Earth in search of Dagny's parents. And at this end, Yu will be conducting a series of tests on all tissue and blood samples he has gathered. Our goal is to learn as much about the aliens as we can to determine their weaknesses. Knowledge is power. Knowledge is key. Knowledge is what we will utilize to outsmart our enemy. And believe me, we will outsmart them. We will obliterate them, and we will take back control of our planet!"

Despite it being a funeral, and one for such a young person, the audience, already standing, gave a thunderous ovation. Someone yelled, "Let's get those aliens!" They felt some encouragement and relief from the pain and hurt of losing friends. Despite the impending battle where there was sure to be more death, it was something for everyone to look forward to. Their lives had attained a purposeful distraction.

"Hello." Yu stepped up to the podium. "We are recruiting for our cause and require volunteers to attend various training classes. Considering we are here mourning the death of a friend and family member, I do not need to warn of the dangers inherent in this fight ahead. We cannot guarantee anything other than the rewards gained from knowing you are fighting for us, for those we care about, and for mankind. Chuck spoke so eloquently of mankind earlier, and I fully second everything he said. Mankind is good, and mankind is here to stay. We will do our part to protect it."

Chuck and Yu nodded at each other.

"Sign-up sheets will be posted outside this room. No one will be forced to help or face any repercussions for not joining. We understand that each person's situation is different, and we would never bully anyone or purport the right to tell anyone what to do. For those who are willing and able to help, we need pilots. We also need fighters. We need people to become proficient at handling a variety of weapons, both hand-held and on-board our ships. For those who are unable to be out in the field, we can use your help in the lab, analyzing alien tissue samples to aid us in discovering as much about them as possible. We need tactical people who can work with Grammy and Brody to plan missions and anticipate the aliens' next moves. We need people who are able to tend to our wounded. I am asking each of you to please let your family and friends all know what we to have to offer. All training is free, and everyone is welcome.

"Our goal, friends, is to learn as much as we can so we can make them go away."

The crowd clapped again as Mr. Castle joined Yu. "Thank you from the bottom of my heart for being with us here today and showing your support for the incredible loss of my son, Nathan. There are many others who would have come from Earth, but it was too dangerous. It is likely that our homes back on Earth are being watched or have been destroyed, and we must protect these headquarters with our lives. The aliens know who we are and have been watching us for as long as we have been watching them. This location must be kept as secret as possible and appear to be just a regular, everyday dojo."

Mr. Castle held up a photo of Nathan and kissed it again. "Nathan— my son, my pride and joy, my life—nothing has made me happier than being your father and watching you grow. You enriched my life, and I know your mother would have been equally proud. You developed from a small, shy boy into a man capable of piloting his own space ship. With your maturity, you became fearless in facing death as you raced with your friends to help loved ones. And you were smart too. Yu told me about how you were able to somehow track Grammy's phone call on that fateful day and tracked us down at the mountain headquarters. Too smart for your own good," Mr. Castle said softly with utter sadness in his voice.

Everyone had remained standing during Mr. Castle's eulogy, and fresh tears graced many faces.

"It is such a damn waste. You were just coming into your own and embracing independence. You were experiencing new and exciting things, and you had cemented adult bonds with your friends that had been nurtured since childhood. You were also robbed of so many things. You will never fall in love, have your own children, or see justice prevail. You will never have a satisfying career or have the opportunity to travel and visit the many different countries on Earth and Eris. You wanted to take up painting, and now that will never be." Mr. Castle's tears were flowing freely.

"But in your name, Nathan, I will see that Chuck and Farley have every opportunity that I would have given to you. I will offer them guidance and encouragement in whatever they choose to do in this life, for they deserve it. They, like you did, have put and will continue to put their lives on the line for humanity, and I will repay them by treating them as though they are my own sons. Nathan—my son, my pride and joy, my life—I love you more than anything. And I will miss you with every aching beat of my shattered heart."

Chapter 2

Mr. Castle stood at the door shaking hands and receiving hugs as the group of mourners filed past him. Many of them assured him they would be signing up to join the fight. Mr. Castle expressed his gratitude and offered his support in any way it was needed. It was 4:00 p.m. He made his way to reconvene with the main team in Yu's office to discuss details of their upcoming missions. Now that he had taken a week to close himself off and be taken care of with no responsibilities, it was time for him to step up to the plate again and take charge. He had strong people working for him who had handled things during his temporary release from command, but it was all hands on deck now.

"Mr. Castle, your speech about Nathan was so touching. And about recruiting, you came across as fierce and determined. I think you've really encouraged almost everyone to help us," Chuck said, removing the first suit jacket he had ever worn and hanging it on the back of a chair.

"Thank you, Chuck. Yours was very moving as well. My son loved you and was happy to have you as his best friend. We'll have him in our hearts every step of the way until we put things back to the way they were before. The whole galaxy will know what we are capable of and that we are not to be messed with. Now, if we can just figure out where they're coming from, we can launch an attack against them." Mr. Castle stared at the ceiling as though it would open up and a map would appear with perfect directions.

"Thank you, Mr. Castle. Grammy wrote it for me. I could never come up with those words."

"I'm sure you could, son. Very easily." Mr. Castle smiled up at Chuck.

Grammy entered the office with Brody and Ronnie and sat on the couch. She had changed out of her blue dress into her work attire—black pants, black top, and black combat boots. They had no intentions of fighting that day—or even that week—but she was leaving nothing to chance after the ambush at the mountain, and she had her cane ready.

"Do you have any ideas at all, Mr. Castle?" Farley asked, also removing his suit jacket and draping it on the arm of the couch.

"What did we miss?" Brody asked before taking a sip of his coffee.

"Farley is asking if we have any ideas about where the aliens come from," Mr. Castle replied.

"Oh" was the unenthusiastic response from Brody.

Farley looked around the room and then raised his eyebrows at Chuck.

"I guess that means no," Chuck surmised, crestfallen.

"Well, dear, not entirely," Grammy answered. "We know they come from outside our galaxy. We also know that they probably don't come from any neighboring galaxies because our scanners would have picked up on that. We've detected nothing other than regular space garbage and small meteors." Grammy looked away as she said that last sentence.

Chuck looked at Farley and paused for a few moments before replying. "Well, your *scanners* didn't detect the aliens but how does that mean we can we rule out neighboring galaxies? I don't mean to put anyone on the spot."

"Yeah, we still don't know everything you guys know. We need to be in the loop on everything now that we're in it with you," Farley added.

Grammy looked to Mr. Castle, who looked to Ronnie, who looked to Brody, who took the look full-circle back to Grammy.

"So, it's safe to say that we really don't have any idea about where the aliens come from?" Chuck asked. Farley's back-up bolstered Chuck. Even though Grammy was his Grammy, he was an important member of the newly-expanded team, and his young-man age of only seventeen wasn't going to hold him back from asking any hard questions.

Grammy shook her head, waving her hands in the air. "Boys, boys, it's not that simple. Oh, girls! Just in time!"

Dagny and Karona entered the room dressed identically to Grammy in all-black, slim-fitting outfits and black combat boots. Both carried canes and both looked uncomfortable carrying them. Farley stepped to Dagny and kissed her cheek. "You look wonderful."

"Thank you!" Dagny blushed. "Was Calliope your grandmother, Farley? You have the same last name."

"No, Fillion is a common last name just like Smith used to be. We weren't related at all," Farley responded.

"You look marvelous, too, darling," Grammy said to Karona, relocating from the couch to the table, motioning for her to take a seat beside her. "Would you like some coffee?"

"Yes, please, Grammy. That would be nice."

Grammy passed her a steaming mug. "Sorry, dear, we don't allow sugar and cream. Straight black is how we do it."

"That's perfectly fine." She took a sip and tried to hide her grimace.

Grammy patted her knee. "You'll get used to it," she said with a smile.

Farley and Dagny took seats across from Grammy and Karona at a large, black table with enough room for ten. Two coffee pots with mugs and two platters filled with sandwiches took up the space in the middle of the table. Everyone dug in. Brody and Ronnie moved to the table while Mr. Castle and Yu took their seats at the ends.

"Grammy? You were saying?" Chuck steered the conversation back on track.

"Oh, yes, of course. Wasn't that a lovely service, everyone? Castle, were you pleased?"

"Most indubitably, Grammy. It was lovely, and I think it was befitting to my son's life. His friends got to speak, I spoke, and that band played a song—that part wasn't so lovely, but it was Nathan's favorite, so what can I say?"

"Indeed," Brody piped in. "I don't really like that type of music either. Do you enjoy it, Ronnie?"

"Ha! Oh, you know I have no use for it," Ronnie said, twirling his moustache around his index finger.

The door opened once again and Josh entered the room. "Good… sandwiches. I'm famished." He dug right in and took the last seat. "What have I missed?" Josh asked with his mouth full.

"Well…" Chuck began.

"We were just discussing the funeral service and how heartfelt it was," Grammy interjected smoothly. "Wouldn't you agree?"

"Absolutely. It was a special service for a special young man. He should be sitting at this table here with us right now. He should be eating a sandwich and…" Josh paused to take a sip of the coffee he'd just poured "…drinking this disgusting coffee. Whose idea was it to cut out cream and sugar anyway?"

Chuck rolled his eyes. "I don't believe this," he muttered.

"It really is awful." Karona joined the conversation.

"Well, it's much better for you without it, and we all need to be in tip-top shape. Everything in those sandwiches is fat-free too. You can barely notice how dry they are," Mr. Castle said, rolling his eyes.

"I'm used to it, and I actually like these sandwiches." Farley took another sandwich as proof.

"Thank you, Farley. Finally, someone's not ganging up on me. We have rules for reasons. Maybe one day we can be gluttons again, but for now, we sacrifice."

"Speaking of sacrifice," Chuck began, yet again, as he looked at Grammy pointedly.

Grammy avoided his gaze and said, "I'll get the sugar-free cakes from the fridge for dessert." Grammy stepped out of the room.

"What is it, Chuck? What are you on about?" Josh asked, wiping a crumb from his lip.

"Well, we're here to plan our attack and everything we need to do to prepare, and Farley and I asked about the aliens. You know, where they come from and stuff, and Grammy talked around it but never really gave us any information. I pointed out that the scanners didn't detect the aliens, and she's been changing the subject ever since." Chuck looked around the room. "What's going on here?"

Farley joined in. "Yeah, we were on that mountain alongside all of you, and we made it out with our lives. And Nathan lost his life. We have the right to know whatever you know and to be as much a part of this fight as any of you are."

Mr. Castle stood up. "Okay, I agree. Quickly, before she gets back with that dreadful excuse for dessert." Mr. Castle paused for a moment. Brody and Ronnie looked at each other shaking their heads.

Josh muttered, "Don't do it, Castle."

"We know nothing," Mr. Castle said simply.

The older people tensed, waiting for the backlash.

The younger people slumped as the reality of those three, plain, everyday words sunk in.

Chapter 3

I *will get out of here*, he thought. *I will escape. This is not how I die.* He felt along the walls for about the eightieth time searching for a door or a window or even a garbage chute, anything through which he could free himself. He didn't dare open his eyes; the light in the room in which he was being held was so blinding, it was worse than if he was in pitch blackness. In fact, he begged for darkness, but no one answered him. He had no clue where he was, who took him, or why. He just knew he had been locked up for several days.

His "dungeon," as he called it, actually was far from it. When he stretched his blue shirt over his face, it provided enough of a barrier to the blinding lights above that he could make out where the washroom was, find the hole where his captors slid his food through (it was too small for him to fit, of course), and see that all the furniture—a table-and-chairs set and a couch—was brand new. The room itself was one big square, at least twenty feet by twenty feet. He had never heard of such a set up. *Aren't dungeons supposed to be wet, dark, and dank with mice and rats fighting the prisoners for the food?*

The dungeon was actually cleaner than his house. In fact, it was spotless, and somehow the washroom was cleaned after each time he used it, though he saw or heard no one. The food was also delicious. Once he realized he had been kidnapped, he did his best to remain calm and keep his wits about him. He ate every meal instead of whipping it across the room in protest. He kept his strength up by exercising every day. He figured out that the blinding lights were probably meant to break his psyche, never being able to open his eyes, or move about freely without using his hands to guide his way.

"I will get out of here! I will escape! This is not how I will die!" He shouted this to the ceiling at least once a day, hoping his jailers would take heed his warning and just let him go. At other times, he'd yell, "I don't care what you want with me! You and your motives mean nothing to me! You are insignificant, and this room is boring. Keep it clean and shiny all you want, with a new, comfy couch for me to sleep on, but it doesn't matter to me. This could be a scurvy dungeon with weeds growing toward me and entangling my legs for all I care. Whatever you're hoping to get from me, you can forget it!"

No response. As usual. He dropped to the ground and did one hundred push-ups. Push-ups were his favorite, and he would do one hundred of them, four or five times a day. After the push-ups, he rolled onto his back and squeezed one hundred crunches into his abdomen. He liked the burn he felt after a good workout. It hadn't always been that way, though. His favorite pastime used to be hanging around like a sloth watching science fiction movies. He longed for the day when he could teleport somewhere. Or send people he disliked to strange places from which they could never return.

Something happened, though. One day he became interested in cooking. It was when he was watching one of his sci-fi movies and the captain of a ship requested a fancy chicken dish from his food replicator, and he was overcome with the urge to try and make it himself. It sounded delicious, with goat cheese and sun-dried tomatoes. His first six attempts were disastrous. He burned it the first three times and the last three, he had the chicken on such a bizarre angle that the goat cheese all leaked out. The seventh time (and seven is his lucky number) was a charm. It turned out beautifully, and he was happy that he had kept trying. After that, he attacked his mother's cookbook with ferocity, making every recipe in the book until he had mastered it. When he began to put on weight from all the rich, gourmet meals he'd made, he offset it by working out. In so doing, he had become strong and fit, and being captured for an unknown reason didn't stop him from eating every bite given to him and maintaining his fitness routine. A determined man was he.

Determination kept him eating and exercising to maintain his physical strength, but he also worked on his mental strength. As he did squats and leg lunges, he said aloud, "My name is Bross David. I live on Eris. My address is 47 Willowbend Roadway, Satellite Station X to the X. I live with Sonny and our two cats. Their names are Kylie and Barbara. We have our three-year anniversary coming up in October. I *will* be there to celebrate it with him." Bross wiped a tear away, thinking about Sonny. He missed him terribly. They were best friends and lovers, and Bross thought about him in every second. He vowed to himself to break out and get home to him.

When he was sufficiently fatigued, he felt his way to the edge of the room where he began his next investigation of every inch of the wall. The room was wide and long, but the ceiling was an arm's length above his head, so it was easy for him to reach the top of the walls. He replayed the last thing he remembered before waking up in confinement. He was in his backyard, planting some purple and blue flowers to surprise Sonny. It had been a beautiful, sunny day, but the clouds were rolling in. Bross was trying to finish the job before the rains came and soaked him. He patted down the soil around the last plant, securing it in place, and rose from his knees as a few drops pelted his face. Then he had been clobbered in the head from behind. That was it. That's all he remembered.

He heard a noise to his left that brought him back to present day. The door covering the little hole slid open. He squinted as freshly laundered pants, a shirt, and socks were pushed through. He also caught a glimpse of a red arm at the end of the clothing pile.

Chapter 4

Only a quarter of Eris had been colonized. The other part would remain barren until more people decided to take the leap and change planets. More jobs would have to be created so people could make a living. Aside from being a novelty, moving to Eris held no real opportunities at that point. However, it was the perfect spot for Yu's dojo as it was on the outskirts of the colonized section and therefore easy to hide their activities.

A silver ship landed on a barren part of the planet, and four human-like beings exited it. They spread out a large, green checkered blanket and from a picnic basket, pulled sandwiches, containers of fruit and vegetables, and a large upright cooler filled with punch.

"We have to do something," a woman with spiked, brown hair said as she poured four plastic glasses of punch. "They need our help, and they don't even know it."

"We're lucky to be alive. I don't think we should interfere. The humans can take care of themselves," replied a short, bald woman wearing a multi-colored sundress.

"I agree with Sulinda." Troy stood seven feet tall with skin black as night, stroking his long, gray beard as he motioned to the lady in the sundress. "Our species was all but wiped out. We need to worry about finding others of our kind and rebuilding."

"Rebuild. Reeee-build. Re-buuiilld," the fourth drawled. "Hmmmmm."

"Out with it, Maywano. What are you thinking?" Sulinda asked, smoothing out her sundress and putting on a hat with a bright blue, two-foot-wide brim.

"Hmmmmm."

Spikey-haired Sparrow snuck up behind Maywano and playfully pinched him on the back of the neck. "Tell us what you're thinking! Do you think we should help our cosmic neighbors instead of rebuilding? I know that's what you're thinking." Sparrow turned to the others. "So, it's two against two. A stand-off. What do we do now?"

Troy stroked his beard as he replied in his high-pitched, squeaky voice. "No one said Maywano agreed with you at all, *Sparrow*, and you shouldn't put thoughts in his head."

"Why not? That's exactly what you're trying to do, Troy. And you know I hate it when you say my name like that. It's a real name, and I love it," Sparrow said, pouting. Troy spoke her name as though it had quotation marks around it.

"I eat now. Then talk." Maywano shoved so much of his sandwich into his mouth that all he could do was grunt as the others badgered him with questions. Maywano did everything in his own time and that one, giant mouthful of food would take him at least ten minutes to chew and swallow. *Digestion starts in the mouth* was his motto, and he took it seriously.

"I'm going back to the ship for a minute. Anyone need anything?" Troy asked. A round of "no's" was the response, so he walked as quickly as he could back to the ship and up the circular staircase.

Sulinda and Sparrow made small talk while they waited for Troy to return and for Maywano to finish eating. He would take another ten minutes to eat the second half of his sandwich. Then he would want to eat a few pickles. After that, he would take a walk for five minutes and then—only then—would he be ready to explain what was going through his head on the topic of help the Earthlings or don't help the Earthlings.

Maywano, being the oldest, albeit strangest of the four, was in charge and made all major decisions for the group. They didn't always like it, but they were bound by their cultural rules to obey. And since there weren't many of them left, it was important to them to maintain their ways.

Troy went to his compartment, which was too small to be referred to as an actual room, and pulled a bag of what looked like peanuts from one of the two drawers he had. They had escaped with their lives on a shuttle that had two compartments they had been using as bedrooms (the two females shared and the two males shared); a small kitchen with a fridge big enough to fit three meals for each of the four of them; the cockpit, which sat two; and a seating area, which accommodated the four. He looked back the way he came, ensuring no one had followed him and quickly shoveled a mouthful of nuts into his mouth. He ate like a ravenous dog and before allowing himself to toss another handful into his salivating mouth, forced himself to hide the bag in the drawer. He checked his teeth in the mirror, confirming no evidence of his hasty meal and went back outside.

"Come and get your sandwich," Sulinda said, holding one up to Troy. At just under four feet tall, Sulinda stood on her tippy toes to reach Troy's hand.

"Oh, no, no. I'm okay for now. Maybe later." He made repeated tossing motions with his hands and arms as though he was trying to shoot a basketball.

"It's actually not okay. You haven't eaten in days," Sulinda responded.

"Let him starve. If he doesn't want to eat it, we surely will," Sparrow said. There was no love lost there. Sparrow and Troy hadn't been friendly toward each other since they met a couple months before. Because they lost their home planet and somehow made an escape on the tiny ship together, they were forced to be together pretty much all day, all night, every day, and every night. If they ever were to live normal lives again, they would gladly part ways and not look back.

Sulinda held the food high above her head, trying to meet's Troy's eyes with her own. "You will take this sandwich," she said forcefully.

"You're such a mother. Fine. Give it here." Troy took the sandwich, trying to hide the look of disgust on his face.

Sparrow, the perceptive one, saw the look flash across his face and jumped all over it. "What's your problem with the food? I've been watching you, and I know you've been purposely avoiding it."

"No problem and mind your own, *Sparrow*."

"Jerk," she replied, imitating his high-pitched voice. Troy narrowed his eyes at her.

"Sparrow's right, though. Do you not like the food? It's the best we can do. Is it making you sick?" Sulinda asked.

"All right! All right! No, it's not making me sick. I just think it tastes absolutely disgusting, and I don't want to eat it."

"Just like a petulant child," Sparrow muttered.

Troy stared down at Sparrow long and hard, his eyes narrowing into slits as his lips peeled back into an evil clown grin. "Watch your step, space cadet. You might find yourself eating something you don't like the taste of either." Troy looked to the others. "You know what I'm talking about. This human food is sickening. How they eat other creatures is beyond imagination."

"Stay away from me," Sparrow said softly, fearing retaliation for her petulant child comment. Troy was not much more than a foot taller than her, but she knew he was much stronger and wouldn't hesitate to knock her to the ground.

"Calm down, both of you. Maywano, are you going to get in on this? Anytime would be good. Troy, we eat other creatures, too. It can't all be nuts and berries, although the nuts and berries we had at home were just scrumptious. We all miss our food, but we must adapt. We have to survive, and to do that, we have to eat." Sulinda then stared intently at Maywano as though trying to *will* him to eat his pickles more quickly.

"I personally think this human food is delightful." Maywano finally broke his silence. "The way they combine meat with cheese and put different sauces on it is so intricate, so delectable. And the different bread options. Wow! Well, there's bread slices, buns, croissants, pita bread, white bread, blue bread, brown bread, bread with their own kind of nuts and seeds in it..."

"Ridiculous." Troy spoke loudly and firmly.

Maywano looked at Troy curiously, as though he had never seen him before.

"Indeed. It is ridiculous, indeed," Maywano agreed, "but I still enjoy it. And if we ever find a food source similar to ours, I shall gladly put some of our nuts between two slices of human bread and eat it. I would probably drink a large glass of milk with it." He tucked his long, braided hair into the neckline of his robe.

Troy made retching noises, threatening to throw up.

"I will take my walk now, and when I return, and am ready, I will let you know what I have decided about what we will do next." Maywano's long robes were patterned with burgundy insects that looked like two-headed dragonflies. He gathered them as he stood up. He slipped matching slippers onto his brown, slim feet and moved away from the others. "Don't squabble while I'm gone. It's very unbecoming of a mother, a jerk, and a space cadet."

Chapter 5

"Nothing? Nothing at all?" Chuck asked incredulously. He stood up so quickly that his chair fell over behind him. He didn't even bother to pick it up. Farley looked down at the chair and decided he didn't feel like picking it up either. It seemed poignant somehow, and he wanted the chair to represent how he and Chuck felt. They had recently—very recently—begun to feel important and worthy and that all seventeen years of their lives were destined for greatness. They were going to be partly responsible for ridding the world of the murderous aliens and saving mankind, and they actually thought they were so close to doing that. To discover that they were just at the beginning was disconcerting and disheartening.

"Well, we know everything that Grammy told you, but that's it. There's no point in trying to mislead you into believing something better or more encouraging. I *can* tell you this: we are going to do exactly what we set out to do, and that's send those aliens home," Mr. Castle said.

Grammy walked in, carrying a tray of purple and green squares. "Well, here we are! Delicious squares and they're good for you!"

"I told them, Grammy," Mr. Castle said.

Grammy looked at him reading his face. "Everything?"

"Yes. And by 'everything,' I mean nothing. Well, the nothing that we know, which is what you've told them already."

"Stop speaking in riddles," Chuck said. "Let's just get on with it and figure out what we're going to do. So you used to meet them at the Planetary Space Agency space station and give them supplies, and you later found some of them just floating out in space. They never wanted your help in the first place, and when you confronted them, they began attacking."

"It's all probably beside the point now since we have to get Dagny's parents back. That should be our first priority." Farley stood beside Chuck, and Dagny smiled up at him. "We should put on disguises and go back to her house to search for clues. There may be something we missed when we were there, and it's just a logical starting point."

"Yeah! Disguises! I like the way you think, Far. I think I'll be a hover salesman, and you can be my assistant," Chuck said excitedly.

"Uh, no. *I'll* be the hover salesman and *you'll* be the assistant. The assistant gets to stay outside and be on the lookout for anything suspicious while the salesman goes inside and scopes out the scene."

"Well, what am I supposed to do while I'm on the lookout?"

"Measure the driveway to see what size of a hover will fit there. Measure the garage too. It doesn't really matter. Just look busy. If anyone comes, just say you're a serviceman and yell into the house for me to come if anything suspicious happens. My stage name will be Rosco. Just yell 'Rosco' into the house, and I'll come right out."

"What a dumb name. You couldn't come up with something better, like Krull or Thunder?" Chuck couldn't have sounded anymore disappointed at Farley's choice of code name.

"Good call. Okay, I'll go by Krull," Farley replied.

"No. I'm Krull."

"Oh, for Froggy's sake, who cares? Let's get on with it," Josh jumped in. "Nicknames are done. You can both be Krull. The likelihood of anyone even needing to know your names is slim. I *do* like where you're going with the idea though. So, it's Krull, Krull, Grammy, and me flying back to Earth."

"Sounds good," said Farley. Then looking to Dagny, he said, "Sorry, Dagny. There was no way we were going to let you go." He looked away before he could see the disappointment on her face.

"If you guys carry on with ridiculousness the way you do, I'd rather Yu take you, but of course I'll do whatever we need," Josh winked.

"I'm having reservations now too," Grammy piped in, rolling her eyes and grimacing at the dryness of one of her "delicious desserts."

"Haha! Sorry, Grammy. Sorry, Josh," Chuck said, giving Farley a high-five.

"No worries. We'll get serious again soon enough," said Josh. "We'll take one of the ships we've borrowed in case the aliens recognize Castle's ship. We should probably not be selling hovers, though, in case nosy neighbors become interested in making purchases. How about we're just there to do some landscaping?"

"Yes," said Dagny. "That's perfect. My parents have always said the front looks too plain and can do with some color. I'll give you the code to the house so you can get in quickly. I know you won't let me go so I'm not even going to ask again, but I do want you to send me images of everything once you're there. We can communicate in code, and I can let you know if anything is out of whack."

"Awesome! It'll be like we're spies or something," Chuck fist-bumped the air above him.

"Now, dear, it could be a dangerous mission, and I don't want you to think like that. This is serious, and you need to have your wits about you constantly. Do not trust anyone. Keep your eyes wide open. I'm glad I'm going too, so I can keep an eye out. I don't want to lose you." Grammy walked around the table and pulled Chuck down to give him an affectionate squeeze.

Brody piped in. "It's a sound plan. Chuck and Farley will go with Grammy and Josh—Josh is the pilot and Grammy is on surveillance. Farley can send images back to us here at the base, and I'll work communications

28

with Dagny. I can scramble the signals so no outsiders are able to interpret the meaning. I think the goal should be to enter the house, gather as much information as possible, and be out within fifteen minutes. Unless the aliens are actually watching the house, that should be long enough to find whatever there is to find and also to get out of there before they show up if they're watching from a distance."

"Agreed," Mr. Castle said.

"What do you need me to do?" Ronnie asked. He casually played with the thick, brown leather band he wore around his wrist that matched his brown leather shirt and brown leather pants.

"We need you to teach as many courses as you can fit in a day. Can you create a course schedule, determine which classes to use, and develop the curriculum and materials for each course? It sounds like a lot, but it's necessary," Grammy said, as she walked back to her seat.

"Consider it done."

"So, when should we leave?" Chuck asked.

"I'm hoping you can leave tomorrow. Well, today would be better, but with the funeral and everything, I'll wait until tomorrow. Please say you can go tomorrow?" Dagny pleaded.

Farley looked to Josh and Grammy for the answer. "Do you think we can be ready?"

"Of course," Grammy and Josh replied in unison.

"Well, take some dessert, everyone," Grammy said, passing the tray to Karona.

Karona helped herself despite Farley shaking his head "no" inconspicuously. "What can I do to help?" she asked, playing with her ponytail self-consciously.

"You've seen the list of courses we're offering. Is there anything that interests you?" Mr. Castle asked.

Karona's face turned red, and she glanced at Dagny before answering. "I, um, have always dreamed of being a pilot. My best friend and I would fantasize for hours at a time about flying around the system. But if it's not possible, that's okay." She shoved a square into her mouth.

"That's a grand idea, and we need pilots. I'd be delighted to have you in my class, Karona," Ronnie said beaming.

"Re-re-really?" Karona's face turned an even deeper shade of red. She looked around the table at the smiling, encouraging faces.

"Absolutely!" Ronnie said. "The way you handled yourself back at the mountain was courageous and valiant, and we're lucky to have you working with us."

"We all agree, dear. We're happy to have you," Grammy added.

"Well, I won't let you down. I'll do my best and will practice constantly!" Karona jumped out of her seat. She hugged Grammy tightly and then dodged around Brody to throw her arms around Ronnie. He laughed and hugged her back.

"I want to do the pilot training too," Chuck said.

"That'll be the day," Farley said, rolling his eyes.

"What's wrong with me flying ships?" Chuck turned on Farley confrontationally.

"Remember 'four on the floor'?" Farley laughed so hard he began choking. Josh poured him a glass of water.

"Ha ha, very funny. Did you just come up with that yourself? Remember how you were on your hands and knees too?"

Farley slumped out of his seat and onto the floor where he got on his hands and knees. "Can I fly a ship? Can I? Can I? Please, I want to be a pilot." Farley laughed, recalling the first time they had flown in Nathan's ship. He had seen a different, less serious side to Nathan as Nathan had quizzed them on how to pilot the ship. Nathan had told them that they needed to understand "four on the floor," which Chuck, followed by Farley, had interpreted to mean they had to get down on their hands and knees for whatever reason. They all had had a good laugh about it afterward.

Mr. Castle leaned toward Josh and said, "These boys are strange."

"They are, indeed," Josh concurred.

Karona went back to her seat, wiping tears of happiness from her eyes as Farley quit joking around and sat down again.

"Chuck, of course you can take the pilot training. In fact, I think it's a good idea for everyone to try all the courses and see if any specialties surface. I'll devise a program designed to pinpoint areas where individuals excel and that can help people decide where they should focus. I hope we don't end up with all pilots and no fighters," Brody joked.

"Actually, being a pilot would be so cool, but I think I'd rather be a fighter. I'll pretend the aliens are all Mike look-alikes and bash their heads in. I already know I'm not a tactical person, so I don't wanna waste anybody's time in thinking I could be an asset in that department." Chuck turned to Farley. "What are you signing up to do? I think you'd make a great tactician."

Farley waited for the punch line while they stared at each other.

"Uh, what are you doing?" Chuck asked, with eyebrows raised.

"What do you mean?" Farley asked guardedly.

"Unbelievable. What. Courses. Will. You. Be. Signing. Up. For?"

"Are you being serious?"

"Yes! What's wrong with you?" Chuck almost yelled.

"Oh, I was waiting for a snide remark. Do you really think I'd be a great tactician?" Farley asked incredulously.

"I do. I actually do. Far, you're the only reason we are even here. You did all this on your own and brought me along. I had no clue what you were even up to all those months ago when you were here working with Yu. You kept it hidden until you were ready to let me in. Once again, I know I'm not the brightest, so it was probably easy to keep me in the dark, but that doesn't diminish your effort and skills."

"Well, Chuck, you *do* pay attention. Thanks, man!"

"It's decided then. Ronnie will create an aptitude test of sorts.... Ronnie, how long do you need?" Mr. Castle asked.

"I'll be ready to begin testing in two days. That gives everyone time to sign up. There are not more than forty people here, so I can administer the test in one sitting. I can make any changes necessary afterward before we extend the program to the residents of Eris."

"Solid," Josh said.

"It's been an emotional day for all. I think we should get some rest and be ready to go first thing in the morning. Chuck, Farley, Grammy, and Josh—good luck tomorrow. Dagny—we will figure out what happened with your parents. Karona—welcome, we are delighted to have you with us. Brody and Ronnie—your skills are invaluable, and I have no doubt you'll prepare everyone fully. Good night, everyone." Mr. Castle left the room, and the others filed out after him to sleep and rejuvenate body and mind.

Chapter 6

The atmosphere inside the ship was hazy, as though a fog machine blew small amounts of smoke around. It was difficult for the humans to breathe because the air was denser than what they were used to. There was oxygen in it, but it felt thick—too thick for their lungs to absorb. They had to breathe extremely slowly and extremely deeply to avoid the sense of suffocating.

Dagny's parents, Luke and Leila Reynolds, were alert and ever watchful. They were no longer bound, but that didn't afford them much mobility; they were locked in a room no bigger than a broom closet, with no discernible door or opening. They had tried speaking once the aliens had left them alone, but the air was so thick they could only focus on just breathing, never mind talking too. They used hand gestures and eye movements to communicate and worked on finding a way out.

The ceiling was too high for either of them to reach, so after feeling every inch of the walls and floors, Leila climbed up on Luke's shoulders and ran her hands along the smooth ceiling. It took no time for her fingers to touch the outline of an exit. The panel slid easily to the side and Luke pushed her up. *Finally, something is going our way,* he thought. He gave her a thumbs-up with a questioning look. "Is everything okay up there?"

Leila glanced around the shaft she was in before nodding and returning the thumbs-up. It was a typical shaft that seemed to be made of aluminum or metal with air just as dense as it was below, but at least it wasn't worse. She reached down, motioning for her husband to give her his hands as she was going to try to pull him up. She was a strong woman, and Luke weighed only slightly more than her 130 pounds. She thought she would give it a try, but there was nothing she could brace her feet against to avoid being pulled back down into the brig.

With exaggerated mouth movements, Luke asked her if she wanted to go back down and push him up. He could go searching for an escape and risk the punishment of being caught. They agreed that there was risk either way. If she stayed behind, the aliens could come and take her away at any time. They agreed that she would explore and try to find a way to free him.

She blew him a kiss, told him she loved him (that didn't require an exaggerated mouth movement), and crawled away, her heart pounding violently. Luke brushed a tear away after she left and continued running his hands along the walls feeling for anything that could help them. He was so thankful that Dagny hadn't been home when her so-called friends arrived looking for Gaz. He was still unsure what happened exactly, only that he had been hit over the head and not by Mike or Gaz. He knew it was an alien, but how it got into his home and why it was even there was the shocking part. He just hoped he lived to see his daughter one more time.

Chapter 7

Chuck, Farley, Grammy, and Josh raced toward Earth in a ship they had borrowed from a new team member. They had it loaded with weapons and everything they felt they would need. All four were dressed in black at Grammy's insistence, but Chuck thought he would be changing that soon enough; he favored blue over black. Chuck had chugged a glass of a natural anti-anxiety liquid, which everyone hoped would prevent his usual freak-outs in space that were followed by a puking session. It was called Calmalot, was a clear greenish-brownish color, and tasted like pooh, according to Chuck.

"The fox is nearing the hen, and the chop chop will soon begin," Farley said, sounding as though he had been communicating in code for years.

"Roger on the chop chop, and zahoo my boys and girl," Dagny responded from their headquarters on Eris, gaining confidence. Her initial communications while the rescue team was on course went something like "Uh, okay."

"Zahoo, indeed," Josh said smiling. He had used that same word back at the school when he had observed Lexi ransacking Dagny's locker. Dagny using the same word was like a confirmation that their lives were meant to link together.

Chuck pulled out a trolley that was filled with "gardening equipment" which would be their cover for going to Dagny's house. They also decided to visit a few of the neighbors to determine if anyone had seen anything. When the trolley was positioned by the door ready for landing, Chuck and Farley put on mustaches so big and garish that it would be the only thing people would notice. Chuck's was a clown red color. Farley sported a salt and pepper mustache that looked as though he had a raccoon tail sprouting sideways from each nostril.

They turned and looked at each other for a few moments before Chuck lunged at Farley, swiping at his face. "There's a rat on your face! Aaaahaha! Get that dirty, filthy rat off your face!" Farley sidestepped and tripped Chuck, grabbing his arm at the same time to lower him, unhurt, to the ground.

"This rat's gonna gnaw your head off!!" Farley jumped on Chuck and pretended he was eating Chuck's face, making loud chomping sounds.

"Rat! I smell a rat! Disgusting!" Chuck punched at Farley, writhing to get out from under him.

Josh and Grammy sat in their pilot and co-pilot seats, shaking their heads while smiling. Grammy got up and checked her and Josh's weapons one last time before they landed. Once she was satisfied, she checked one last time that her cane was fully loaded and fully operational. Grammy's cane was not unlike a loaded gun, and it fired bullets just as effectively. It was always her main weapon.

As they neared their destination, Josh scanned the ground for movement and signs of life. Several people were out walking the street, going about their business. It was Saturday, and there was a market nearby that sold fresh fruits and vegetables. Most people stocked up at the market every Saturday, and today appeared to be no different. The number of people walking casually was a good sign. Though there was no sign of danger, they kept their guard up. The aliens had only attacked a small number of people, but enemies were often known to become more aggressive over time. They were taking no chances.

"The bark is becoming close…as does the tree," Josh spoke to Dagny.

"What's the music like at the hop?" she responded.

"The crowd is plentiful. Looks like a good turn out, and everyone is shining."

"Roger to the shining. Enjoy the stage and come on back, ya'll." There was tension in her voice, but she was trying to be positive. Chuck and Farley began to tense up, and their facial expressions became serious. Things appeared to be safe and normal, but that still didn't mean aliens weren't lurking in Dagny's house, waiting to lash out with their lightning-speed, snake-like tongues.

"Come on, get up, you weirdo," Farley said, climbing to his feet.

The boys consulted the map of Dagny's house and went over their plan of entry one last time. Grammy inspected the trolley that carried the "gardening equipment" and said, "You're sure you know how to activate this stuff if you need to?"

"Yup, we're good, Grammy," Chuck assured her.

"Yo, D. Can you hear me in stereo?" Farley spoke into the communicator clipped to the inside of his jacket collar.

"Roger on the stereo, and the music is sweet."

"Let's jiggy," Farley said.

Josh gently and deftly landed the ship in Dagny's driveway. Grammy gave the boys good luck hugs. They wheeled the trolley down the ramp as it lowered, casually glancing around the area and up to the front door where Farley keyed the pass code to enter the house. It worked, which gave them comfort, either false or real. They would soon find out.

"Rock and roll," Farley said to Chuck.

"Rock and roll, buddy."

Farley quickly heaved the trolley into the house, and Chuck closed the door behind them. The house was dark and quiet. They perked up their ears, listening for intruders to give themselves away. Everything seemed clear, so they parted ways. Farley moved the trolley into the center of the main level where the living room met the kitchen and left it there before soundlessly taking the stairs up three at a time. Chuck watched him dash upstairs and shook his head in amazement. Months ago, Farley would have sounded like an elephant falling down those stairs. Now, he was like a ninja.

Chuck peeked through the curtain and saw Grammy demonstrating the power of the hover-cleaning supplies they were "selling" to a couple who seemed duly impressed. She glanced his way, and he made a circle with his thumb and forefinger, indicating things were okay inside. She gave a slight nod of acknowledgement. He cocked his cane and moved toward where he pictured the basement door to be from the map Dagny had drawn them. The light on the end of his cane flashed across something on the floor, and he focused the glow on it for a better look. It was blood, the blood that had been spilled by the aliens a mere week or so ago. The blood that made their search necessary and put fear in their hearts as the owner remained unidentified.

It was dried up and appeared dark brown against the cream-colored carpet, almost as though someone had spilled a Coca-Cola. Chuck respectfully stepped around it and through the basement door. When he reached the bottom, it was exactly as Dagny had said, just a few boxes pushed against the far wall. Exploring the basement would only take moments. He pulled the boxes away from the wall to be thorough, and deciding that there was nothing hiding or unexpected, he went back up to the main level.

"Far, can you hear me?" Chuck whispered.

"Yes. Anything?"

"Nope. Bottom is glorious and checkin' out the sound at the main hopster."

"Yo, D. Did you catch that?" Farley asked.

"Roger on the glorious bottom, and hopster is in check. Yo, yo, yo," Dagny replied.

"Yo," Chuck said in a low voice, as he heard Grammy say in a loud voice just outside the door, "This is a restricted area. Do not take another step!"

Then there was a sharp knock at the door.

Chapter 8

Bross changed into the red and black silky outfit he had just been
given and wondered why he was being treated so well, considering
he had been stolen and locked up. The food was scrumptious, he had fresh
clothes at least twice a day, and the room was somehow always spotless
despite his efforts to mess up the bathroom. He would smear soap on the
mirror using his fingers to write nasty messages to his captors and the next
time he checked, the mirror would be clean as new. He expected that his
messages would have negative repercussions or send an angry person his
way, but his threatening messages had no effect.

And he had seen that red arm as his clothes were passed through the
slot. He now knew who had him and was floored by the discovery. He
had heard about the aliens and every account except one indicated that
the aliens were killing humans. He didn't know why he had been "saved."
Maybe they're going to probe me, he thought grimly. He was terrified of
being probed or cut open and dreaded that he would be fully awake while
it happened. Bross blinked several times quickly to keep the tears at bay.

When Bross had pushed his emotions back down, hardening his
heart, his throat suddenly felt as though it was heating up, and his ears
became itchy. *Great time to get a cold.* He walked the ten memorized paces

to the bathroom with his eyes closed against the blinding lights to get some tissue for his nose, which had begun to drip. When the lightheadedness overtook him, he thought he was coming down with more than just a cold and wished he could have a hot tea. Just like that, Bross heard the slot open and went to see what he had been given, hoping for medicine. A hot tea presented itself. *Now they're reading my mind.*

He brought the tea to the couch, sat down, and enjoyed it. This treatment was so incongruent with the alien behavior they had heard about on the news. Bross, deep in thought, could come up with no explanation for it. He breathed deeply, and then more and more deeply, until his need for air dragged him from his reverie. He opened his mouth and took a huge breath, sucking in the air until no more would squeeze into his lungs, and it still didn't feel like he was getting enough. He threw what remained of his tea—cup and all—across the room, thinking he had been drugged. He had hoped for medicine, not the feeling that he was being strangled by a lack of oxygen.

Bross got up off the couch and almost fell to the floor. Despite feeling drained of all his energy, he crawled along the floor to the slot and pounded on it. He couldn't speak and was beginning to panic. Shielding his eyes with his shirt, he opened them slightly and realized that the brightness of the room had been replaced with a hazy, scentless, foggy substance. His eyes shot open wide, and his panic worsened. *They're suffocating me,* he thought in a panic.

Bross clawed at the slot, trying to open it. He was desperate to fill his lungs, yet his mind raced, wondering why the aliens bothered to keep him so comfortable (aside from his pinched eyes) only to kill him in such a way. His strength drained rapidly, and he was no longer able to work at breaking through the slot. Just then, a regular-sized door opened, one that he didn't even know existed, and a woman was shoved through. The door slammed behind her as a voice said, "You know what you're supposed to do. Do it."

Chapter 9

"This is Rod Walken reporting for Planet Talks. Funeral services for Nathan Castle occurred yesterday amid a small group of close family and friends at an undisclosed location. Others lost were also remembered and their lives appreciated. Beautiful holographic images of Nathan graced the room we are told, and his favorite band also performed in ten-definition holographic mode."

Nathan's photo flashed on the screen for a full minute, honoring his life while Rod sat motionless in the background. His black hair was slicked back in its usual style, and his peacock blue tie had Nathan's face embroidered into it. Rod had just won Anchor of the Year and was intent on keeping that title by manipulating the viewers with his fake displays of connectedness to "his public."

"After the turmoil and emotional times we have had these past few months, I regret deeply that I have other bad news to pass on to you, my friends. The bodies of Luke and Leila Reynolds have been discovered, intact, which is shocking as it is not the usual modus operandi of the aliens. We are unsure what to make of it, and police are conducting a full investigation. The bodies don't appear to be damaged in any way, and in fact, are smiling. If it is someone's idea of a joke, it is a sick one. Police are asking for any information from the public—anything anyone may have seen or heard, last known whereabouts of Luke and Leila, or where they were headed."

Rod Walken adjusted his Nathan-adorned tie and cleared his throat.

"At this time, the police department is not releasing details of where the bodies were found or who found them so as not to compromise the investigation. Here is a picture of them with their daughter, Dagny, taken about a year ago. Dagny has been notified, and the people close to her are asking that you respect her privacy in this sad and devastating time for her. If this is the work of the aliens, their message is obscure, and we can only surmise that they are mocking us, telling us they can do with us what they want, telling us that we are indispensable."

The camera zoomed in on Rod's face.

"Such death and destruction in our worlds, after decades upon decades of peace and harmony is incomprehensible, and yet here we are. What is it all coming to? When will it end? Will we ever be able to return to the times of playfulness and tranquility? I am afraid I cannot answer these questions. In other but related news, Castle Enterprises has analyzed all video recordings available of the alien attacks in Newfoundland, as well as the tissue samples of an alien they killed. They have concluded that the aliens are, in fact, eating humans. We are food. I am just as stunned by this knowledge as I am sure you all are, and I need some time to absorb it. This information raises so many questions; it's hard to determine where to begin in seeking answers."

Rod shuddered and held his arms around himself protectively, for effect.

"Are they eating us because they've run out of food wherever they are from? Are they eating us because they are malevolent and that's simply the way they kill? If we are food to them, why have they taken some people away with them instead of eating them on the spot like they have most of the time? Remember the Wright family and others who had been reportedly 'mesmerized' into following aliens onto their ships? We may never know what happened to them. That is a whole other series of unanswerable questions and makes me very anxious at the thought of what is being done to them. The mind reels. Clothing clearly does not offer us protection against the violent lashes of the aliens' tongues. Analysts with Castle Enterprises continue working with the tissue samples, hoping to find something to make humans repulse the aliens and send them away from our beautiful planet. We wish them all the luck there is."

Rod paused dramatically, running a hand through his hair.

"Reporting for Planet Talks, I'm Rod Walken, bringing you the news the second I get it. Good night, friends."

Chapter 10

They waited as patiently as they could, trying not to squabble with each other. Troy braided his long, gray beard in fourteen braids—fourteen being his favorite number. Sulinda busied herself by ripping the hem from her sundress and twisting it into a band she wrapped around her hat; she fancied herself a fashion designer. Sparrow stretched out on the blanket, enjoying the hot sun beating down on her. Her eyes were closed, and she wore a content smile as she hummed to herself.

Maywano held his robes up around his waist, displaying the matching shorts he wore underneath as he danced his way back to his group. He beamed at the three staring intently at him, waiting for his decision. And waiting. And when it seemed like he would never speak, Troy said, "Out with it. What are we doing?"

"We will help the humans," Maywano exclaimed triumphantly. He then spun and spun. His robes flew out at the waist like a skirt. Troy and Sulinda groaned with disapproval.

"We'll meet our death!" Sulinda cried.

"That's it for us. Why'd we even bother escaping the aliens if you just want to kill us anyway?" Troy stepped toward Maywano and grabbed him roughly by the shoulders.

"Hey, hey, now. Let him go!" Sparrow jumped to her feet and attempted to pull Maywano free from Troy's grip.

"Always so quick to jump to conclusions," Maywano said, no longer spinning but still doing a little dance with his feet on the spot. "We are not taking up the fight. We will not go after the aliens. We will help insomuch as they want us to and insofar as we are able…*with information.*" Maywano had a flair for drama and spread his arms wide as he said those last two words.

"What does that mean? 'With information.' You need to give *us* more information. And I say that respectfully, Maywano." Sulinda was frustrated but didn't want to overstep her place in the hierarchy. She had taken off her hat and was wringing it with her hands as though it was soaked with water.

"Well—and I think you will all agree with me—we are a superior race despite our current situation, and it is incumbent upon the stronger to assist the weaker. That's just the way it is. But seeing as we are only four, we cannot physically fight. We do not have the means. We are smarter than the humans and can offer to them, for a fair price, everything we know about the aliens. Maybe they will have better results against them than we did. Not helping could mean that sooner or later, their species, too, will be all but wiped out, as are we. Where does it end?" Maywano looked each one in the eyes until he saw acceptance.

"What's the price?" Sparrow asked, breaking the uncomfortable silence.

"We need a home. I think this should be it. Most of this planet is uninhabited. Aside from Troy disliking the food, I believe we can make it work."

Maywano acknowledged nods from Sulinda and Sparrow before turning to the always hesitant Troy.

"Troy, do you have any better ideas?"

"I've said it from the start that I think we need to find others of our kind to strengthen our numbers. Staying here does not accomplish that. We came here looking for our people, and it's obvious none of them are here. I say we leave and keep looking." Troy sounded confident, but he was blinking quickly; he didn't agree with Maywano but felt awkward expressing his conflicting views to their leader after laying hands on him.

"I see, and you do make a point. However, for how long do we search? We can send encrypted messages into space from here, and if there are more of us out there, they'll recognize and locate our beacon," Maywano said reasonably.

"Sulinda, what do you think?" Troy sought a partner.

"Well," she replied uncertainly, "I guess we could try that. We should give it a month or a specific time period before we move on. I don't know that staying here indefinitely is the best idea. We could have people out there who need our help and are unable to respond to our signals."

"That's right!" exclaimed Troy.

"You make a valid point as well, Sulinda. It's settled then. We will stay here for six months incognito, subtly advising the humans by way of dropping hints during casual conversation. I think it is prudent to try to pass as humans ourselves for protection. We don't want the aliens catching on to us or for the humans to inadvertently expose our existence. The aliens don't take kindly to failure, and if they learn that some of us are still alive, they will be ruthless in their hunt."

Sparrow jumped up and down clapping her hands and yelping in delight like a puppy while Sulinda and Troy groaned at the thought of their lengthy stay in Earthling territory.

"I'm going back to the ship to work on our signal. If you need me in the next six months, that's where you'll find me," Troy said bitterly, stomping off.

"What's our first step?" Sulinda asked. The tone of defeat weighed her words down.

"Well, we've just eaten and six months is not a long time at all, so I think we get started. Troy is okay to stay here and attempt contact with other survivors and, frankly," Maywano said, "I think the less interaction

I have with him, the better. He can fly us over to the habited side of the planet and drop us off."

"Let's go!" Sparrow gathered up their blanket and basket and ran to the ship with Maywano dancing along behind her and Sulinda bringing up the rear, dragging her feet and her hat.

Chapter 11

They huddled in a corner, Mike's arm around Lexi's shoulders and Gaz with his head between his knees. Mike knew Lexi was on the verge of a panic attack, and he tried to soothe her as best as he could. Mike was a bully and usually preyed on anyone he considered to be weak, but he genuinely loved Lexi and wanted to protect her. Gaz hadn't spoken since that morning, and that was only to blame Mike for their predicament. "This is your fault. Why you wanted to go with the aliens is beyond me. They'll only kill us too," Gaz had said with venom in his voice. It had surprised Mike because Gaz had always known his place and had never spoken to Mike in that manner. Under normal circumstances, Mike would have laid a beating on Gaz to put him back in his place, but Mike was willing to let it go—at least for the time being. Mike sensed that Gaz no longer feared him and would only put up with it for so long. Lexi did little more than stare ahead and eat whenever the aliens brought them food.

Mike, on the other hand, was in his glory. He was in love with the aliens and was quite at home with them. He marveled at everything on their ship and was convinced that he and the alien leader had become as close as best friends. He whole-heartedly believed that he would have a place in their ranks sooner than later. All he had to do was find Chuck and Farley. It would be easy, he had told the aliens with a smile. He had hoped he looked convincing and not patronizing. Mike had a hard time not being an arrogant, controlling know-it-all but knew enough to not overstep his bounds. As quick as the lashing tongues of the aliens were, so were their hands. The smile was erased from Mike's face with one sharp smack. His face had immediately begun to burn as the aliens' skin was toxic to humans, but he had been just as quickly given an ointment to repair the burn. Mike learned respect all in that one instant and kept the pain and humiliation of that violent act against him in the forefront of his mind when interacting with the aliens.

It had been over a week since the aliens had snatched Mike, Lexi, and Gaz from Dagny's house, and Mike was beginning to squirm. He hadn't been able to deliver the boys and had begun to worry over how much time he had left. It was hard to admit that he had failed, and his hatred for Chuck and Farley grew deeper. He didn't think it would be possible, but for two losers to evade him so successfully made him see black. He knew he had to think of something quick or his perceived high-standing among the aliens would falter, and next time he might not receive just a simple slap across the face.

They had maintained constant surveillance of Chuck and Farley's homes, but unbeknownst to Mike, Chuck's mom was on Eris and Farley's parents had left town the day the aliens at first attacked. Neither home would be occupied until the aliens had been obliterated. School was closed for the summer, but they searched it every few days in case the boys holed up there to hide. Mike reiterated to his new friend whom he called "Chief" that Chuck and Farley were stupid and would show their faces at any time. Frequent visits to the comic store, coffee house, and Nathan's father's home and office proved fruitless.

"Chief, what about Chuck's grandmother? I think she lives in Newfoundland. We should check that out." Mike thought he'd finally come up with a good idea.

"You are useless. It was an error on my part to bring you with us," Chief responded coldly.

"Wha...wha...what do you mean?" Mike stuttered.

"It was reported all over your planet that we attacked that place and blew it all up. You wish to serve us, and yet you did not even follow our movements reported in your news. Imbecile."

"Please, things are going so well between us. I feel I was meant to be with you and your kind. I will deliver. You'll see. I know I can find them. Just give me more time. And, very respectfully, you also have not been able to find them." Mike paused after that last sentence long enough to confirm he was still alive before continuing. "I've been thinking about it, and we should probably look farther away."

"Obviously," Chief said icily.

"I don't mean searching their hangouts locally or anything like that. I mean leaving Earth. I used to see Farley getting on the interplanetary shuttle, which only goes to Eris. Maybe we should go there and search. They really aren't that bright, and if they were still on Earth, I have no doubt that we would have found them by now." Mike stood straighter and taller, regaining some confidence at his new idea.

Chief slowly licked his thin, red lips, the warning apparent. "Do you hope you are right?"

Mike couldn't move his eyes from the snake-like tongue and stammered, "Y...y...yesssss."

"Good."

Chapter 12

C huck froze in his tracks as Farley moved stealthily down the stairs. Farley held up a hand, holding Chuck to his spot, and approached the front door with his weapon trained on it. Chuck motioned upstairs. His eyes widened questioningly. Farley gave the "okay" sign with his thumb and forefinger, indicating that all was clear on the upper level. They had only to check the backyard when there was a sudden knock on the door, which meant that someone had been somehow, unbelievably, able to get past Grammy and Josh.

Chuck whispered into the communicator pinned to his collar. "Grammy, what's going on out there?"

She didn't answer, but he could hear her yelling at someone. "I'm warning you. Step away from that door and move on!" Chuck and Farley both strained but heard no one respond to her.

"Grammy!" Chuck whispered more urgently. "Josh! Where are you? What's happening out there?"

Chuck moved to the window and peeked out, seeing only Grammy in a combat stance pointing her cane at someone he couldn't see. Farley tiptoed to the front door and pressed his ear against it. He could hear only Grammy as well.

"Josh! Someone answer me!" Chuck raised his voice, no longer caring who heard him.

Grammy suddenly began firing. Chuck and Farley heard three quick shots and were ready for anything. They had all agreed beforehand that if anything was going down, they would await instructions from Grammy or Josh before they stepped in. Chuck joined Farley at the door and put his hand on the door knob, ready to whip it open. Farley, being the better shot, was ready to fire when needed.

"Blow the door!" Grammy shrilled. Chuck jumped back from the door so quickly, he would have knocked Farley over if Farley hadn't also leaped at the same time.

"Chuck, move!" Farley yelled. While Chuck ran to the couch and pushed it away from the wall, creating a barrier to hide behind, Farley pushed the trolley into the kitchen, well away from the front door. He grabbed two of the canisters from the trolley and ran back to the living room. From what he hoped was a safe position behind the couch, he twisted off the lid from one of the canisters and yelled, "Fire in the hole!" Farley whipped the canister at the door. He and Chuck spread themselves flat on the ground behind the couch, convinced they were about to die.

They could hear Dagny screaming in their ear pieces as the door exploded. The sound was deafening, and bits of wood bounced off the walls and ceiling. Some of it was aflame. A burning chunk of door landed on Farley's back. He quickly rolled to his side, and it fell off. Chuck used a pillow to brush Farley's back, ensuring he wasn't going to catch on fire. The two young men stood up and aimed their weapons at the blown opening, scared of what they might see. Neither of them expected to be fighting with the aliens again so soon after the mountain battle, but they did feel more prepared. At least they had had time to plan the search of Dagny's house and what they would do if attacked.

"Farley! Chuck! Are you there?" Dagny's voice pierced their ear drums.

"Dagny! We're okay. I have no idea what just happened, but we blew the door wide open."

The guys moved slowly toward the opening when they heard Josh near the blast-hole call, "Clear!"

Grammy rushed in poking and prodding Chuck first and then Farley. "Are you hurt? You're both okay?" Chuck and Farley nodded. "Well, we suspected this wouldn't be an in and out sort of job." Grammy looked at Josh, "Report?"

"That was Henry Wright. About six months ago, he and his wife and two kids were reported missing, assumed taken by the aliens. They've never been found, but I guess we know now what happened to them. He was under some sort of spell. Rod Walken often reported that people had seen others being led onto alien ships in a trance. I guess it's safe to say that maybe some of the others are still alive, although who knows in what state? Henry had obviously been controlled somehow, and if he was here, that means the aliens might be onto us." Josh held his weapon at the ready as his eyes darted back and forth, searching for more unwelcome surprises.

"We need to get out of here fast in case they're on their way. There's no way we can protect all the people out walking around today. Some of them are already watching us, curious about the explosion. Castle is sending some of his people to cordon off the area, and he's alerted Rod Walken to report that the aliens are to blame. Chuck and Farley—did you find anything to indicate where Dagny's parents are?" Grammy asked.

"Dagny," Farley said with sadness in his voice, "I'm sorry. We didn't find anything. But we'll keep looking," he continued fervently. "Maybe the false report we released about them being found dead will slip up the aliens and lead us to them. Or maybe those idiots, Mike and Gaz, will make a mistake and point the way. Wherever they are, they're with your parents."

They heard Dagny crying softly. Then she said, "I can never go home again, can I?"

"Don't think like that, dear. We aren't done-for yet. If Henry Wright just came back and we haven't found any indication whatsoever that your parents were killed, then we have every reason to believe that they were taken away like others were. Let's not despair yet." Grammy spoke soothingly as she motioned for Chuck and Farley to board their ship.

"But that means that they've probably," Dagny paused for a few seconds, "*changed* my parents too. What if the aliens keep them forever? What if they do come back but they don't know me or…or…*or they try to kill me?!*" Dagny was beginning to go off the deep end.

"Sparks? Are you there?" Josh asked.

Chuck looked at Farley and could see he didn't know what to say to Dagny. He was staring at Chuck desperately, but Chuck only shrugged his shoulders also not knowing what to say or do. Chuck turned away, feeling inadequate, and focused on securing the remaining explosive canisters.

"I'm here," responded Sparks. "What do you need?"

While preparing for takeoff, Josh said, "We have a Dagny situation, and she needs your help. Can you get her a sedative for now and arrange for her to talk to a specialist? She's not handling the disappearance of her parents very well, and I fear she'll be useless to us in this fight if we don't address her mental state now."

"She'll be well-cared-for, Josh. See you when you get back," Sparks said competently.

"Thanks, Sparks. Can you also compile a list of the people who have gone missing over the last six months? The aliens seem to be using them as pawns against us." Josh turned to the rest of the crew. "Are you ready for takeoff?" He heard three "yes's" and lifted the ship skyward.

"Yes, this could be a tricky situation. We need to be aware of who else may be after us under the aliens' influence," Grammy piped in. "We need names, descriptions, and pictures of each and every missing person. The more organized and prepared we are, the better chance we have of not needing to kill another one. Dagny, if your parents are under some kind of mind control, we'll find a way to snap them out of it. Trust me."

"Thank you, Grammy," Dagny said quietly. "Sparks is here. I'm signing off."

"Full radars have been initiated, so if we're being followed, we'll know about it immediately," Josh advised as they broke Earth's atmosphere and headed for Eris.

And not a split second later, an alarm sounded in the cockpit.

"What's that??" Chuck shrieked. If he hadn't been belted in, he would have reflexively jumped right out of his seat. Farley uttered a small cry of surprise at the sudden, unexpected wail of the alarm.

"Oh, great. What do we have now, Josh?" Grammy asked, scanning the dashboard full of multi-colored lights and dials.

"We have a fully-functioning system and the perfect sign that our radars are working," Josh replied. "Is everyone ready?"

"Ready? Ready for what?!" Chuck turned to Farley and began screaming and clawing at his seat belt.

Farley wailed, "He didn't drink the damn Calmalot!" Farley smacked Chuck hard across the face. Chuck continued screeching.

"Smack him again!" Grammy shouted.

Farley whipped his head around, completely astonished, but smacked the woman's grandson again. Unbuckling his own belt, he moved behind Chuck and grabbed him tightly around the neck. He squeezed until Chuck fainted. "Damn, damn, damn! We can't forget to make him drink that stuff ever again. I know he did it on purpose too. He says it tastes like bunghole."

Josh began turning the ship around as though heading back to Earth with the ship's alarms still sounding at full volume. "Tower one, this is tower two. Do you read?"

Sparks responded. "Dagny is resting, and she'll be fine."

"Good. Thank you, Sparks. We may have another guest hoping to be invited to the shindig. I'm responding to their request." Josh dipped the ship sharply, Earth hovering in front of them, and then dodged to the right, away from Earth and in the opposite direction of Eris.

Their pursuer followed.

"I can't believe they're onto us already. And they're not even trying to hide it!" Farley yelled incredulously. "What kind of ship is that anyway?"

"Looks just like one of ours. We can't rule out that it may be more of the missing people. The aliens are proving to be quite crafty." Grammy was busy expertly activating the ship's weapons. Farley marveled at how little they still knew about the lady.

Farley grabbed a pail and stuck it between Chuck's legs. "What do you need me to do?" he asked.

Josh did an about-face, turning the ship once more toward Eris. They were still being tailed.

"We should save the ship's weapons if we can, so get the explosive canisters from the closet," Grammy replied.

"What are we going to do, blow ourselves up and hope to take them with us?"

"Preferably not," Grammy said. "Get them and take them to the rear of the ship and wait for my instructions."

They had initiated cosmic speed in an attempt to get away. In no time, they had passed Mars, and on-screen, Farley could see Jupiter in the distance.

Farley's eyes widened in fear, but he did as he was told. He hated to admit to himself that he felt unnerved leaving the cockpit. He felt as though, should anything bad happen, he'd die. Alone. In space. He looked inside the closet and saw four white canisters that resembled fire extinguishers. He grabbed two of them and made his way to the end of the ship farthest away from his best friend, who was sleeping peacefully for a few more minutes before the need to vomit awoke him. He was going to die and Dagny was sedated millions of miles away; he couldn't tell her he loved her. He would never hear her say it back to him.

"Farley, where are you?" he heard Grammy ask.

"I'm at the back of the ship. What do you need me to do?"

"Just hold your position. The other ship has got some power, and it's caught up to us. There's no doubt we're being followed. Just trying to determine by whom. We don't want to be hasty if they're friendlies."

"Okay."

Sparks replied to Josh. "Roger. The party is full. Tell them maybe next time."

"Roger that," Josh replied.

Farley waited for almost a whole eternity before being poked in the back. He jumped and a frightened sound from deep in his gut escaped.

Chuck put down two more canisters and said, "Sorry, man. This is crazy. When does it stop?"

"You better now?"

"Yeah."

"Good. Next time drink the damn Calmalot. Fine time you picked to freak out."

"I know. I know. It won't happen again."

"Did they tell you what to do?" Farley asked.

"No, just to bring more explosives and hang tight with you."

"Chuck and Farley, are you ready?" Grammy's voice was loud and clear over the speaker system.

"Uh, yes?" Chuck asked uncertainly.

"See the hatch?" Grammy asked.

Farley and Chuck looked at each other questioningly. "You want us to go through it??" Chuck asked, nearing a panic state again.

"Goodness, no! You watch too many movies. It's got two doors—one where you are and one on the outer side of the ship. Open it and put all the canisters inside. Then close it up again. Make sure you close it properly or we'll all be blown to smithereens."

Chuck found the lever for the hatch and began to turn it. He expected it to be tight, but it moved easily, as though it had been recently greased up. Once it was turned as far as it would go, Farley pulled the hatch door open and slid the canisters inside. The hatchway was slanted downward and the canisters slid gently, clanging metal on metal to the far end to Farley's relief. He quickly closed the door and nodded at Chuck. Chuck turned the lever in the opposite direction as tight as he could and nodded back at Farley. Farley pulled on the hatch door and couldn't budge it.

"The package is on the chop chop, and the party is sealed tight," Farley said.

"You don't need to talk code on the ship, but we get your meaning. Good work, boys," Grammy said.

Both boys breathed a deep sigh of relief and shook their bodies, starting with their heads and working their way down as Yu had taught them to release stress. Chuck and Farley had both been wound tight, scared by the thought of a canister exploding on the ship right in their faces. Chuck bent over at the waist and let his arms hang loosely while he shook out the tension before suddenly standing at attention. He lightly patted his hands on his hair.

Farley stared at him.

"What?" Chuck asked, careful not to move his head.

"I know what you just did."

"I don't know what you're talking about, but I feel much looser. You should try it. Just let your arms hang."

"Yeah, I know that's the best way to get the most oomph behind your hair flicking. That feathered-hair look is not in style anymore. It's so high school, and you're livin' in the past. Since you're not gonna stop doing that, I'll assume you no longer want to be cool like me," Farley said with a high-and-mighty tone.

"Cool with that rat's tail hanging off one side of your face?" Chuck swatted at Farley's face and then doubled up with laughter.

"Damn! I forgot I still had it on!" Farley laughed too, and with a quick yank and a short yelp, he pulled it off. "Where's yours?"

"I guess I lost it when I did a face-plant behind the couch back at Dagny's."

"Too bad it didn't improve your face," Farley said, rubbing the spot above his lip where the mustache held on so tightly.

Josh continued his evasive maneuvering, and he and Grammy smiled, listening to the boys' banter. Josh's smile quickly disappeared, however. "Here we go! That ship is definitely not friendly, and we haven't been able to determine who's on it. They've got our position locked, and I can no longer evade!"

"Chuck! You need to find the release pulley beside the lever you turned. Do it now!! Pull it!!"

Chuck scrambled to the lever and searched the wall for the release. Farley joined him, also searching.

"There's a metal ring. Is that it??" Chuck yelled frantically.

"That's it! Pull!!" Grammy and Josh shrieked in unison.

Chuck and Farley looked at each other, gave a quick hug, and then squeezing his eyes tight and looking away from that metal ring, Chuck jerked hard. The ring came out in his hand, and he stood there waiting for something to happen.

"What are you doing? Pull the damn ring!" Grammy was almost hysterical.

"I did! I did!"

Farley glanced at the pulley. The ring was indeed missing, but the rod it was attached to was still in place in the wall. Farley pulled on it, but there was just the tiniest loop and his big fingers couldn't grasp it. Chuck looked at the ring stupidly, unable to comprehend what had just happened but then realized the ring wasn't the important part—it was the rod that Farley was clawing at. Chuck tried to reattach the ring but he was so frantic his fingers were shaking. He was fumbling too much. Wasting no more time on the ring, he tossed it to the ground.

"The ring has broken off! Wait! Just give me one minute!" Chuck shrieked, his long, blond hair flying out behind him. He leaped to the opposite wall where there was an ax and smashed the window with his elbow to remove it. Grabbing it with both hands he hurriedly moved back to the wall with the pulley. Eyeing it steadily and with his greatest force, he took a swing and connected on the very edge of the pulley. He made a slight dent, but it wasn't enough. He aimed and swung again. And again. He wildly swung the ax over and over, losing confidence in what he was trying to do.

Josh stared at the image on-screen and watched as the other ship fired upon them. It would be mere moments before impact if the boys were unable to eject the canisters. "Grammy, we're going to have to fire back. I don't think we can outrun their weapons, and we have no idea how many they have." Josh's voice was steady, but she could see the underlying tension in his grip on the controls.

"We only have two. If we miss, we're done for. Let's give the boys another minute to do whatever it is they're doing. If they can release the canisters, that's our best bet. You're doing a fine job, Josh, and we'll get out of this. We always do," Grammy said encouragingly. "Chuck? How are you doing back there? Farley? Any updates?" She spoke calmly, not wanting to stress them out any more than they already were.

Farley answered. "Almost. One more hit should do it."

"Hit? What does that mean?" she asked. "You can't hit the pulley; you have to pull it. It's a *pulley*, not a *hittey*."

No one bothered to respond to the bad joke.

"One more, Chuck, you can do it. Aim in the same spot. You got this, buddy."

Chuck closed his eyes, took a deep breath, felt the weight of the ax in his hands and the power behind each swing and imagined all the energy on the ship being channeled for one last purpose.

He slowly opened his eyes, looked at Farley, who gave him a slight nod, and swung with all his might, true and strong. He connected and the metal wall surrounding the rod buckled away from the rod. Farley, fast as a bullet, snatched the rod from its place. They heard a whoosh sound from the far end of the hatch.

"We did it! The hatch is open!" Chuck jumped up and down, unable to contain himself.

"Woo hoo! Yes!" Farley yelled, bouncing up and down the hallway.

"Now, Josh. Blow it up now!" Grammy commanded.

Josh and Grammy unblinkingly stared at the monitor and watched the canisters floating in the dark behind them, the enemy ship in the distance. Josh plotted his weapon's trajectory, aimed at their deadly life-savers, and fired as Chuck and Farley ran into the cockpit.

"Boys, strap yourselves in; this could be rough," Grammy instructed. They obliged.

Chapter 13

Mr. Castle sat in his office, wearing a peach-colored robe. A cup of black coffee laced with a shot of scotch was cradled in his hand. He took small sips as he looked at, but didn't really see, the contents saved from Nathan's ship before it had melted away. The aliens had killed his son and then had killed his son's ship for good measure, unintentionally or not. Yu had been piloting it, trying to save everyone when they were on Earth the day Nathan's young life was taken. He had succeeded in blowing up the alien ship, but it had burst into burning, swampy pieces all over Nathan's ship, melting it so quickly that it was unstoppable and unsalvageable.

Chuck and Farley and a couple of the others there that day had rescued as much of Nathan's belongings on the ship as they were able, and those items covered Mr. Castle's desk. He felt it was time to go through them, as hard as that may be, and tried to take solace in the idea that he would have more mementos of his son.

He picked up the first item and put it on his head. It fit perfectly, and he thought it would be divine to wear it every day for the rest of his days. It was a black-and-white-checkered ball cap Nathan had bought at the hover races the year before with a picture of his favorite racer on it—Trippy Stevens. Mr. Castle recalled that Trippy came in last place last year, but

Nathan's loyalty never wavered. Maybe, one day, he would take Chuck and Farley to the race. He thought they would enjoy it.

Mr. Castle picked up the next item, the owner's manual for the ship. The ship no longer existed, so he didn't see much point in keeping it. Into the trash can it went.

Nathan's portable holograph device was also saved. Mr. Castle turned it on and played the last song Nathan had listened to. Grimy Toes came on singing "Skull Crush Skull Mend," and Mr. Castle put it at full volume. He pushed the desk against one of the walls to make room for the holographic image in the middle of the floor. The four band members wailed away on their instruments while the singer screamed into his microphone. Mr. Castle danced circles around the band trying to do the same moves he had seen Nathan do. Catching sight of his reflection in the glass of a cabinet, he laughed out loud. He looked insane bouncing in a peach robe with a ball cap suitable for young, exciting men, not a middle-aged man such as himself. He danced anyway.

The song ended, and Mr. Castle stood at the desk, looking at the remaining items. Picking up Nathan's red jacket, he thought it would be too small for Chuck or Farley to wear but that it might fit Karona. He went through the pockets and found two pictures, one of Nathan with Chuck and Farley and the other was of Nathan's mother when she was pregnant with him.

Mr. Castle choked back a sob. He had no idea that Nathan had carried the photo around with him. Nathan's mother, Maggie, was seated by a window, the sun dancing on her waist-length, dark brown hair. Her head was thrown back in laughter, and Mr. Castle remembered how sweet the sound of her giggles had been to him. He remembered taking the picture; it was only a month before Nathan was born, and they had no idea that it would be the last time they ever were to dine at her favorite restaurant. It was their sixth anniversary, and she'd been wearing a new, blue dress. She had been laughing at how big the maternity dress was and how she could have it made into two or three dresses once she'd given birth. Mr. Castle had kept that dress hanging in her closet, and though he smiled, he wiped a tear away as he savored the memory of their last night out for a fancy dinner. He kissed the image of his dear, departed wife and put the photo in the pocket of his robe.

He looked at the other photo and decided the boys were around ten or eleven when it had been taken. He made a mental note to have copies made so he could give one to Chuck and one to Farley. Nathan was standing in the middle separating his friends who had been horsing around just moments before. Chuck had his tongue stuck out at Farley, and Farley was reaching around Nathan grabbing at it. *Oh to be young and free again*, he thought. Those were certainly simpler times.

There were other items of clothing that Mr. Castle would give away at some point and Nathan's laser gun for playing laser tag that he would give to Josh, but that was all they had been able to salvage. He was thankful that Nathan didn't live on the ship because there wasn't much stuff saved. At least his son had still lived with him, so Mr. Castle had a house full of mementos of him.

Mr. Castle decided it was time to shower and get dressed. He had much work to do. Sitting around drinking coffee laced with scotch would result in another drunken waste of a day. Walking toward the door to leave the office, he caught sight of the ship's owner's manual he had discarded. Though he had dismissed it as useless earlier, he now wondered why the boys would have felt the need to rescue it. He pulled it from the trash can and leafing through it, discovered pages and pages of notes. His son had written more notes in the book than what had actually been printed in the book by the manufacturer. Nathan had always been conscientious, but those notes included mathematical calculations, instructions on how to trace calls and track people, super easy instructions on how to operate the ship, and on and on.

Mr. Castle was stupefied; this was a side of his son he did not know. He read further and discovered Nathan had somehow boosted the power to his engines—something he should not have been able to do on an entry level ship—and managed to cut the travel time from Eris to Earth in half. Mr. Castle pondered this and came up with no reason why Nathan wouldn't have shared the fact he possessed such skills with his father. He had always wondered how Nathan and his friends had gotten to Gros Morne before him and Josh on that fateful day, and now he had the answer. Nathan had traced Grammy's call that day, despite all the security and scrambling systems they had had in place, and his ship was twice as fast as it should have been. Nathan's own brilliance had played a part in his death. Before Mr. Castle began tearing up again, he shook his head violently, warding off another slump of depression, and read on.

Nathan's handwriting was neat and structured, not messy or hastily written. To Mr. Castle, this meant his son wasn't hurriedly trying to get something down on paper before he forgot it. He already had it in his head; he *knew* the things he was filling the pages with and merely wanted to pass the information on to others. Everything was written clearly and was accompanied with drawings where needed so that almost anyone would understand and be able to follow along. He would read more after his shower, he decided. He left the rest of Nathan's belongings on the desk but took the book with him.

Yu was rushing down the hall toward Mr. Castle when he stepped out from the office.

"Mr. Castle, we have a situation."

"Of course we do."

Chapter 14

An intermittent beeping sound marked the progress of the ship they were monitoring, becoming quicker as it neared its target. They sat in darkness, watching as the two ships danced in space, one mirroring the other's movements. It was evident the lead ship knew it was being followed. It was also evident the lead ship knew it could not lose the follower. The lead ship almost seemed to slow, surrendering. The watchers hoped they'd see a white flag extend from the stern of the ship before it went up in flames.

There were three of them. Their bulbous red heads were as motionless as their expressionless faces while they waited. Reports they had received from their puppets on the tailing ship indicated that there were two young men, an elderly lady, and a middle-aged man on board. *It had to be them,* they thought. It had to be the ones responsible for outwitting them in their efforts to take Earth and eat everyone on it. They had never had to endure such capable adversaries before, and despite their commonly expressionless faces, they were becoming increasingly frustrated. And hungry.

They had to be smart about things and not just come in with all their troops, tongues blazing. They had done that with the food supply on their home planet and again with the last species they wiped out. They were now on the verge of starvation. Desperate as they were, it was hard for them not to eat everyone in sight; they had to nurture part of the human population for breeding purposes to ensure their long-range survival. Those who had been lucky enough to eat a human thought they were delectable, more deliciously intoxicating that any other being upon which they had feasted. It became increasingly difficult for them to contain themselves, but the threat from their higher-ups loomed and gave them pause.

The aliens had captured ten men and ten women and had successfully managed to not eat half of them. The other half, except Henry Wright, who was just blown up by the humans, were contained and about to be paired up—a male with a female—and bred. With their understanding of the human anatomy and ability to manipulate it, human babies would be born within mere weeks instead of months. Once born, the infants would also grow at an accelerated rate, being edible within two months. The aliens estimated that each couple could produce three babies each year. That wasn't enough—they would also begin experimenting with the aim that each woman would bear multiple offspring with each birth.

The few people they held captive wouldn't yield enough sustenance for the alien population, even with multiple babies. They would have to capture at least five hundred more humans and have space to store them in order to maintain a viable farm. They had a crew on a nearby moon currently building such a space underground where the prying eyes of the humans could not find them. The humans would be kept in the holding area until they had enough to transport back to their home planet.

They had to get it right the first time. They had to have enough humans to fill their mothership for just one delivery as they feared the humans and their unanticipated power. If they failed to bring food home, their species would die. Most would die from starvation. But a select few, the few who were charged with securing a new food source—the few who were on Earth and on Eris and who were also trying to kill the group of people who were after them—would die a different kind of death if they were unsuccessful. And it would be painful.

The beeping quickened, amplified in the otherwise silence of the cockpit. The three watched on. The largest one stood at almost six feet tall and an inch-wide vein in his head pulsed rapidly as he leaned closer to the screen, watching the dots blink on and off, closer and closer together. The stillness was interrupted as the door slid open and someone entered. Screams filled the room. The aliens all turned around. Their species was already a scrawny one, but the female who stood there with thin, blood-looking tears coursing down her gaunt cheeks looked like no more than a child's stick-figure drawing. And the screeching, starving baby she held was no better off.

"She's hungry…so hungry. Na won't live much longer. I need to feed her. Please let me have one of the humans, or at least part of one," she said.

"Kla, you know we can't do anything. Shabay will let all the babies die if he thinks it becomes necessary. Babies cannot help us fight. They cannot help us survive. We can always have more babies," Jambay, the tall one, told her. "Babies are dispensable." The vein in his head throbbed almost violently.

Kla hung her head, hiding the baby in her skeletal arms as she began to sob. Her pointy shoulders lurched up and down, and her cries were short barks, like the sound of a human coughing up bronchitis. Jambay went to her and put his arm around her neck, trying to console her. After a few moments, he lifted her head with a jagged finger and turned her gaze from her baby to the screen.

"See that?" he asked.

Kla nodded, her slimy, tear-soaked face glistened in the dim light.

"That is our future. That is our ship chasing them, and we're going to kill them. We believe their ship holds our strongest opponents. Believe me, they will not escape. Once they are dead, no one will stop us. We can repopulate our food supply and eat again." Kla thought Jambay sounded convincing, but she was still doubtful. They had never had anyone or anything fight back before. While her baby screeched the sounds that only come from complete helplessness and an empty stomach, Kla couldn't let herself believe that everything would be okay.

The sound of a snort erupted from across the room. Kla and Jambay turned to look. Rebay and Besbay stood eyeing Na. Rebay's tongue licked his thin, red lips slowly.

"Shut that baby up, or I'll eat it," Rebay said in a gravelly voice.

Kla gasped and clutching Na, ran from the cockpit. The door opened swiftly to let her through and closed just as quickly behind her.

The beeping on the monitor suddenly sped up to the point where it sounded like one long, solid beep. Jambay, Rebay, and Besbay all focused back on the screen. The two ships were now so close to each other that they appeared as one. They stared intently at the images, their red, gooey faces practically begging for the destruction of that ship they hated most. In a heartbeat, a bright flash of white light filled the center of the screen. An explosion! In unison, the three aliens sucked in their breath and waited for the outcome.

Chapter 15

Leila Reynolds tucked her short, sweaty, blond hair behind her ears and tentatively began crawling along the length of the air duct. She moved slowly, unsure if the shaft would hold her weight. She also didn't want to make any noise to alert the aliens of her actions. She kept images of Luke and Dagny in her head to hold her fear at bay and to distract from the pain in her arthritic knees. Her heart thumped strongly in her chest, reminding her that she still had a life to live.

As she inched forward one hand in front of the other, she concentrated on her breathing. The air was thick but seemed clean. She was grateful that she wasn't claustrophobic because the shaft was, typically, very narrow and only allotted enough space to crawl. As she moved farther away from Luke, who was waiting patiently locked in a small room several feet behind her, the light began to dim. She knew she'd soon be in total darkness but had faith that she'd be able to find her way out somehow.

Leila began counting in her head every time she put her left hand forward. Once she was without light, she wanted to have some sort of idea of how far she'd gone. She paused a moment to wipe down her oily face with her sleeve. Crawling was very hard on her knees, so she also repositioned herself so she could roll up her yoga pants and create makeshift knee pads. She began to move again.

She thought of her sweet husband. Luke would have died for her to be safe, and while some people might wonder at the contradiction of him letting her risk her life trying to find an escape for them, he understood that she needed to be in control of her own destiny. For Leila to stay behind in that small cell just waiting helplessly would mean she had given up everything for which she stood. She loved him with everything.

One hundred left-hand moves forward she counted in her head. *Whatever that means,* she thought. Her next move forward brought her to a wall. She felt along it with her hands and discovered that she could choose to go left or to go right. Being right-handed, she chose right. There was no logical decision-making process she could employ since she had no idea where she was. Turning right, she began counting all over again intent on remembering every turn she made and how many "steps" she took.

Once in a while, light would filter through tiny holes in the corners of the air duct but not enough to illuminate her surroundings. Her hearing seemed to sharpen in the absence of sight. She heard a baby crying. As she inched along, it became louder, although it didn't sound like any baby she'd ever heard cry before. She kept going, still counting, and listening more and more intently. She suddenly stopped. She heard voices. Aliens. At once, she realized she was very close to them—almost above them. It sounded as though a mother was trying to comfort a baby. Both were crying, or at least what Leila assumed was crying.

Leila stayed in place, breathing slowly and evenly, despite her heart beating dangerously fast. Her ears pricked as she waited to hear more. She wiped away more grease from her face and rested sideways on one hip to ease some pressure from her knees. She desperately wanted to see what was happening below her, but there were no holes or cracks that she could find.

The only sounds she could hear were coming from the two aliens below, and briefly—very briefly—she wished she would crash through the shaft and kill them. The baby should be no trouble, and she would have the element of surprise on her side. She pictured falling directly on them, knocking out the mother. Within reach, there would be a hammer or a knife or some other kind of weapon suitable for murder, and she would take hold of it, fiercely driving it right through the mother's deserving head—once, twice, as many times as she needed to. She would be as relentless toward the baby too. *It deserves it*, she thought. It would only grow up to kill humans just like the other aliens. She would bash its skull in.

Once she was satisfied they were both dead, she would see that there was a blueprint of the ship on the wall, conveniently, and she would analyze it to determine where Luke was being held and the quickest way to get there. Weapon in hand, she would stealthily make her way to him, killing every single alien she encountered. She could almost feel their blood soaking through her shirt and dripping off her chin. She would rescue Luke, and he would figure out how to fly the ship and take them home where Dagny would be waiting for them.

A voice below brought her out of her violent day dream.

"It's going to be okay, Na. Mommy is here, and I will save you. Rebay won't get to eat you; no one will. Don't cry, my baby. This will all be over soon."

The alien mother sounded as though she was choking on her sobs, while the baby's cries sounded like a sickly dog barking in short, pained barks.

"You won't be hungry anymore, baby doll. Mommy promises to fix everything."

The baby's sobs sounded abruptly muffled to Leila, and her ears strained even more.

"Mommy loves you, Na. Mommy loves you so much."

Moments later, Leila could only hear the mother alien. She held her breath as she grasped what had just occurred.

Suddenly, she felt as though she was going to be sick. She had never wanted to kill anything in her life. She even let spiders live in her bedroom if she saw them. And she recognized that she had just been witness to one of the most intimate acts of love she could imagine. The love of a mother toward her child—that she killed it to save it from starvation or from being eaten—was unaccountably powerful in that act. Leila knew that if she found herself in that situation with Dagny, the outcome would have been very different. She would not have been able to do the same thing.

Leila wished she had turned left instead of right. She felt almost crippled by disgust at herself for her killing spree fantasy and could go no farther. She struggled to back up until she reached the first length of shaft that she had crawled through and returned to Luke.

Chapter 16

When the air cleared, Bross sucked a lungful of it in deeply. He would never take the simple act of breathing for granted again. He lay on the ground with his eyes closed, breathing in and out frantically until he no longer felt as though he was suffocating. He rolled over, climbed up on his knees, and opened his left eye just a smidge. There was no blinding light. He opened his eyes fully as he stood up and saw her standing on the other side of them room. She was shaking.

She wore a long, red ball gown and her jet-black hair was piled on top of her head. She didn't look at him, but he could see her face. It was covered in make-up, and she looked clownish. Despite her bizarre appearance, Bross guessed her age to be around the late-thirties. He wondered what kind of joke was being played on him and to what end. As Bross took a step toward her, she let out a scream. He leaped back, putting his hands up in front of him in a surrendering, appeasing way and said, "Okay, okay, I'm not going to hurt you."

The woman slowly turned to look at him, revealing a deep gash on the side of her head. It had been crudely sewn up, Bross assumed, only to stop the bleeding because no self-respecting plastic surgeon would have done such a botched job. It looked pretty fresh as though she had been cut open and stitched up sometime in the past couple of days. The stitches themselves were hideous; thick, black pieces of thread held her skin together unevenly. Her eyes were swollen and red-rimmed, but she was no longer crying.

"Who are you?" he asked softly, sitting on the far couch. He wanted to show he was not a threat to her.

She pressed her back against the wall, eyes skirting this way and that. She didn't respond.

"My name is Bross David. I was captured at least a week ago, and I've been locked in this room the whole time. When did they take you?" He spoke very gently and didn't use the wild hand gestures he usually employed when having a conversation. In fact, he sat on his hands to ensure he made no aggressive moves at all.

She glanced at him but still did not speak.

He tried a different tactic. "Are you thirsty? The water here is quite good. All the food they've given me has been delicious, surprisingly. I really don't understand it. Maybe we should order steak and lobster. We are, after all, dressed as a lady and a gentleman might be on a special night out."

That instant, the slot door opened and a tray laden with two steaming, whole lobsters, two filet mignons, and two loaded baked potatoes was pushed through. The tantalizing aroma of the meal filled the room. The tray also held a bottle of red wine and two wine glasses. Bross hadn't had a drink in days, and his mouth was watering. He jumped up and practically ran to the food. The woman yelped in fear at his sudden burst and dropped to the floor cowering.

Upset with himself for scaring her, Bross stood awkwardly, not sure if he should get the food and appear insensitive or go to her in an attempt to calm her and show he wasn't the enemy. He saw her covering her head and her gash protectively with his hands and decided it was best to maintain his distance. He went to the food. He carried the tray to the coffee table and placed it down gently. He thought about bringing her plate to her but the way she was trying to hide against the wall made him think of a beaten animal. Instead, he sat at one end of the table and put her plate at the other end. It was only three feet away from him, but he was determined to find a way to break through to her and help her if possible.

Bross found the corkscrew and opened the bottle. He guessed they had no fear of him using it as a weapon against them. He sniffed the cork, although he had always thought that was something pretentious people did, and slowly reached over to place it on the table beside her plate. He breathed in the mixing scents of the food and despite everything he was going through, very much looked forward to eating every last bite. He cut into the steak and saw that it was cooked medium rare, exactly as he liked it. Blood spread the short distance and touched the potato, but he didn't mind that. He wanted to eat slowly and enjoy, but he found he was ravenous and chewed bite after bite as fast as he could. The second he had a piece cut, it was in his mouth. Once the steak was done, he picked up the lobster and immediately dropped it again; it was burning hot. He dug into the potato instead, making sure every mouthful had some cheese, bacon bits, and sour cream. When the inside was scooped out and devoured, he picked up the skin with his bare hand and bit off half of it.

Lifting his eyes from his food, he noticed the lady in red was watching him.

"This really is divine, and if you want any chance of surviving this ordeal, you need to eat." He spoke with his mouth full and didn't even care. Before the first half of potato skin was swallowed, he popped the other half in his mouth. While he chewed like a beast that hadn't been fed in days, he poured two glasses of wine, placing one near the lady's plate.

She stared at the food and then looked at Bross. He sensed she was sizing him up and kept to himself, allowing her to take the time she needed to develop some sort of trust in him. The woman rose slowly and took one step toward him.

"Come on and get it while it's hot," Bross said, ripping the lobster in half. He busied himself splitting the tail open and pulling out the meat. The aliens had been considerate enough to also provide garlic butter, so he dipped the meat in the bowl and tore a chunk off with his teeth. Butter dripped down his chin, and he promptly wiped it away with a white linen napkin, also provided by the aliens.

She walked directly to the table, no hesitation, but sat down on the floor away from Bross. She ignored the knife and fork and picked up the steak with her bare hands and ate the way cave men had. She no longer paid any attention to Bross and in no time had gobbled down the whole steak. And about a minute later had puked it up all over the floor beside her.

She broke down sobbing.

Bross jumped up. "Oh dear, come to the bathroom and let's get you cleaned up." He held out his hand to her and was surprised when she actually took it. He realized that was the moment when she had fully given up. Given up on hope, on life, on escape, on everything. She had, in that instant, been reduced to a shell. He led her to the bathroom and ran the water, filling a glass. He held it to her lips and said, "Rinse and spit." She did as she was told, and he wiped the spittle from her mouth. "Again." They rinsed and spit a few times, and by the time they returned to the coffee table, the puke had disappeared and a bowl of clear soup and some plain toast was where her meal used to be. There was also a tube of antibiotic ointment on the table.

Bross sat her on the couch and sat beside her. He tasted the soup. It was warm but not scalding. He fed it to her, half a spoon at a time, and she let him. Half a bowl later, he stopped and said, "Let's wait a bit and then have a little more."

She nodded distantly. She was like a child who needed to have everything done for her.

He picked up the ointment and read the label. "Heals beautifully and painlessly."

"I'm going to put this on your cut. If it hurts tell me and I'll stop."

Again she nodded, staring into space.

Bross opened the tube, squeezed a bit of it out onto the tip of his forefinger, and very gently began smoothing it onto the jagged gash on the side of her head. She jerked ever so slightly but then nodded for him to continue. He made sure that the whole cut was sufficiently covered and fed her the rest of the soup. Tears rolled slowly down her face the whole time. Since the soup stayed down, they moved on to the toast. Her stomach managed to keep it down as well.

Pieces of her hair had come loose from their clips so Bross carefully removed all the clips and combed her hair with his fingers. He was so thankful to have human contact, even if it was a woman. He thought of his lover, Sonny, again and reaffirmed that he would do everything possible to see him again. He continued stroking the woman's hair, which hung down almost all the way to her waist. It was naturally jet black, and he thought it was beautiful. Turning her face toward his, he held her hair back and was shocked and yet not shocked at the same time to see her cut had already begun to heal. The stitches were growing out, the skin was pink instead of the angry red it had been, and it was all but closed up. Bross knew that in another couple of hours there would be little sign that she had ever been sliced open. If only humans and the aliens could work together. He sighed.

"You're healing," Bross said to her. "I don't even think there's going to be a scar on your lovely face."

He saw that she was no longer crying and went to the bathroom. A few minutes later he came back with a towel and began wiping the smeared make-up from under her eyes. The white towel was blue and black and red by the time he finished cleaning her up.

"Will you just look at us? All dressed up with nowhere to go. You've got on your fancy red dress, and I'm wearing this delightful red and black outfit to match you. We'd be the envy of the town. We'd go out for a nice steak dinner....Oh, we've had that! Sorry, that was insensitive. Forget the steak; forget the lobster. We'd go out and get some maple-smoked salmon with seared capers and steamed horse radish risotto. And asparagus puree soup to start, of course. I like cracked pepper in my soup. How about you? Now, I'm not a big dessert eater....I have to watch my figure, you know! But I can see you have no worries in that area!" Bross paused and looked at her. She was unresponsive and didn't seem to know he was even running off at the mouth.

"Can you even hear me? You haven't spoken once, and I want to know you're okay. Can you at least tell me how you got here? Do you know why they dressed us up?"

She finally spoke. "My name is Chrystal Wright, and I've been here forever. I don't know how I got here, but I know why I'm here. I'm to have your babies."

Chapter 17

Chuck and Farley scrambled to buckle themselves in when they were suddenly, violently kicked out of their seats. Grammy wasn't kidding when she said things could get rough. The force of impact after Josh fired at the ejected canisters shook their ship. One by one, the canisters exploded. Chuck smashed face-first into the back of Grammy's chair. He let out a loud, surprised cry as he crashed to the ground and landed painfully on his knee. He tried to get up but the ship lurched. He decided to stay on the floor and held onto Grammy's chair to keep from being flung about. His blond hair hung in his face, and he tried to blow it out of his eyes, too afraid to let go of his anchor.

Farley fared better. His training with Yu had taught him to prepare for almost anything, and at the mention of things going rough, he was ready. He stumbled a bit but recovered and was able to plant himself and do up his seat belt. He held onto the arm rests of his chair, closed his brown eyes, and took five deep breaths before opening his eyes again. He looked down at Chuck and stretched out his long leg.

"Grab my foot. We need to get you strapped in," Farley said calmly.

"Not a chance. I'm good here." Chuck was jerking back and forth. He didn't know how long he'd be able to hold on, but he thought he was better off not letting go. He was still trying to blow his hair out of his face.

"Told you to cut your hair. It should be no more than one inch long, like mine." Farley tried to make light of the situation because he could see pure fear in Chuck's eyes between the sweaty strands of hair shielding his face.

Chuck rolled his eyes but said nothing.

"Chuck, are you okay?" Grammy asked. "You hang on, Chuck. Everything is going to be fine." Grammy rarely lost her composure, but she undid the top button of her black combat shirt. Her eyes were wider than usual with her forehead creased and glistening under a layer of sweat.

The ship pitched to the left and to the right, and the hull groaned as though under pressure of caving in. Josh looked up at the ceiling apprehensively. The main lights had gone out, but the generator lights dimly lit the perimeter of the cockpit. Farley's outstretched leg swung back and forth. Chuck watched his friend's leg, thinking, *There's no way I'm letting go now.*

"Chuck? You with us?" Grammy pressed.

"I'm good. I'm okay, Grammy. That blast was insane." Chuck had his eyes squeezed shut and tried to tighten his grip on the base of his grandmother's seat. The ship continued rocking like a deep-sea fishing boat on Earth, struggling to stay upright in the massive, rocky waves.

"Status report, Josh," Grammy asked with the slightest of quivers in her voice.

Josh had been monitoring the screens and controls since the explosion, but the dials were spinning out of control, indicating nothing. "I'm not entirely sure," he said, shaking his head. His wild, sandy hair stuck off all sides of his head like a mad scientist. "These dials won't settle, and none of the sensors seem to be detecting the ship's activity. I can't tell if we've sustained any damages. I'll keep monitoring, but if this control board doesn't start operating properly, I'm going to have to physically check the ship myself. I didn't expect the blast to be that powerful. I hope we got the

aliens, but I have no way of knowing that without our visuals." Josh's deep
voice was usually soothing—Chuck thought it sounded more doom-filled.

The cockpit was filled with the sounds of metal scraping and bending,
but at least the air was clear. Chuck could smell no smoke.

Farley was staring at Chuck, his head shaking. He suddenly undid his
own seat belt and dropped flat on the floor. Like Chuck, he slid around a
bit with the swaying of their ship, but he was able to get a strong hold of
Grammy's seat which was right in front of his. With his feet, he clutched
onto the base of his own seat.

"Hey, Chuck, check me out. I'm a ladder."

"What?" Chuck asked, eyes still closed. Farley saw that Chuck, despite
being rocked by the ship, was also shaking his own head from side to side,
as though he was saying "no" to their predicament.

Farley held on tight but was close enough to Chuck to head butt him
in the arm. "Chuck!" Farley yelled. That snapped Chuck out of his reverie.

Chuck looked at Farley as fear popped through his eyes.

"I'm your ladder. Climb across my back and get yourself up into my
chair. I've got a good grip on everything here, and then you can help me
get to your chair. Okay?" Farley smiled in a "we can do this" sort of way.

Oddly, Chuck let go of Grammy's chair with one hand and, arm
thrashing in the air momentarily, grabbed onto Farley's black shirt with
a tight grip.

"That's it, buddy. Keep going." Farley urged him on.

As the ship thrashed, Chuck's body slid along the floor and smashed
into Farley's. He quickly threw a leg over Farley and squeezed tight. Farley
managed to hang on with his hands on one chair and his feet clasped
around the other. Chuck awkwardly held on, the length of his body
covering the length of Farley's. Chuck released Grammy's chair with his
other hand and held only onto Farley. His face was pretty much pressed
into the back of Farley's head, and he asked, "Now what?"

"I guess you'll have to shimmy backwards somehow. You can try to
turn around, but I think going backward will be easier until you can get

a good enough grasp of my chair to pull yourself up. Hurry up, though. You're heavy!"

"That's ironic. Or a metaphor. Or something," Chuck retorted.

"Hey, man, I've lost almost thirty pounds!" Farley groaned in time with the ship's constant groaning.

"Teasing, man, teasing."

Grammy and Josh smiled distorted smiles at each other as they rode out the uncontrollable thrashing of the ship.

"Just get shimmying," Farley ordered.

Chuck grabbed onto Farley with both hands gripped as tightly as he could muster and did a sort of backward, inchworm-type movement while the ship tried to buck him off. He screamed as he was jerked about. Farley screamed too. "Don't dig your knees in so hard, man! You're killing me!"

As luck would have it, the ship jerked in such a way as to toss Chuck backward right to the chair. He scrambled to his feet and sat down with a hard thump. He buckled his belt before he was thrown around the room again. Looking down, he saw that Farley was still hanging on tight on both ends.

"Farley, I'm okay. Swing yourself around and I'll help you get into the other chair," Chuck said encouragingly.

Farley unclamped one of his legs from under Chuck's feet, expecting it to run wild, but surprisingly, finally, the ship settled. The group collectively held its breath for a few moments, waiting for the shaking to start back up, but the aftershocks had really subsided. Farley jumped up quickly and strapped himself into the seat.

"Well, I'm glad that's over!" Josh exclaimed.

Grammy let out a deep, relieved sigh while Chuck and Farley high-fived each other.

The dials on Josh's control board began slowing down as well, and he studied them to check for damages. All sensors appeared normal as the main lights blinked back on. "The oxygen system is fine. The engine seems undamaged. The hull appears to be uncompromised. I'm going to walk around just to confirm." Josh began undoing his seat belt when the screen came back to life. The four onlookers stared wide-eyed.

"Whoa! Now what's that?" Chuck asked, undoing his belt and rising to his feet.

An oblong-shaped planet floated in a purple haze off in the distance. Whenever Chuck neared Earth's atmosphere, he always thought his planet was big, but this one was at least triple the size of Earth. "What's that?" Chuck asked almost in a whisper.

No one answered.

Planets were always round. No oblong-shaped planets had ever been discovered before. Some had rings around them and some had one or more moons, but they were all round.

Josh began pressing buttons on the control panel, and the rest of them could hear the weapons system loading. "Better sit down, Chuck, and everyone hold on tight."

"Josh, where are we?" Grammy asked, her brow furrowed and her hands tightening on her cane in her lap.

Josh played with the dials and scanned all the frequencies for what seemed like forever to Chuck. At last, he answered. "Wherever this is, it's not in our system. Or any other system we've ever identified."

As they all stared on, hearts racing, a ship—the enemy ship, to be exact—floated into their line of sight.

Chapter 18

Their silver ship was pointed to a tip at the front and widened to the back like a long, thin triangle. There were only two seats in the cockpit. Troy sat in one, being the pilot, while Sulinda sat in the other. He wasn't a fan of the others, but since Sulinda was the only one who liked him, he was fine with her sitting with him. She was almost half his size and called him her giant. She asked him regularly to put her up on his shoulders because she wanted to know what it was like to be tall. Sometimes he obliged; sometimes he didn't. Troy's skin was black as night and Sulinda's was white as a ghost. She always wore dresses of many colors and brightly-colored hats while he preferred plain, solid colors. While he had fired up the ship, Sulinda had changed from her "lunching outfit" to her "flying outfit."

"You changed? I can't even tell," Troy said. "Too many colors. Can't distinguish from one dress to the next." Troy still wore his long, beige dress that he had been wearing for a straight week.

Sulinda laughed him off. He knew his insults never hurt or upset her.

"Are you guys done back there?" Troy asked Sparrow and Maywano.

"Everything is secure, and we are strapped into our seats," Maywano yelled toward the front of the ship. "We're ready when you are!"

Troy then heard Maywano say, "Boy, do I ever love flying! Take off is so exhilarating, don't you think?" He shook his head when he heard Sparrow agree.

From the cockpit, Troy began his countdown. "All systems are a go in 14, 13, 12, 11…" He counted all the way down to one and then yelled, "Blast off!" Being afflicted with obsessive-compulsive disorder, he pressed the Start/Stop button fourteen times, turning the ship on and then off again with each push. Then he motioned for Sulinda to press it once more to start the ship. It was their routine since they had met while escaping the aliens two months prior. Troy sometimes threw her a bone and let her help him; it made her happy and ensured she would do whatever he told her to do.

Slowly, the tip of the ship began to rise so that it stood up tall and straight on its back end. The four passengers were facing the sky. Troy glanced in his mirror and saw Maywano swinging his legs playfully as they dangled. It irritated Troy seeing Maywano's face lit up with excitement. Sparrow was giggling, irritating Troy even more.

The pointed, silver ship began to lift from the ground. The engines grew louder and louder as the ship rose, gaining speed.

"Wee!" Sparrow screamed.

Maywano smiled and said, "Wee!" along with her.

Troy listened to them and shook his head while he operated the controls and adjusted dials. Sulinda caught him and also shook her head. From the shoulder strap of her dress, she pulled a red scarf and passed it to Troy. "Here, Troy, I found this for you to wear. It can be a part of your flying outfit."

Troy looked at it and ignored the offering. Sulinda shrugged and wrapped it around her own bald head instead, tying a bow in the front. Once they had reached an altitude to Troy's liking, he maneuvered the ship so it was flying back on its side, pointy tip leading. They were about a mile above the ground and moving swiftly.

"Can you be quiet? I'm trying to concentrate on flying this thing."

Sulinda stopped humming immediately.

A mere twenty-five minutes later, Troy flew in large descending circles to lower the ship. Once they were low enough, he engaged the ship's gyroscopes so they hovered just above the ground. A door slid open on the side of the ship, and its staircase extended out until it touched the ground. Maywano, Sparrow, and Sulinda all released their chair straps and said their goodbyes to Troy.

"Wait—when do you want me to pick you up?" Troy asked.

"In six months," Maywano responded.

Troy grinned

"Six months?! That's too long!" Sulinda protested.

"But that's what we decided just earlier today. I think it may have only been a couple of hours ago, in fact," Maywano pointed out.

"I didn't think that was serious. I'm going to go back with Troy," Sulinda said.

Troy's eyes bulged. He was antisocial at best, and his expression stated that he wanted solitude, not company.

Maywano looked up at the sky and then down at the ground and then up at the sky again, seemingly considering Sulinda's statement. His mouth was wide open the whole time. Sparrow watched him with a look of admiration on her face while Sulinda's frustration began to kick in. "Say something!" she yelled.

Maywano suddenly twirled, his robes flying up around his waist, and said, "There is no way to contact Troy, so we must decide now when he shall return for us. We need you, Sulinda. We will go now." Looking at Troy, he said, "See you in six months." Looking back at Sparrow and Sulinda, he said, "Say goodbye to Troy."

"Goodbye, Troy!" Sparrow said, her eyes twinkling.

"Goodbye, Troy," Sulinda said sadly. Her eyes teared up big, yellow tears, and she hugged him around his legs. He rolled his eyes but reached down and removed her red scarf from her head. She looked up and beamed when she saw him tying it around his neck. He bent over at the waist and wiped her tears away with his giant finger and then turned away. Maywano, Sparrow, and Sulinda watched while he boarded the ship.

"How about three months?" Troy asked.

"Agreed!" Maywano replied.

Troy turned away, the stairs retracted, the door closed, and the ship took off. Yellow vapor trailed behind but soon dissipated.

"Let us be on our way. It should not be more than half a day of walking before we get to the people." Maywano spun around on one foot, his other leg extended out in front of him. He lost his balance, so he spun around again. Again he lost his balance. This went on several more times until he felt he had done it right. He smiled brightly at the others and began dancing toward civilization. Sparrow picked up her satchel and followed. Sulinda stared off into the distance even though Troy and their ship were long gone.

"Sulinda, let's go!" Sparrow called back to her.

Sulinda swung her dress-filled bag over her shoulder and slowly put one foot in front of the other as though begrudgingly. Sparrow had stopped to wait for her. "Are you going to be okay?" she asked. Sulinda did not reply. "Fine," said Sparrow. "We'll tell everyone that you're one of those people who doesn't speak."

"Catch up, everyone." Maywano sang his words as though music were playing. "I'm getting so far ahead of you." Maywano danced everywhere he went, and the happier he was, the faster he danced. Sparrow quickened her pace while Sulinda trailed behind, sulking.

An hour went by. Then two, three, and four. By that time, they were close enough to hear the music that was continuously playing in the human-inhabited part of Eris. Maywano stopped to spin in "circles of joy," as he called it. When he was dizzy, he spun around the opposite way faster and faster until he fell to the ground.

"For someone so old, you sure act like someone very young," Sulinda said under her breath.

Maywano heard her and replied, "Yes, well, 218 years is still not very old, and with your attitude, you'll probably not see half my age. But I hope you do anyway."

In the distance, they could see ships landing and taking off. The ships were saucer-shaped, tube-shaped, and a combination of saucer with a tube off the back end. They didn't see any that had a pointy tip at the front, so they were relieved at their choice to let Troy leave with their own ship. Without knowing a whole lot about humans and their cultures and the way they thought, they wanted to be as inconspicuous as possible.

"Almost there. Let us keep going. The sky is darkening, and we want to get there before we cannot see any longer." Maywano pulled a small brick of cheese out of his pocket and offered it to his companions. Sparrow bit off a mouthful and surprising both her and Maywano, so did Sulinda. Maywano then took a bite, and the three of them passed it around until it was all gone.

As they walked on, the music became louder and louder, and Maywano tried to sing along even though he didn't know a single word. Eventually, he made up his own lyrics. "I dare say it is us coming along. Coming along to meet you. Maybe all of you. I'm not sure." Sparrow bopped her head from side to side, grinning as she walked.

"There!" said Maywano, twirling. "I see someone!" They all came to a halt and stared on wide-eyed.

Chapter 19

The small, square room had one desk that ran the full length of its ten feet. Its walls were baby blue and its ceiling had a giant brown nose painted on it. Two of the three chairs in front of two of the three screens were occupied by Yu and Sparks. The sign on the door to the room read, "Monitoring Room." Yu and Sparks looked at each other, stunned, before Yu rose from his seat. Staring almost blankly, he slowly, as though in a trance, walked across the small room and closed the door. Returning to his seat, he began turning dials in his work area. Where before, he could hear Chuck, Farley, Grammy, and Josh speaking—or screaming—the speakers now emitted static. He tried every frequency, but their voices did not resume filling the room. Sparks also twisted dials and pressed buttons, trying to help Yu regain contact with their friends.

"This does not make sense," Yu spoke to the room.

"I know," replied Sparks. "They've disappeared. The aliens too."

"Yes, but do you see? The sensors are still picking up their four vitals. We should be able to see the ship onscreen. It's as though they're still there, but they aren't." Yu flipped switches and scanned the screen, waiting for their friends to reappear. "Grammy, can you read me?"

Sparks lit a stick of incense that smelled like camp fire and inhaled its scent deeply. She had always said that the smell helped her think better. "Can the vitals just be a residual heat signature?"

"No. Our technology is more advanced than that. It will only pick up signals from what is actually there. Sparks, run a diagnostic on all the systems to rule out a failure." Yu coughed on the incense.

"I'll put it out," Sparks said, picking up the stick.

"No, everyone needs you at your best, and you need it to be your best. I'll be fine."

As Sparks typed codes into her panel, a series of blips and bleeps filled the room while the system searched itself looking for problems. "This will take a few minutes. I'm going to get us some water." She stood up and left the room.

Yu watched his screen intently, waiting for some indication of where the two ships may have gone. One at a time, each program name appeared on his screen with a check mark to indicate that it was operating properly. He stood up and walked to the adjacent wall where he did a handstand. Resting his feet above his head against the wall, he lowered himself so he was standing on his head. Yu folded his arms across his chest and inhaled slowly through his nose until his lungs were full. Then he exhaled just as slowly. He tuned out the beeps and blips coming from the computer system and just let his mind go blank while he breathed. Yu was great at thinking on his feet, but he also did well while on his head. He knew they were missing something. How can something be there but not there at the same time? He pondered the possibilities.

Yu let his mind fill with ideas. He considered alternate dimensions, the aliens doing something to mess with their computer systems, their computer systems not functioning properly but thinking that they are—nothing made sense to Yu. The blood flowed through his upside-down head, and he opened his eyes when he heard the door open. Sparks and Mr. Castle walked in, appearing as though to be walking on the ceiling. Yu dropped his legs and stood upright, coughing as the incense hit him in the face.

"Hello, Castle. How are you feeling?" Yu asked, searching Mr. Castle's face for signs of depression.

Mr. Castle was dressed in a pink paisley robe that bunched around his feet, and he held a book in his hands. "I'd have to say I feel shocked… haunted…proud…lost…overwhelmed…all in a mostly-good way. Do you see this book I'm holding in my hands?" Mr. Castle looked down at the book nestled in the crook of his arm.

Yu looked at Sparks, and she nodded.

"Yes?" Yu responded, confused.

"This was Nathan's book. This is the key."

Yu thought Mr. Castle looked positively euphoric as he gazed down at the book. Yu recognized it as the owner's manual to Nathan's World's Mustang that had been destroyed by the aliens when they were in battle against them back on Earth. "In what way is Nathan's book the key? To what is it the key?" He looked again at Sparks, and she was still nodding. Yu thought she probably hadn't stopped nodding from when he looked at her moments before. Seeing the look of almost reverence on her face, Yu knew Mr. Castle had revealed something to her about that book. He held his breath waiting for the answer.

"My son was a smart boy," Mr. Castle began, "but I had no idea how smart. Had he lived, we would have benefitted greatly. Everyone in the system would have benefitted greatly. I haven't had the time or wherewithal to read through and understand everything in Nathan's book, but what I've read so far gives me pause. I think it's the key to helping us fight these aliens."

"Please, go on, Castle," Yu urged, placing his hand on Mr. Castle's shoulder encouragingly. He still had no idea where Mr. Castle was going with his reference to the contents of a book explaining how to operate a ship that no longer existed.

"It might all be in here," Mr. Castle continued. "Nathan was very precise, and I'll never be able to talk to him about what's in here or thank him for it. It may be what saves our lives."

Yu needed something more definitive at that point. "Mr. Castle, it's the manual for a ship that has been destroyed. How do you think it can help us?" Yu coughed again as he inhaled the incense.

There was a dramatic pause before the computer bleeped one last bleep and reported, "All systems functioning as per code."

Sparks stepped in and gently removed the book from Mr. Castle's grasp, opened it up to the page with Nathan's picture posing as a book mark, and passed it to Yu.

Yu accepted the black book with both hands, meeting Sparks's gaze as he did so. She was still nodding, but then, with a dip of her head toward the open pages, broke their gaze and stepped back. Yu looked down, expecting nothing, but his brow wrinkled as his eyes widened while he read the unexpected notes that were neatly written in every margin. He absorbed every word on the two pages and then flipped to the next page and did the same there. Page after page, Yu flipped and read and flipped and read. Finally, he looked again at Sparks, who nodded again.

"They're in a parallel realm??"

"Yes," said Mr. Castle.

"Can we get them back?"

"Yes," said Mr. Castle, who tugged gently on his nose.

Yu tugged in response on his own nose. "How? How do we do that?" Yu asked, taking his seat at the computer again, preparing to do anything Mr. Castle told him. Sparks took her seat as well.

Mr. Castle shuffled toward the desk. His paisley robe rustled as though made of crinkly paper. He fanned the pages of Nathan's book a few times, letting the wind it created blow in his face. He fanned the book one more time and stopped halfway through. He took a deep breath and then read every handwritten word on the two pages on which he landed. "We need to determine exactly what triggered their jump into the parallel realm. Something specific must have happened, and we need to recreate whatever it was. Can we figure it out, Yu?"

"Of course we can. We already know. They caused an explosion that was supposed to kill the aliens that were chasing them. It was a split second later that they disappeared. It must have been the explosion. Castle, are you saying we just need to blow something up out in space and they'll miraculously reappear?" Yu's eyebrows were both raised. He hesitated to believe it could be that simple.

"Pretty much." Mr. Castle shrugged his shoulders as though it would be super easy. "We just have to do it in the exact same spot where it happened in the first place. Provided they are in the exact same spot on the other side, it should work according to Nathan's theories. It's like it'll be opening a door." Mr. Castle pulled a red apple from his robe pocket and took a huge bite. The crunch of it filled the room.

Yu and Sparks looked at each other before she said, "Let's give it a whirl, shall we? We can go back through the footage and calculate precisely where Grammy and the rest were at the time they set off that bomb or whatever it was, and we'll just send a drone ship out to do the rest." Sparks stared at Yu, who was unresponsive. After what was becoming an uncomfortable silence, she said, "Right?" The tone of her voice indicated that she was no longer sure of the plan she was trying to create to save their friends.

"On the surface, yes. That is the gist of it, Sparks. Considering it realistically, however, there is much left to chance. As Castle said, they must be in the exact same spot in the parallel realm as they were when they were on this side of it. What if they've moved? What if they aren't even alive anymore? We don't know if that explosion injured or killed them. Or if a new explosion will injure or kill them." Yu was worried, not his usual self-assured self.

"Valid…but if they're injured, we have to try to get them help, and if they're dead, we have to bring their bodies back for their families. Or, at least provide some sense of closure. I'd hate to go on forever never knowing what had happened to my loved ones." Sparks looked to Mr. Castle, her eyes asking for support.

"Of course," Mr. Castle agreed. His eyes misted over as though he were thinking of Nathan. "We need to move on this quickly and take whatever risks necessary. We can't worry about 'what ifs' because they may never happen. Maybe this time, we come out on top, but we have to get out there and blow something up."

Yu laced his fingers together and pushed his hands out away from his body, cracking every single knuckle in his hands before he began madly typing away on his keyboard. His eyes were squinted as he concentrated on his calculations. Yu valued precision and accuracy, and he checked and double-checked every formula, angle, equation, and possible outcome of them blowing something up.

"Sparks, can you arrange for the drone ship? We know Josh and Grammy ejected four explosive devices, so ensure that you load it with at least triple that amount just in case our first attempt is unsuccessful. We'll use our remote access to release and detonate the cans."

"Sounds good, Yu. And I guess that if our people don't reappear, we set off a couple more cans?" Mr. Castle asked.

"As many as we need to until we get them back," Yu said somberly.

Sparks jumped up from her chair. "Yes! We can do this! I'll go and get started." Sparks ran from the room, waving goodbye as she went.

Mr. Castle lowered himself into Sparks's chair and pulled a pear from the other pocket in his robe. He held it out to Yu who declined it with a slight shake of his head. Yu's fingers kept banging away at the keys, planning how they would save their friends. Mr. Castle ate the pear as he watched Yu work. "Can we really do this?" he asked.

Yu stopped typing and looked Mr. Castle in the eye. "I have a few ideas based on Nathan's notes. One of them is bound to work."

Chapter 20

The voice-activated camera floated toward a lone man sitting tall and straight-backed behind a large, mahogany desk with a single sheet of blank paper set atop it. He opened and closed his mouth wide over and over and then made a bunch of animal-sounding noises louder and louder. A woman at the back of the room rolled her eyes. The man hadn't noticed, he was so wrapped up in staring at his reflection in the mirror he held while a hair stylist flitted around his head with a fine-toothed comb, ensuring his black hair was slicked back just so.

From across the room, they heard, "In five, four, three..."

The man waved the woman away, and she almost tripped over her own feet to move away from him.

A spotlight then shone on him, and after a dramatic pause, the man said, "I'm Rod Walken reporting for Planet Talks. Good evening, friends. Not too long ago, we announced that the bodies of Luke and Leila Reynolds had been found dead. While Castle Enterprises has been assisting the local authorities with their investigation, the police remain stumped. We are now asking for the aid of the public. Anyone who may know something about the whereabouts of the Reynolds couple in the days leading up to their demise is asked to come forward. Even the smallest detail may be useful."

Rod adjusted his lavender-colored tie, ensuring the camera could see that Luke and Leila's images were stitched into it. Rod took every opportunity to look like a man who cared, whether he did or not; he enjoyed the status and perks associated with being Anchor of the Year and wanted to win again.

"These continue to be trying times. Though there have been no further attacks on Earth directly, we do report that there was an explosion outside of Earth's atmosphere earlier today. Several ships have been dispatched by the Planetary Space Agency to investigate, and I have no doubt that Castle Enterprises will be assisting their efforts as well. I, Rod Walken, would like to speak on behalf of everyone here on Earth and on our inhabited, neighboring planets when I thank all those who have fought for our lives and who continue to fight for our lives and freedoms."

Rod cleared his throat and flipped the blank piece of paper over. He regarded it for a moment before slowly and dramatically holding it up to face the camera. It was a beautiful, colorful picture of Earth and its solar system. "This image represents every one of us, and I am going to offer it to anyone who knows the whereabouts of three inseparable teens named Mike, Gaz, and Lexi. We are still trying to determine their last names and how they may be connected to the aliens that have been killing us, but we have received information that they may be working against humanity." Rod stared into the camera penetratingly while he let that tidbit settle in with his faithful audience.

"It has been suggested by several students who attended classes at Campfire Collegiate Institute, a high school in Toronto, that Mike, Gaz, and Lexi—also students at Campfire—were notorious for bullying others at the school. The three apparently bullied Nathan Castle, may he rest in peace, and no one we've spoken with would be surprised if they have now aligned themselves with the aliens. I cannot comprehend why anyone would do such a thing, but we can still be hopeful that it is not true. Anyone knowing the whereabouts of Mike, Gaz, and Lexi are also asked to come forward as this information may be crucial to the ongoing investigation. I'll pass you over to Terry, our most excellent weather specialist. Signing off, my dear friends, I am Rod Walken reporting for Planet Talks. Good night and be safe."

Chapter 21

Brody pulled the sign-up sheet out of his desk. He sat in a large classroom with windows along one side, a chalkboard that ran the length of the front of the room, and pictures of different spaceships and space shuttles on the other two walls. There were six pairs of chairs and tables spaced out evenly on the floor to accommodate twelve students. He would be teaching the pilots, beginning in a mere twenty minutes. He stood and wrote "The History of Aviation" in white chalk on the black chalkboard. He knew time was of the essence and wouldn't dwell on the centuries of advancement in flight and then space flight, but he did feel he'd be remiss in not touching on it at all.

The door opened to the classroom, and he turned to see who was there. He smiled. Karona entered and then blushed.

"Uh, sorry," she stammered. "I'm early….I'll come back." She carried a red backpack and swung it over her shoulder as she backed out of the room.

"Nonsense, Karona, come on in and take whatever seat you wish." Brody smiled at the young woman welcomingly as he gestured to the empty seats.

Karona immediately took a seat in the back row along the wall closest to the door. When Brody finished drawing a picture of an old plane from who knows when and turned to look at her, she said, "I figure I'll let others sit near the front since I have excellent eye sight."

Brody knew she was shy and was not surprised that she would sit at the back. He used to choose seats near the back when he was in school many moons ago. He didn't want to make her feel uncomfortable with her explanation so he pretended to consider what she said and then nodded vigorously. "I do remember seeing a kid wearing glasses. Maybe he's taking this class and needs to be close to the board. That's indeed considerate of you, Karona."

She turned red again and smiled back but then looked away and appeared to be interested in the images on the walls.

"Why did you choose to take this class, my dear?"

Karona's black hair was in a long ponytail, and she began to play with it, twirling it around her forefinger. "Ahem," she cleared her throat as another girl strode into the classroom. In a small voice, she said, "Well, I want to be a part of the fight. Since I know I'm no good at hand-to-hand combat, I thought that transporting the people who *are* good at it would be the next best thing." She didn't make eye contact with Brody or the new girl.

"Sounds like just as good a reason as any," Brody said, smiling gently. He stared at Karona for a few more moments. He saw her blinking rapidly as she focused on the chalk board and twirled her ponytail. Brody sensed she was uncomfortable with the attention and turned to the new student. "And who might you be?"

"Well, hi y'all!! My name is Katie, and I'm so excited to be here! I can't wait to kick some alien ass! Oops, pardon my French," giggled Katie. Her orange hair was made up of big curls that bounced as she laughed. She took her seat front and center, smiling and addressing other new students who were now walking in. "Hi! How y'all doin'?" Some students nodded hello back and others looked away.

The class filled completely.

"Good morning, everyone. It's nice to see you all here. We have a full class and a full agenda and a full need to learn everything as quickly as possible. We'll call this a 'crash' course if you pardon the use of that word as we indeed do not wish for anyone to crash." Brody searched the faces for signs of fear or hesitation. When he saw fierceness, enthusiasm, and intelligence, he continued. "Our goal is to get everyone working in the flight simulators in the next day or so."

A man in his late twenties jumped up and shouted, "*Yes*" as he pumped his fist into the air. He beamed around at his classmates and had his grin returned by most. He sat back down, giving the impression of being completely satisfied with himself.

"Thank you for your exuberance, Kyle, is it?" Brody asked.

"Yes, sir, Kyle is my name, sir." Kyle flexed his muscles under his tight black shirt. The material strained against his arms.

Brody wondered if he chose a uniform shirt that was a size too small on purpose just to show off. He glanced at Karona and saw that she was unimpressed.

But Katie spoke up. "My, my, Kyle, aren't you a sight for sore eyes?" She winked at him, and he winked back.

The rest of the students seemed to shift uncomfortably in their seats before Brody spoke up. "Okay, okay, everyone, let's stay on track. As I said, we have much ground to cover. I appreciate the energy, and just so everyone knows, it was a requirement to pass a physical fitness exam before being permitted entry into this training, and you have all passed. It was also a requirement to undergo a psychiatric evaluation. We must all be mentally fit as well as physically fit, and we must keep our heads in the game. I don't mind joking and jocularity after we leave this room each day, but while we're here, let's focus."

"Sorry, sir," Kyle and Katie both said simultaneously. His expression was pleasant but serious. Her expression was serious but pleasant.

"No worries. My name is Brody, and that's how you may all address me. I am in no way qualified to teach you how to fly ships. I am here to give you the basics on space flight and give you a series of tests to determine where your best skills are and assign you to tasks that best suit your abilities." Brody paused for questions but there were none, so he went on. "I'm going to give you all information about the history of aviation. Some of it will be written on the board, some will just be me telling you things, and we'll start with a hands-on exercise using these space flight models." Brody lifted a box from a table at the front of the room and passed it to the nearest student. "Take one and pass them along."

The box contained a dozen toy spaceship models that were already built. "These models are for you to play with. I want you to take yours apart and then put it back together. Once you have it assembled perfectly, take it apart and do it again. You have three attempts to disassemble and reassemble your model in less than one minute. It looks complicated but it can be done—I've accomplished it."

Brody watched as each student examined his or her model turning it upside down and right-side up again, paying attention to how the pieces fit together. Karona turned her model over and over and smiled as she inspected the little spaceship. Brody knew she didn't even realize she was smiling, while among strangers, no less. That was huge for her, considering how timid she was around others. She had the look of someone who was lost in a pleasant memory, and he wanted to know what it was. He made a mental note to ask her once the class was over.

"I'm going to start the timer now that you've all had a chance to check out your models. I'm not going to monitor your first go at it, but you'll have a minute which will give you a base as to how quickly you have to work inside that time limit."

Brody's words snapped Karona out of her own head and back into the task at hand. Her eyes were wide and her face serious as she held her test. She stared at Brody who was walking down one aisle, holding a stop watch and waited to begin.

"Everyone ready?" he asked.

After a series of "yes's," he said, "Go!" and pressed the button on the timer.

The sound of a collective intake of air filled the room and then silence, save for the shuffling of the classmates working their wooden and metal pieces, trying to get them apart as quickly as they could. Brody witnessed Karona take hers apart so deftly that she appeared to be convinced she had broken it. She glanced at Brody but looked away to keep working. There were twenty-two pieces, and her fingers moved quickly to reassemble them. He marveled at her natural ability because in no time, she had the ship back in one piece. Karona rolled it over and over in her hands, doubtful. She glanced up at Brody again and saw that he was fixated on her. She went beet red.

Brody looked at his watch and then back at Karona. He made his way to her desk where her desk-mate was struggling to separate the last couple of pieces from each other. Brody watched the last twenty seconds count down and said, "Time! Put down your models." He looked around at the students and watched them hesitantly obey—some of them quite frustrated.

"Put up your hands if you were able to take apart all twenty-two pieces." He watched as all but two students raised their hands.

"Good. Keep your hands up if you started putting it all back together." Six hands dropped leaving six in the air.

"Now, only keep your hands up if you completed the puzzle." Brody listened to the brief but loud groans as all hands went down. Karona's hand also went down even though Brody had witnessed her success. Brody was aware of Karona's insecurities and did not single her out, and he knew she would be eternally grateful.

"Not to worry. As I said, that was a test run. You have an idea of what you're supposed to do. Put your pieces back together, and then we'll try again. Let me know if you need help at this stage and then we'll get going."

Karona fiddled with hers, Brody figured to make it seem as though she hadn't completed it in under forty seconds like a pro.

"It looks as though we're ready to go again, so on your mark; get set; go!" Brody started the timer again and made no bones about watching Karona's progress from start to finish. She had the model in pieces and put perfectly back together in about half a minute. Brody had never seen a novice do it that quickly before, and he was duly impressed. He knew that Karona was special and marveled at how they had "met" her. It had seemed like eons ago to him back when they were on their home planet of Earth and their headquarters in Gros Morne Mountain in Newfoundland had been blown to smithereens by the aliens. Brody was lucky to be alive and was thankful that Grammy had saved him. Karona had just so happened to be living/hiding in the woods, and they had taken her in. Grammy had seen something special in Karona, and now Brody had too.

"Time!" Brody walked the room and noted that five students were able to complete the task. "Good job, people. Finish putting it together if you haven't already, and we'll go one more time."

One the third and final test, Karona had beaten her last time by shaving eight seconds off. Brody thought that was probably a record or maybe tied with Yu's time. Out of twelve students, seven had completed the take apart and rebuild of the model within the one minute. Brody thought that was an acceptable number. He then spoke for about an hour on how aviation had come to be and its advances. After that, he filled the whole chalk board with notes on how to work the flight simulation machine. Some students yawned as they read what he wrote, and others paid strict attention, appearing to Brody as though they were memorizing each word. No one was permitted to take notes during any portion of the class, which he could tell frustrated some of the students, and that was part of what he was monitoring.

When he was finished with the notes, he put down the chalk and said, "Well, I suppose it's time for the test."

Brody caught Karona's smile. He had a feeling she used to do well in school and was excited that there would be a surprise test. She had been the quickest with the model, and he was anxious to mark her test and see her results. He walked through the room, passing out a piece of paper and pen to each person and winked encouragingly at Karona as he set hers down on her desk.

"You're sitting with partners, but this is an individual test, and I want everyone to keep their eyes on their own papers. The questions are based on the information I have imparted to you here today, and I will mark your answers before we are dismissed. After that, I'll break you out into groups based on your results, and you'll head to the applicable room to begin the next step of training. Some of you will even head right over to the simulator room." Brody looked at his watch. "You may begin now, and we will be here until you are finished. There is no time limit."

One by one, each student walked their completed test to the front of the class and dropped it on Brody's desk. He marked them as he received them—Karona's was first, and she received a perfect mark. In terms of reading skills, listening skills, and practical skills, he considered her to be a triple threat. When all papers were marked, Brody divided the class and instructed Karona and four others to begin training with the flight simulator. Karona couldn't stop blushing or smiling. Brody asked Karona to hang back for a moment, and once everyone else had left the room, he brought up that she had been smiling and seemed to have been lost in a memory earlier. He asked what she had been thinking about.

"Oh! Um, my best friend, Desiree. Desiree was three years younger than me and like a sister to me. We used to dream of becoming pilots together when we grew up. Now, my dream might actually come true. By some great twist of fate, I'm here and about to experience flight in a simulator. I wish Desiree was here too." Karona stared off as though back in the past.

"Where is Desiree now? Was she left back in the woods?" Brody asked, concerned.

"No, she wasn't. I haven't seen her in almost two years. I ran away from home without telling anyone." Karona began to cry and wiped at her eyes. "I feel terrible! If I ever see Desiree again, by some fluke, I hope she forgives me for taking off without warning or word."

Brody felt sympathy for the girl and said, "You can do this fight for her. I haven't heard her name in the news. It's likely that she's alive and well. You will see her again one day. I'm sure of it!" Brody exclaimed confidently.

Karona lifted her chin and said, "This one's for you, Desiree."

Chapter 22

They peered through the purple haze at the alien ship, wondering what was going to happen next. Chuck, Farley, Grammy, and Josh dared not speak as they watched from their seats. The alien ship seemed to no longer have interest in them. It raced toward the oblong planet. They frantically searched the screen for signs of other enemy ships. Four sets of eyes darted this way and that as four hearts beat violently. Chuck ran his fingers through his hair, slicking it back with his own sweat. The alien ship became smaller and smaller until it was just a tiny dot. Then it disappeared.

"Well, this is an interesting twist," Grammy said.

Josh made a whistling sigh noise that dripped with doom. Chuck and Farley looked at one another, unsure of what to say. One by one, they freed themselves from their restraints and began pacing the cockpit while their ship seemed to float on the spot. All four were quiet until they began to all speak at the same time.

"We need to discuss our options," Grammy said.

"We must determine where we are," said Josh.

"We can figure this out," Farley said with a hint of optimism in his voice.

"Oh man, we're all gonna die out here!" Chuck yelled.

Farley strode to Chuck and grabbed him by the shoulders firmly but compassionately. "We are *not* going to die out here. We haven't died yet. Now get off your guff."

Josh went to the main control panel and scanned their coordinates. "If these readings are accurate, we should be orbiting Eris, but we know that isn't true. Wherever we are, our coordinates are identical to those when the aliens were trying to kill us." Josh looked at the stunned faces. "Clearly, we are in a parallel universe," he stated as though it was obvious.

"And that doesn't concern you?" asked Farley. He released Chuck and went to look at the screens Josh was regarding.

"Of course I'm concerned, which means it's no time to panic. We need to keep our heads together. Grammy, brainstorm our options, if you please."

Grammy cleared her throat, tilted her head back so her face was aimed at the ceiling, closed her eyes, and in a monotone voice, began to speak. "Do some knitting. Fly backward. Drink enough Calmalot to kills ourselves. Go to the planet surface. Chant. Try all the frequencies in an attempt to reach Eris or Earth. Activate a pulse beacon. Duplicate the explosion that brought us here…"

"That's it! Great job, Grammy!" Josh ran from the cockpit, leaving behind a smiling Grammy and two confused young men. Grammy did a bit of a hop, jumped and clicked her heels together in the air, and landed into a curtsy. Then everything turned serious again. Grammy yelled at Chuck and Farley to search for more canisters.

They ran from the cockpit with Chuck running down one hallway and Farley running around the opposite corner. They opened every door they came across, almost savagely rummaging through every box, carton, and crate. Chuck returned to the cockpit with a box of bullets but no gun. He passed the box to Grammy, who placed it beside two pocket knives that sat side by side on the counter. As Chuck was heading back out to keep searching, Josh ran into the room carrying what appeared to Chuck to be two broomsticks. He glanced back as he kept walking and watched as Josh leaned them against the counter and saw Grammy nodding approvingly.

"Any luck, Farley?" Chuck yelled down the hall.

"Not yet!" was the response.

Josh ran past Chuck again. He had sweat soaking through his shirt, darkening his arm pits, and his hair was wild. He told Chuck he was going below deck and to meet him down there once he was finished searching that level. "Bring Farley with you!" he called as he disappeared through a doorway.

Chuck looked through the remainder of the rooms on "his" side of the ship, but his search yielded nothing. He met up with Grammy in the cockpit again to let her know he was heading downstairs. Farley entered the room just then with two canisters identical to the ones they had ejected and blown up, attempting to kill the aliens.

Chuck grabbed one of the canisters from Farley and hugged it. "This canister is my most favorite thing in this weird world right now," Chuck said before laying a peck of a kiss on its "cheek."

Grammy took the canister from Chuck and said, "I couldn't agree with you more." She also kissed the canister. "Now, both of you, go and help Josh. We need strong enough weapons to blow these babies up. Keep your fingers crossed that there's something we can use."

"On it!" Farley pushed past Chuck. After finding the canisters, Chuck noticed that Farley was as buoyant as one could be, considering they had seemingly teleported—despite teleportation having not been invented. Even more unsettling was that they had no idea where they were or how to get home. They had one idea of what to do, and they were all counting on it working. They left Grammy fiddling around with the controls.

The two young men rounded the corner and found the staircase. Descending, Chuck asked, "Far, do you think this is going to work?" Chuck's voice trembled slightly. He immediately regretted asking the question. He knew Farley was going to say what he was supposed to say, and he also feared that his question might cause whatever optimism Farley had to falter.

"I know I'm going to see Dagny again, so yes, this will work. Or something else will work, but we'll get home again. We just have to work as quickly as we can because I don't want to be stuck over here for years. Maybe she won't wait for me that long."

Just then, the ship shook slightly. Chuck and Farley halted and grabbed the railing to keep from falling down the last few stairs. "What the..." Farley started.

Grammy's voice came over the speaker system. "Well, they're firing at us, boys! I don't see a ship, though. I think they're firing from the planet's surface. Fortunately, they don't seem to have much range. That shot exploded far enough away to do us no damage but close enough to shake us up a bit. Keep doing what you're doing, and I'll keep you updated."

"Get over here and help!" Josh yelled. He was struggling with what looked to be a very heavy missile. Josh was dragging it across the floor, bent over at the waist. Chuck and Farley ran over and each picked up an end. Josh stood upright and massaged his lower back as he stretched backward.

"Are we taking this upstairs?" Chuck asked.

"No, take it over to that wall. See that opening? Put it in there, Farley's end first. That's the launch space. It's directly below the hatch on the upper level that you guys opened earlier. If we can get our timing right, we can blow up those canisters and maybe get back home."

The ship shook again. Chuck dropped his end with a girly scream. He spun around and dropped to the ground covering his head. Moments later, he realized he was still alive and peeked up to see Farley and Josh staring at him. "Are you okay, Chuck? Do you need a tissue?" Farley asked sarcastically.

Chuck looked at him resentfully but picked up his end of the missile without a word. Though it was heavy, he moved more quickly than he had before, dropping it trying to redeem himself.

They heard a buzz as the loud speaker was turned on. "Everyone fine down there?"

Josh ran to the wall and pressed a button. "We're good, and we found a missile. We're moving it to load it into the shaft. There's only the one. We better make it count."

"Roger."

They finished loading the missile, took one last look around for anything else they could use, and when they were satisfied that there was nothing more, they went back up to Grammy. They found her busy gluing the bullets and knives to the canisters. Chuck tried to help, but she shooed him away. "I'm just about done. There's only one way to do this—my way." The ship rocked gently as another shot came from the planet, again nowhere near close enough to touch them. The crew was mindful that they had to get out of there soon.

"Grammy, can I ask you something?"

"Sure, Chuck. What is it?" She glued the last bullet and focused on him.

"You've known the aliens forever and you used to meet with them. Was it here?"

"No, I've never been here, wherever 'here' is. We only met at the Planetary Space Agency space station. We'd give them the means to grow food, and they would leave. We never actually knew where they were going. They always said it was too far away, and we accepted that. Huh, blind trust—not always a good thing as it turns out." Grammy shrugged as though passing it off; there was nothing they could do to change anything.

"Not to question you or anyone else you worked with but why would you just accept that it was too far? Weren't you curious as to where they lived? Where they came from?" Chuck pressed on.

Farley shuffled foot to foot appearing uncomfortable at the questions, but he stole looks at Grammy, also wanting to know the answers.

Grammy looked at Josh who said, "It's neither here nor there at this point. They already know most of it."

Grammy nodded in agreement.

"Well? What is it? Is it scary? What's the rest of it? Farley and I deserve to know everything, and I mean *everything*."

"We did try to follow them. Countless times," Grammy admitted. "Each and every time we did, their ship suddenly disappeared as soon as we were on the edge of our solar system. They no longer appeared on any of our radar systems, and eventually, we accepted it. We chalked it up to them not fully trusting us, so we gave them more supplies, trying to build on what we thought was a healthy relationship." Grammy paused, thinking. "Chuck and Farley, you can never be 100% sure of what anyone else is thinking, and that includes what's in the minds of those of another species. We've learned that lesson the hard way." Grammy sighed and shook her head.

Josh cleared his throat and ran his fingers through his wild hair, taming it ever so slightly. "I witnessed it once. There was a bright flash of light that blinded me for a few seconds. Only after blinking at least twenty times, could I see again. The alien ship was gone without a trace." Josh picked up one of the canisters. It looked as though it had been decorated with diamonds as the light bounced off the shiny bullets. He nodded his head. "This could work." Josh addressed Chuck and Farley further. "We asked the aliens how their technology worked. We wanted to know if they were using some sort of cloaking device, if they had discovered how to teleport, if there was something else even more mysterious happening, but they were always evasive. They were clearly not interested in sharing anything with us, and we eventually gave up."

"LOOK!!" Chuck yelled all of a sudden. Farley, Grammy, and Josh all jumped at the unexpected outburst and turned their heads in unison in the direction in which Chuck was pointing.

The screen showed a giant ball that appeared to be made of purple fire hurtling directly at them.

"Brace yourselves!!" Grammy yelled as she pushed Chuck into his seat. Farley followed suit, strapping himself in while Josh ran to the control panel.

"This might be bumpy!" Josh yelled as he frantically adjusted dials and knobs before engaging the steering mechanism. He jerked it hard to the left trying to evade the oncoming attack. It worked! The purple fire bomb sped past, merely shaking the ship, but then seven or eight more came flying toward them. It was like playing a game of dodge ball. The fiery balls came from the same starting point, but each one had a different trajectory. "I've never seen that kind of weaponry in my life!" exclaimed Josh.

"Neither have I!" answered Grammy.

Chuck knew he couldn't help and would soon be nothing more than another burden. He dug into his pants pocket and found a tube of Calmalot and drank it all down. Within minutes, he was out cold.

Josh expertly piloted the ship, avoiding everything that came at them until two sources on the planet's surface began firing. His jaw was clenched, and his knuckles were white. He successfully dodged every glowing ball, but the ship was moving as if in slow motion and the attack on them was growing. "I don't know how long I can keep this up!" he yelled. "We need to deploy the canisters and missile, and I mean now!" The ship shook with each fire ball that nearly hit them.

Grammy twisted around in her seat and saw that Chuck was sleeping peacefully. She appeared both shocked and relieved once she realized it was for the best. She then looked at Farley who gave her a wink. She winked back. "You ready, Farley?"

"Yes, my lady."

"Let's go!"

In unison, Grammy and Farley unbuckled their seat belts. They moved slowly toward the counter where, as luck would have it, the canisters hadn't budged. The bullets had created enough friction against the surface of the counter to keep them in place. They each grabbed one, and finding their "sea legs" made their way as quickly as they could down the long hallway toward the hatch at the back of the ship. Time was of the essence, but the hatch door opened smoothly. They tossed the canisters down the chute and slammed the door again, ensuring it was closed tightly.

"Are we good?" they heard Josh scream toward them.

"Yes!" both Grammy and Farley responded.

"Release!" Josh yelled.

Grammy grabbed at the beaten-up pulley and yanked.

"Done!" she yelled.

"Fire in the hole!" Josh fired the missile.

Grammy and Farley stared wide-eyed at each other as though having no idea what to expect next. "Let's go," Grammy said, taking Farley by the hand. They walked hastily back along the corridor to the cockpit to await their fate. They made it in time to watch the missile meet one of the canisters. There was a burst of white light and the ship shook, but only one of their targets was hit. The second canister floated away in the opposite direction. Josh fired the rest of the ship's ammunition but could not make contact with the rogue canister.

The three who were awake were crestfallen. Chuck snored softly. Grammy went to him, smoothed his hair back, and gently kissed his forehead. Farley couldn't take his eyes away. A tear tried to escape, and he wiped at it as he swallowed a giant lump in his throat.

Josh continued his evasive movements trying to avoid being hit. "There are only two sights firing on us, and they're pretty close to each other. We aren't done yet, people," he said.

"But I don't know what else we can do," Grammy responded. "We had to blow up four of those canisters to end up here. Now we have none left. There's nothing left on this ship to simulate how we got here."

"So we find another way," Josh said with conviction.

"Yes! We find another way. What was that you did earlier, Grammy? Brainstorming or something—do that again. What were the other ideas you said?" Farley asked encouragingly.

Grammy's eyes searched the ceiling of the cockpit as she tried to recall what her brain had randomly thought of earlier. "Most of it was gibberish...no help at all."

"There had to be something else. Think! Please."

Grammy sighed. "This is hardly an idea, but it's the closest thing we've got to one. I mentioned something about going down to that planet."

Josh was already watching the planet on the screen, but Grammy and Farley both turned to gaze at it as well. "Let's go with that. Let's play out

112

that scenario. We know hardly anything at all about that planet, but let's focus on what we *do* know," suggested Josh.

"The aliens went there immediately," said Farley. "They're firing at us from the planet, so maybe this is their home. I mean, you guys said you never knew where they were going or how they disappeared. Maybe this is where they went." Farley's point made sense.

"If that's true, we probably shouldn't land there. I just don't see what choice we have. We certainly don't have enough fuel to just fly around out here until they're able to shoot us out of the sky," Grammy said.

Josh piloted the ship a little closer to the planet, steering away from the area where they had been fired upon. "Agreed. Maybe we can find a remote area on the other side and regroup while we come up with a plan. Knowing Yu and Castle, they're working on getting us home as we speak. There has to be some kind of radio frequency we can tap into that will connect us with our world. I'll play around with that once we land and see what we can do." Josh sounded believably optimistic.

"Yeah! We can do this!" exclaimed Farley with a fist pump to the air.

They slowly but deliberately flew closer and closer to the planet, all eyes searching for incoming enemy fire. Josh continuously scanned all frequencies, trying to connect with their own world or pick up signals from the aliens. They were desperate for any contact with anyone—or anything—because they could use whatever information they could pick up as a way to somehow help them get home.

"Josh, try hailing the aliens. I want to speak with them," Grammy said out of the blue.

"Are you nuts? Are you off your guff now, Grammy?" Josh's eyes were wide as his head whipped around to look at her. "There's no reasoning with them. Surely you know that."

Grammy gestured at the screen. "They can't reach us with their weapons, and they're no longer firing. We might have a chance to talk our way out of this. Maybe I can play on their heart strings, assuming they have feelings, or maybe have a reasonable conversation with them about what had gone wrong. If the aliens would at least entertain talking to me, I might be able to get them to open up and reveal why they turned on us."

Though Chuck stirred, his eyes remained closed. Farley's head moved from left to right and left again as he looked from Josh to Grammy, listening to their debate. He remained quiet.

"I think it's a terrible idea." Josh's head wouldn't stop shaking, and his lips were pursed. He took off his black denim jacket and dropped it on the floor beside his chair. It was warming up inside the ship, and the purple haze surrounding their ship began to swirl.

"What choice do we have?" Grammy asked.

Josh, still shaking his head, said, "I know what you're saying, but even if they say they'll help us, we can't trust them. And what are the chances they're even the same aliens we used to deal with? I'm betting that they're not because the ones we know wouldn't be risking their lives out fighting."

"Farley? Do you think you'll weigh in here sometime soon?" Grammy put him on the spot.

Farley shifted from foot to foot and stared at the swirling, bubble-gum-looking mist that seemed to be thickening. He cleared his throat for a good thirty seconds before Grammy snapped at him to get on with it.

"Well, I can see both sides…"

Both Grammy and Josh signed heavily in frustration.

"Do you want it?" Grammy asked Josh.

"No. You take it," he replied.

"Be a man and speak your mind, Farley. We have neither the time nor the patience for your wishy-washy, don't-want-to-hurt-anyone's-feelings attitude. Take one minute, and then I'll ask you what you think again."

Farley's face said it all—he knew that they were in crisis mode and that he *did* have to step up. Only twenty seconds later, he quickly cleared his throat again and gave his opinion. "I think that we should continue scanning all frequencies while we circle around to the other side of the planet, and if no contact is made, we land—as long as it appears safe. If there's any sign of danger, obviously we keep flying. But we need to find more fuel for the ship, and unless Josh can stay awake indefinitely, we'll have to rest."

Josh and Grammy were listening intently, and Grammy nodded for him to continue.

Farley, fueled by Grammy's encouragement, said in a hurried voice, "We can find something to cover the ship to hide it while we go out and search for anything that can help us while we take turns resting. If we seem to be getting nowhere, we make contact with the aliens. If you guys can convince them somehow to help us, great. If they kill us, not so great. We'll be the 'ones who disappeared,' and we'll become part of history."

"We're already a part of history."

Farley, Grammy, and Josh turned around to see Chuck in his seat as calm as was humanly possible under their current situation. One might think that he was still somewhat sedated from the Calmalot, but Calmalot was instant when it made someone fall asleep and also when it wore off—it was either there or it wasn't. Chuck was fully awake and lucid but yet there was no panic in his face whatsoever, despite their dire circumstances.

"Right you are, my precious grandson," said Grammy. She went to him and kissed his forehead. "How much did you hear?"

"Enough to agree with Farley's ideas. The aliens won't be expecting us to land on their planet. I think it's the only play we have to buy us time."

Grammy looked at Josh. "You okay with that?"

"Yes," Josh replied simply.

"Let's do it," said Chuck.

Chapter 23

Luke heard Leila's faint scratching on the metal shaft above and jumped to his feet. He climbed up on the narrow bench, careful not to lose his balance. As quietly but quickly as he could, he opened the latch and removed the door. Leila's sweat-and-tear-streaked face appeared in the opening. Luke began to cry in relief and concern at the sight. Leila twisted around and lowered herself feet first. Luke reached up to help her down. They threw their arms around each other and clung on for dear life, both sobbing. He covered her whole face with about a hundred kisses, and she kissed him back. They had been together since they were nineteen years old, and Luke thought about their upcoming twenty-year anniversary. He hoped they would be alive at the end of the year to celebrate it.

Luke pressed his forehead against Leila's and held it there. They didn't need to say it; the words "I love you" were understood. After a couple more minutes of tenderness, Luke pulled away and spoke. "Are you hurt?"

"I'm fine, my love," Leila replied. "I'm just shaken up is all."

Luke stroked her hair from her face and then guided her to sit down on the bench. "Tell me what you saw."

Leila began shaking her head. "Oh, Luke, it was awful. Even though I found no way to escape, I'm going to try again. I ended up above a room where an alien mother was with her baby. I couldn't see anything, but I could hear the mother. Luke, she killed that baby. She strangled it or suffocated it or something, but she killed her own baby." Leila's voice shook as she began crying again. She wiped the tears away and continued. "She was talking to it while it cried, and I heard her say that no one was going to get to eat it. Luke, they're eating their own kind! We have no chance!"

"Shh, baby, shh." Luke's own wide eyes watered again as his mind raced. Things seemed even more hopeless to him. If the aliens were able to kill each other, what chance did the humans have? *Stay positive*, he told himself. "We can't give up, baby. What else did you see? Did you find anything at all that can help us?" He had desperation in his voice.

Leila squeezed her eyes shut and was silent for a few moments before speaking. "It was so dark and I didn't want to lose my way. I counted each crawling step forward until I hit a wall and then went to the right." She rubbed her eyes before continuing. "I didn't get very far before overhearing that poor mother and her baby." Leila looked at Luke. "I know; I know; I shouldn't have sympathy for them, but I do. There are good people and there are crappy people. Maybe the aliens also have good people." Luke kissed her forehead, acknowledging that his wife was one of the good people.

"Didn't you hear them crying? They can't be more than a room or two away from us."

Luke said he had heard nothing.

"So the rooms must have some good sound-proofing then," Leila said. "Maybe if we can get somewhere, we can use that to our advantage." The air was still thick, and Leila took a pause for a few minutes to catch her breath. They sat in silence, each in his and her own thoughts.

"I know I can get back to that room, and if no one is in it, I can check things out. I can get you out of here!"

"Let's not get ahead of ourselves, Leila. We have no idea where we are. Every now and then, it feels as though we're moving. I'm sure we're on a ship because the aliens wouldn't be able to stay on Earth for very long before we blew them sky high." Luke rubbed his chin, thinking. "We do

117

need information, though. Information may help us greatly, and perhaps we can find something to arm ourselves if you go searching again. Are you sure you're up for it?"

Leila smiled wearily at him, but he saw a glimmer of spark in her eyes. It was the spark he fell in love with all those years ago.

"When do you want to make a move again?" Luke asked.

Leila looked up at the ceiling at the opening in the shaft. He could see that she dreaded going back up there but that she tried not to let it show. It was easier for her to get up inside it and move through it than it would be for him. She already knew what to expect—unless she came face-to-face with an alien. That would surely mean her instant death. Luke did not want to cloud his limited optimism with thoughts of his wife's death.

"Just hold me for a little more. I'm going to try to get into that room, but we should give it just a bit more time to ensure that alien has cleared out of there. I don't imagine she'd want to get caught having killed her own child."

"One less alien to kill," Luke said quietly but firmly.

"I guess you're right. It was just sad to listen to. I'm glad I wasn't able to watch it."

"I can only hope that other aliens do the same thing. The whole lot of them can kill each other off as far as I'm concerned. We have Dagny to think about. We need to stay strong for her. She's home, and she's waiting for us. Actually, she's like you, Leila. She has your spirit. She's probably out looking for us as we speak. If anyone can rescue us, it's her." Luke tilted Leila's face up toward his, and he smiled at her. "You know I'm right."

Leila smiled a weak smile back. "Yes, she's on her way into space right now."

They had no idea how close that was to the truth.

Chrystal stared ahead as though avoiding eye contact with him. She touched her head where the gash used to be and felt nothing that would indicate she had ever been sliced open. Whatever that ointment was that had magically appeared, it had worked perfectly. Chrystal smiled wryly at the thought of looking presentable for Bross as the aliens had wanted her to.

"Excuse me?" Bross asked, his brow furrowed. He stood up in front of Chrystal and asked her to look at him. She did. "What did you just say?" he asked.

Chrystal gazed at him for a few moments before looking away. She stared at a far wall, not really seeing it. "I'm 38 years old. I've had my children. I don't know where my boys are, but they exist. And I don't want more children. They're twins named Jack and Jim. My husband is Henry. I don't know where he is either. They took him away a few days ago." Chrystal spoke in monotone. "Would you pass the wine please?"

Bross obliged and watched as Chrystal drank down the whole glass. He ran to retrieve the garbage can from the bathroom and placed it on the floor in front of her. She had thrown up earlier. Chrystal held the empty glass out to him. "More. Please."

He poured more red wine into the glass, filling it halfway. He put it on the coffee table slightly out of her reach. She wanted the wine, though, and leaned forward to grab the glass. She took a big swig but sipped the rest. When she finished the glass, Bross automatically filled it again.

"I'm really sorry to hear about your family, Chrystal. You poor thing." He sat on the couch beside her and drank from his own glass of wine.

Chrystal looked at the bottle and noted it was almost empty. She surprised herself by wanting more. If she was to be locked in a room with a man whom she was to bear children for, she thought it would be a good idea to drink as much alcohol as possible. Not surprisingly, the little door in the far wall opened up and a bottle of wine appeared. She wished that she had lived in an "ask and you shall receive" sort of environment back home. Despite being held captive, she had never been so pampered in her whole life. She watched as Bross walked over and picked up the bottle. He had it opened by the time he crossed the room. "We'll let it breathe," he said.

Chrystal looked at him, poured some into her now empty glass, swirled it around a bit, and said, "Looks like it's breathing to me." She drank down a large gulp. "Ugh, I'm sick of wearing this dress. It's completely ridiculous." They both looked toward the little door on the far wall, waiting to see what clothing would magically appear. Bross took off his tie and unbuttoned the top three buttons of his shirt. He had already taken off his suit jacket.

As predicted, the door opened and two black fleece sweater and pant sets lay in a neatly-folded pile. Bross moved to get the clothes, but Chrystal stopped him. "I can get it."

She was steady on her feet. She even took her glass with her, drinking it while she walked.

"We should have a party at their expense!" he said abruptly. "It's too bad we don't have any music. Really get us into the swing of things."

Crystal snapped her head in Bross's direction. "What do you think you're talking about?" she asked him heatedly.

Bross winked at her. "You know, we seem to get everything we ask for. Might as well take advantage of our situation. In another life, I think I would've liked to hang out with you. I sense a youthfulness in you—a bit of a wild side." He paused, and when she did nothing but stare, he exaggeratedly and very slowly mouthed the words, "I'm not being serious, but we should get what we can while we can. Let's milk this!"

Her eyes widened as she understood. "You know? Music would be nice right now. I can't tell you what the last song I listened to was. I'm going to use the bathroom and change. I'll be right back." She tossed his comfy clothes at him, and he changed into them right there. There were no speakers though music suddenly filled the room. Bross sipped his wine and bopped his head, waiting for Chrystal to return.

She came out of the bathroom, wearing the black fleece suit. Her long, black hair hung in messy waves down her back and framed her face. She held up her empty wine glass before doing a somewhat unbalanced yet graceful spin.

Bross laughed. He picked up the fresh bottle of wine and danced his way over to refill his new companion's glass.

"Thank you, kind sir," she said.

"Most welcome, my lady," he replied.

He, too, did a spin and then reached for her hand with his free hand. She grasped it, and they clinked glasses. He slowly spun her around, making sure she really wasn't going to be sick again. Satisfied, he yelled, "Let's dance!" And they did, vigorously, neither caring if wine sloshed from their glasses as they jumped and spun around and stepped from side to side, finding their rhythm.

They both smiled and laughed as though they had no cares in the world. It was the release they both needed, the escape from their grim reality. The aliens were going to give them everything they wanted that night, and they were going to enjoy it as only true existentialists could. They recognized in each other a desperate need for normalcy. They were determined to achieve it, if only for that one night.

"Say, we didn't get any dessert!" Chrystal winked at Bross.

"Right you are!"

They automatically danced their way to the little door, waiting to see what sweets would appear. They were not disappointed. A tray covered in slices of chocolate cake and cheesecake with various toppings accompanied fresh strawberries, blueberries, and chunks of pineapple. There was also a dish of warm caramel sauce that Chrystal spooned all over her chocolate deliciousness. Bross dipped a forkful of cheesecake into the caramel sauce and plopped a strawberry on top of it before filling his mouth with it.

"Mmm, mmm," he murmured in delight. In that moment, though it was temporary, they were happy. Bross watched her chew the cake with her eyes closed. They both needed that night, that escape from what their reality had become in the new alien-invading world.

Bross plopped down on the couch and said, "Man, I'm pooped!"

Chrystal did the same, and within minutes, they were out cold, leaning against each other with just faintest hint of smiles on their faces.

The door opened as Luke lifted Leila to the opening in the shaft above them. Luke jumped, almost dropping Leila, but she held on tight.

"Luke?" Leila called down.

"Go, Leila, go!" Luke pushed her legs up, trying to push her to safety. He glanced behind.

An alien stood there watching him, unmoving. Its head was large, misshapen, with big bumps on it as though it had four or five brains struggling to get out. The bumps pulsed faintly. Its face was red and seemed to have streak marks running down from its eyes through the slimy skin. "*Tears*," Luke thought. The thought made him happy, albeit fleetingly.

"She must come back down. We are moving you." The alien spoke in monotone. Luke thought it sounded female.

"Leave my wife alone. I'll do whatever you want, go wherever you want." Luke was shaking in fear, not for himself but for his wife. He wished he hadn't let her go exploring again because who knew what the alien would do now that it knew they had been trying to escape. He felt something hit him in the head and turned back. It was Leila's legs coming down out of the shaft. She was coming back down! He screamed, "No! Go back, Leila!"

She dropped out of the hole and put her arms around her husband, who had begun to cry. He sobbed unabashedly. Leila stroked his head soothingly. The alien stood motionless, watching.

"Why didn't you go?" Luke asked, his voice shaking with his tears.

"I could never leave you, my love. Whatever happens next will happen to both of us. Do you really think I could just crawl away? Never know what had happened to you? Always thinking the worst? I will never leave you." Leila looked at the alien and met eyes with it. "Do what you're here to do. Get it over with, heartless monster!"

The alien regarded Leila for a few moments. "Heartless. Would that it was so." The alien sighed and said, "Let's go." It turned away and began walking down the hall.

"Come on, baby," Leila whispered to Luke. "Keep your eyes open for anything that will help us get out of here. He reluctantly let her lead him over the threshold by the hand. They followed the alien, paying attention to everything they saw, which wasn't much. The hallway was long with the walls, floor, and ceiling all painted stark white. It was brightly lit, and no doorways could be seen. Their own doorway had closed behind them seamlessly. When Luke looked back, he couldn't even tell where it had been.

Luke could smell nothing. When he strained to listen for signs of other people, he also heard nothing. He saw Leila dragging the palm of her hand along the wall, trying to feel for any deviation that may be a hidden door. He did the same, but the wall had been completely smooth. The hallway curved to the left as though they were moving in a big circle.

"Where are you taking us?" Leila asked.

"You are going to help us," the alien replied. "You may even be our saviors."

Luke and Leila looked at each other in wide-eyed surprise.

"I don't see how that would ever happen. If you wanted our help, you should have bloody well asked for it. What gives you the right to steal us and hold us captive? You've *killed* us!" Luke was becoming increasingly angry. He let go of Leila's hand and grabbed the alien by the shoulder. His hand slipped off in the slime that covered its skin.

The alien whipped around and said, "You fool!! Our skin is toxic to you humans!"

Within seconds, Luke began to feel the skin on his hand burn. A few seconds more, his skin was raw and began sloughing off. "Make it stop!" he screamed. The alien had disappeared around a corner but had now returned with a bowl of liquid and a towel.

"Put your hand in here now!" the alien commanded.

Luke hesitated but then realized he had no choice. The skin on his hand was literally beginning to fall off in small chunks. The pain was unbearable. He pushed his hand into the bowl so violently that the cooling liquid sloshed about. Almost instantly, the pain began to subside. The liquid was clear and odorless and had the same consistency as water, but Luke knew there was more to it than that. It had some sort of medicinal agents. He stared at his hand and watched as the redness lessened. Then he watched as the liquid appeared to bond to his hand. It was growing skin!

"Leila," he said.

"I know. I can't believe it." She stared unblinkingly.

Luke looked at the alien. It continued to hold the bowl but was distracted; its eyes were glazed as it stared at nothing. Luke blinked twice because he thought he saw another tear slide from one of its eyes. Luke made eye contact with Leila and nodded his head toward the alien. She saw that something was off with it.

"What's your name?" she asked. The alien had no reaction, as though it didn't even know it had been spoken to.

Leila tried again. "My name is Leila, and this is my husband, Luke. We have a daughter named Dagny." Leila saw the alien's eyes flicker at the word "daughter." Being an intuitive person, she asked, "Do you have any children?"

The alien suddenly became enraged and threw the metal bowl against the wall. Most of the liquid was gone. It had somehow turned to skin and bonded with whatever skin had remained on Luke's burned hand. His hand was fully repaired and fully healed. The bowl clanged as it bounced off the wall and down the hall.

It was as though the alien couldn't hold it in any longer. It began to shriek over and over. Then it ran head-first into the wall. Red goo oozed from it and smeared the stark whiteness. It backed up and ran at the wall again, still shrieking. Luke had never heard such a wild, pained sound in his life and hoped he would never hear such a sound again. He knew that Leila's hunch was right; this alien had killed its own child not that long ago. Leila went to the alien and was about to put her arms around it before Luke stopped her.

"You can't touch her," he said gently. Leila stopped in her tracks, her arms still stretched out in front of her.

Leila put her arms down at her sides. "Stop it!" she yelled at the alien.

It hesitated and glanced at her for a brief second before diving head-first into the wall again.

That alien had helped Luke. He felt that they had a short window of opportunity where they could use the alien's despair to their advantage. "Please, stop hurting yourself," Luke begged. "Talk to us. I doubt you want any of your kind to see you doing this."

"I do not care any longer. There is nothing left for me." The alien finally stopped bashing in its own head and slumped to the ground instead. Blood flowed freely from its forehead and from a couple of spots on the top of its head.

"Then help us. Please. We have done nothing wrong, and yet we're prisoners here for no reason. Help us get out of here," Luke implored.

"We have a daughter. You know that. Please give us a chance to be with her again. I know you would do anything to have your child back, and so will we," Leila added.

The alien slowly turned its head upward so it could look Leila in the eye. "What do you know about it?" it asked suspiciously.

"I guessed it was you. You saw me trying to go through the air shaft just now. I was in it before, trying to find a way out, and I heard one of you doing the unspeakable to its own baby. It was you, wasn't it?" Leila hesitated but the alien looked back down and held her head in her hands. She made no more wailing noises, yet her body convulsed. She was still crying.

Leila crouched down in front of the grieving mother and quietly said, "I'm so sorry you felt you had no other choice. I can't even imagine having to do what you did." She waited a few moments, but the alien offered no response. "Don't make your baby's death be for nothing. Don't make it mean nothing. You did what you had to do to save your baby from something far more horrible than what you did. You did it to save your baby from your own species. You know what they're doing to us is wrong, and you can help us."

The alien remained silent. Leila slowly stood and stretched her legs. The three of them said nothing until the alien stood and broke the silence.

"Get moving." She pointed down the hall, not meeting their eyes.

Luke began to protest, "But…"

"I said get moving," the alien reiterated. She had stopped crying and her voice was full of force.

Luke took Leila by the hand. They took a step down the hall and then another. They walked slowly and full of fear, anticipating that they were on their final stroll together. Luke thought of Dagny, hoping that she was not on her way to find them—they didn't want her anywhere near the aliens. After what had seemed like an eternity, the alien said, "Stop here."

They stopped.

They faced each other, both certain they were about to be eaten in that stark, white hallway, and they waited to catch a glimpse of their own blood smeared across the wall like the alien's blood had after she had bashed her own head against it. Without warning, a door opened.

"Go in the room," commanded the alien.

"What's going to happen to us in there?" Luke forced a tone that sounded both fearful and reckless at the same time. Leila squeezed his hand.

The alien sighed. "You are not going to die today. You will stay alive for as long as you are useful to us. Surely you have figured that out." The alien continued to speak in monotone. She was doing her duty despite having slipped into depression over the loss of her baby.

The door opened silently as Bross and Chrystal remained asleep on the couch. Leila stared at them. Luke didn't think that he and Leila were the only humans on the alien ship, but he also didn't think that they would ever see any others. He stared in surprise at the empty wine bottles and plate of desserts, all of which had had bites taken from each piece. He stepped further into the room. When Leila followed him, he held his hand up to her, indicating for her to stay put. He moved through the room, eyes darting every which way, searching for danger. He made his way to the couple on the couch and was relieved to see by way of their chests rising and falling that they were alive.

Because his hand was no longer hurting him, Luke inspected it closely. He was astonished to find that it had healed entirely. It had actually healed so perfectly that a scar he used to have was nowhere to be found, and on a certain level, it saddened him. Luke was becoming attuned to the fact that what used to be was no more. The life he had shared with his wife and with his daughter had ceased to exist. All they had left was fear and the fight for survival. His only desire was to see Dagny again and to protect her and Leila for as long as he possibly could.

Leila walked over to stand beside him and to take his hand. They watched the sleeping couple in silence.

Chapter 24

Searching for a safe area to land, the ship made its way sluggishly through the dense atmosphere. Its passengers watched the screen anxiously. Muscles were tense and tight. Eyes were wide and held nothing but terror. There was no room for hope—their lives depended on the terror. Smokey, swirly haze filled the screen and then cleared again. The ship filled with a subtle hint of the scent of cotton candy from the surrounding fog. It was oddly comforting to the passengers onboard. The planet grew in size as they neared it. From what they could tell, there appeared to be nothing on the planet surface. It appeared to be a giant black ball. They flew toward it anyway.

Chuck unbuckled his seat belt and stood. "Have you scanned the surface for life?"

"Yes," replied Josh.

"What about scanning for any heat sources? Have you done that?"

"Yes."

"Hmmm, is there a way to scan for food or something?"

"Yes," replied Josh. "I've done all those things."

"And?" Chuck asked.

"Nothing."

Chuck walked to Grammy, who had also stood, and hugged her. She hugged him back. "Don't worry, Chuck, dear. We'll find something to help us. And I have to say, I'm impressed with the way you're thinking. It shows you've got insight to ask such questions. Keep it up."

Chuck squeezed her harder.

"Well, don't crush me." She laughed as she pulled from his embrace.

"What are we going to do when we get down there and there really is nothing?" Chuck looked down and met Grammy's eyes with his own.

"What do you think we're going to do?" she countered.

Chuck looked at the screen and saw the purple swirling mist gather just outside their ship again. It looked both ominous and seductive to him at the same time. He managed to take his eyes off it to find Farley. Farley just stared back at him as if waiting for a response. Josh also stared back at Chuck's gaze, waiting.

"Survive?" Chuck asked, his voice filled with uncertainty.

"Pardon me?" Grammy asked, her brow furrowed.

"Survive."

"Couldn't hear you, dear." Grammy turned to Farley and Josh. "Could you guys hear what our sweet Chuck just said?"

They replied "Nope" in unison.

"Survive!!" Chuck said with force and conviction.

"That's what I thought," Grammy said, nodding her head.

Josh sat down in the pilot's seat and patted the co-pilot's seat next to him. "Come here, Chuck. I'm going to teach you how to do the scans of which you speak. We need to all be able to run this ship. Sucks you have to learn on the fly, so to speak." Josh smiled at his own pun. Chuck shook his head but took his seat.

Chuck regarded the screen as though it was the first time he had seen it. He was trying to see something new, something that might help them figure out the best place to set their ship down. They needed to land undetected. They needed to fall off the radar of the aliens who were no doubt watching their approach.

"Whatever happened to the canister that didn't blow up?" Chuck asked.

"It floated off into space. Why do you ask?" was Farley's response.

"We need a distraction. We need a wild goose chase. We need a red herring." Chuck tried to come up with other ways to say that he wanted to throw the aliens off their mark, but that was all he could muster.

"You think we need to trick the aliens?" Farley asked.

"Most indubitably," Chuck responded. "If we just head straight to the planet, even in a zig-zag pattern, they'll be able to follow us or track us down easily once we land. We need to blow up that canister to create a diversion."

Grammy looked thoughtful as she nodded her head slowly. Josh also nodded as he began pressing buttons on the control panel in front of him. The view on the screen changed and presented the images being captured behind them.

"There!" Josh announced excitedly. "See it?" The purple haze had dissipated again, and they were able to see the space surrounding them.

Chuck, Farley, and Grammy saw what was barely bigger than a dot but knew it was the canister. Their hearts all began to race, as did their minds.

Farley spoke first. "How do we do it?"

Chuck answered, jumping from his seat. "We shoot it just before we see the next fog roll in! Then when we're under cover, we punch it on a different course and get to the surface as soon as we can. We'll have to improvise once we're on ground. Our first action should be to hide the ship. Anything we can find to cover it up."

"But we fired all our weapons already. What are we supposed to use to shoot it?" Farley despaired.

Grammy spoke up. "Josh, we still have our smaller ammunition, don't we? Wasn't the ship equipped with mini-armor shots when we boarded? I don't think we used it because it wouldn't have been powerful enough."

Josh nodded vigorously. "Yes!"

"So we can use it to shoot that canister now?" Chuck asked.

"We can try," answered Josh.

"What are we waiting for?" Chuck looked around at the group.

"Chuck, switch seats with me." Josh stood and sat in the co-pilot's chair when Chuck got up. Chuck looked confused but took the pilot's seat. He stared at Josh and awaited instructions.

Josh walked Chuck through how to access the weapons control. They had only five mini-armor shots, but they could be fired in rapid succession, which is what they figured was required under their circumstances. The canister was miles away but still close enough for them to make contact with it and explode it. They hoped that the blast would be large enough to mask their getaway.

Red lights flashed in the cockpit, announcing that the weapons were live and ready to be deployed.

"Press this button when you're ready," Josh pointed.

Chuck's hand hovered above the button. He looked questioningly at Grammy. She nodded in silence. He turned his stare to Farley, who gave a nod and a thumbs up. He saw movement on the screen and directed his focus there. The purple fog was rolling in again.

"Now?" Chuck directed his question at Josh.

"I'll get us out of here but yes, NOW!" Josh prompted.

Grammy and Farley dropped into their seats and strapped in. Josh was busy with his side of the control panel, ready to get them out of there.

Chuck took a deep breath. As he watched the purple haze thicken in the distance while it floated toward them, he slammed his palm down on the button.

The ship lurched to the right as they heard five "pops." The weapons were released from their holsters. Soon, all they could see was purple as their ship became engulfed. They hoped for the best. The atmosphere was dense and they weren't surprised when three full minutes had elapsed before the weapons made contact with their target. Their ship shook briefly. The fog on their screen illuminated as though a giant lamp had been turned on. Their faces glowed purple with the reflection off the screen. It faded after a few moments, and they knew that whatever headway they had been gaining in throwing the aliens off their track would fade away as the fog thinned.

Grammy spoke first. "How long until we reach the planet's surface?"

Chuck didn't know how to answer and remained silent as he scanned the lights blinking on the panel in front of him. He had no idea how to interpret any of it and was losing confidence.

Josh went to Chuck's rescue and said while pointing at the distance meter, "Twenty-eight minutes. Is that right, Chuck?"

Chuck, stunned, looked from Josh to the reading and back to Josh before saying, "Uh, yeah."

Grammy caught on and didn't skip a beat. "Good work, Chuck. Take us down."

"You got it, Grammy." Chuck looked questioningly at Josh, who pointed to a lever and motioned with his hand for Chuck to pull it toward him slowly. Chuck obliged. Slowly but deliberately, the trajectory of the ship changed to put it on a more direct route to the alien planet. Chuck's chest puffed out a bit as his self-assurance grew in equal measure.

Josh pressed buttons, flipped little switches, and maneuvered levers as Chuck paid attention. He was learning how to steer the ship and watched as the images on the screen changed to show every angle of their surroundings as they descended. No enemy ships could be seen. They thanked their lucky stars that they were still alive. Chuck knew that they had a chance at survival because they each had someone for whom they wished to live. Chuck was desperate to see his mother again, and he had no doubt that Grammy also wanted to see Sheila. He knew Farley thought of nothing other than seeing Dagny again, and he was sure that Josh had someone in his life too. Chuck also thought of Lexi, but her face quickly changed to the face of Karona, surprising Chuck. He had never paid much attention to Karona outside of her being part of their fight to live. And yet, her pale face and black hair stuck in his mind as the minutes counted down to their landing. He felt his face warm up and tried to ignore it.

Whether their attempt to create a diversion worked or not, they had no idea. They could still see no enemy spaceships and wondered how that could be. If they were about to land on the alien planet, surely there would be ships coming and going, but they saw nothing. Maybe luck was on their side, and they actually weren't about to potentially commit suicide by landing right in enemy territory. Maybe the ship that had been following them was also in unfamiliar territory, and they, too, had no idea where they were or how to get home. Chuck thought that was a nice idea and chose to go with it.

The oblong planet loomed before them. They were anxious and hopeful at the same time.

"Okay, Chuck, I'm switching the controls back to you." Josh regarded Chuck with raised eyebrows. Chuck nodded acceptance of the responsibility.

Grammy watched Chuck staring intently at all the dials and controls. His lips were moving as he regarded each mechanism individually. Just then, he looked back at her. Grammy unclasped her seat belt and went to him.

"Is everything okay, Chuck?" she asked.

"Valiant."

Grammy wasn't sure she understood. "What do you mean, Chuck? What's 'valiant'?"

"Valiant is what I want to be."

Farley held his breath, waiting for the rest of the conversation.

Chuck continued. "I have always loved the word 'valiant.' I love the sound of it, the meaning of it, and especially the fact that it's not a regularly-used word. Like 'noble.' You don't hear that word much either, but it's completely rock and roll. Wouldn't you agree, Far?"

"I want to be valiant, too, Chuck." Farley swallowed the huge lump in his throat.

Grammy put her arms around Chuck. She was short, but with him sitting down in the Captain's chair, they were almost at eye level. She found his ear and whispered something. Josh looked away, perhaps recognizing an intimate moment—maybe one of the last between grandmother and grandson. Farley, however, couldn't take his eyes off his best friend and Grammy.

Grammy kissed Chuck's cheek. "I love you, Chuck. I will put down my life for yours." She smiled lovingly at Chuck, and while his eyes teared up again, hers remained clear. Grammy did not cry. Grammy was hard as nails.

"I love you too, Grammy. I want you to live forever!" He squeezed her tight. She laughed, embracing him for a few moments more. Then, slowly, she turned his head until his ear was right in front of her mouth. His face clouded when she finished whispering.

Farley was mesmerized. He didn't blink. Grammy locked eyes on her grandson for another moment and then turned her focus on Farley. Farley's eyes widened as she walked toward him. Chuck knew how important and intimate that moment was, and he looked way, paying rapt attention to the screen ahead.

The haze had once again disappeared without a trace. Chuck's heart raced as the planet neared. He knew it had been time for him to step up his game to an even greater degree.

Grammy reached Farley and pulled at his shirt to bring him down closer to her. Farley had to bend over at the waist almost halfway down to hug Grammy. They held each other tightly, and she told him she loved him before whispering something in his ear too. Farley swallowed hard and blinked rapidly over and over, but tears formed nonetheless.

Grammy went back to her seat as Farley looked over at Chuck. He could see Chuck's shoulders moving up and down and knew that he was crying. He moved to stand behind Chuck and bent over to wrap his arms around his best friend. Neither could speak, but Chuck accepted the embrace and they both let loose, crying freely, unabashedly. A minute later, Chuck patted Farley on the hand gently, indicating that they needed to get back into survival mode.

They were only minutes from landing. The planet's surface was displayed on the screen in front of them. It appeared to be covered in black rocks and dust. It was dreary and didn't look as though there would be anywhere to hide their ship. The good news was that their ship wasn't overly big and maybe they could stack enough rocks around it to make it less visible. The ship shook, and the lights flashed as they passed through the planet's atmosphere. They flew lower and lower, and when they found a flat enough spot, Josh aided Chuck in setting the ship down. The air was so dense that the ship landed as though it had fallen into quicksand and was slowly sinking.

They were overwhelmed to be on a strange planet. It was anyone's guess as to how far away from Earth and Eris they were. All they could do was count on each other and hope for the best.

Chuck spoke first. "I think these are the gauges for our oxygen levels and reserves on the ship, and these ones measure the O2 levels outside. Is that right, Josh?"

"Yes, what do they tell you?" he asked.

"I think we're good for two days onboard, but when we go outside, it's going to feel the same as having asthma," Chuck answered. Farley looked duly impressed.

"And do you think we should risk going outside?" Josh asked.

"No question. I have no intentions of sitting around playing cards for the last two days of my life. We have no time to waste. I suggest we go out in pairs, except when one of those pairs includes Grammy—she stays onboard always."

Grammy looked amused as she shook her head. Chuck was sure she had plans other than sticking around the ship—she wanted to explore!

Grammy had joined the Planetary Space Agency when she was merely twenty-two years old. It had seemed like a lifetime ago to her. She recalled her first day when she got her own desk and learned how to monitor activity both within the Earth's solar system and beyond. The job had been quite a bore for her. She had been expecting all kinds of top-secret activities—visitors from other galaxies, learning to fire every kind of laser

135

and weapon, and piloting her own ship. She wanted to reach the outer limits of the universe, and if there was a universe beyond that, she also wanted to race there! She had been naïve only to the extent of *when* those things would happen. She had been a bit ahead of herself, but eventually, all of those dreams had come true. Now, some forty years later, she reflected on how she had gotten almost everything she had ever wanted. *And*, she had had a child and a grandson.

Grammy had lived a full life and had no regrets. Well, she wished she had learned to make banana bread. She blamed the oven time and time again when all her attempts failed miserably. She often told people that it didn't get hot enough, and the bread was undercooked. She also told people that the oven got too hot and burned the bread. She told both accounts to the same people and delighted at their instincts to always sympathize with her. It wasn't that she was manipulative or needed people to go along with or follow her but more that she was so far away from what most people would consider reality that the discussion over not-the-greatest banana bread ever gave her a sense of normalcy. The fact that others even entertained conversation about said crappy bread meant a lot to her.

Grammy knew that the sense of normalcy she needed was the reason why she had had a baby. Sheila was planned, but she never knew who her father was, nor did her father know of Sheila's existence. His name had been Russell, and he had died in a brutal explosion during a laboratory experiment involving new weapon technology. They had been too bold with the chemicals they were mixing, and it resulted in five deaths. Grammy mourned his passing briefly but never felt the need to talk about him at any length with anyone; it hurt her too much.

Grammy had never loved again after that. She threw herself into raising her daughter and living her secret life as a rising leader at the Planetary Space Agency. She was a visionary and always knew that they would encounter other life forms, as most people assumed they would, but she helped design the first ships that took humans beyond their own solar system. Grammy also led the team that first landed on Eris. She had designed the transport ship that carried materials to the planet with which they built their infrastructure of homes, power-generating devices, and refueling areas for their ships. She helped in refining the planet's limited natural resources to make the fuel as well as identified areas of the ground that were suitable for plant growth. They were able to grow food on Eris but still needed to transport water from Earth, both for drinking and to water the plants they were growing.

Grammy had watched the expanding colony on Eris for decades and treated it as though it was her second "baby." Her heart had always swelled at her impact on mankind and its pursuit for knowledge—until recently. Grammy was filled with mixed emotions as her part in advancing mankind also brought them to the aliens that were now killing them. She had honestly thought that theirs was a mutually-beneficial relationship that would flourish forever. She had no idea what had gone wrong. All she knew was they were all fighting for their lives. If they didn't beat the aliens, humans could be wiped out entirely.

Grammy sighed.

Chuck finished displaying all angles of their surroundings on the screen and determined that they were alone. It did not appear as though they had been followed or tracked. He unbuckled his seat belt and went to the closet to retrieve two space suits and oxygen tanks.

"Who wants to go first?" Chuck asked. He flicked his hair back and tried to sound upbeat but came across as flat and unsure.

"Why don't you and I go, Chuck? Josh and Grammy can monitor everything from here since they know the ship's operations better than you and I do." Farley's point made sense.

"That's some sound logic there, Farley, but I'm going to go ahead and recommend that Chuck and I go."

Grammy's suggestion surprised Chuck because he felt that staying separated would give at least one of them a chance at survival in case they were either attacked on the ship or hunted on the ground. He began to protest when Grammy stated her case.

"We all know that I'm an old goat and this might be my last adventure—not that merely being here with you nuts isn't adventure enough—but this is something I'd like to share with my grandson. You guys can go out after we do the first scout. We'll try to camouflage the ship, and then you two can search for—I don't even know what." Grammy looked from Josh to Farley and back to Josh.

"We can do that," Josh agreed.

Chuck didn't even bother to argue and passed one of the suits to Grammy. She stepped into it. Chuck also put on his suit. Farley checked him over, ensuring there were no holes or openings while Josh checked over Grammy. Josh then checked the oxygen tanks and confirmed they were full. "You'll have four hours of air. It should be plenty, and you're likely not going too far away." Grammy nodded.

She and Chuck put on their dome helmets, but Chuck yelled, "Wait!" Farley stopped clasping the helmet in place. Chuck lifted it up on the front and scratched his nose. Once satisfied, he said, "Okay, you may continue."

"Sheesh!" Farley said, shaking his head but grinning.

The last step was to attach the tanks to the built-in carriers on the backs of the suits and connect the hoses to the helmets. Josh showed Farley how to do it and then double-checked to ensure there would be no leaks.

"Are you crazy kids ready?" Josh asked.

Chuck turned to Grammy. When she smiled at him, he said, "Yes." Josh could barely hear him and realized they hadn't turned on the communicators. He flipped a switch on the neck of each suit and asked them both to speak. Grammy and Chuck could then hear each other, and both said they were ready to go.

"Do you want anything to eat before you head out? Are you sure you want to just go right away?" Farley sounded like a worrying old goat.

"I'm good," Chuck laughed. "You, Grammy?"

"I'm good, Chuck. You two make us a fine feast for when we return, and then it'll be your turn to head out."

"Roger that on the chop chop, Grammy," Josh said enthusiastically. "Finest meal you've ever had!"

Josh pressed the button to open the first set of double doors. They slid open with the slightest *whoosh* sound. Chuck and Grammy stepped through, and Josh closed the doors behind them. *Whoosh.* The seal against the outside was secure again. The pair stood there and took a couple deep breaths absent-mindedly before pressing the next button. The outer doors slid apart, making their suits feel as though they had shrunk two sizes. Grammy took the first step. She thought it was like trying to walk against the waves coming in to shore from the ocean. She staggered a bit and regained her footing. Holding out her hand, she felt Chuck grasp it, and he then took his first step. They walked together to the ramp that had lowered and walked down it, stepping onto the ground in unison. Their last adventure together had begun.

Chapter 25

Mike was pushed through the door where a man and woman were passed out on a couch. Another couple sat close together on a different couch. Mike recognized the second couple immediately, although he had only met them briefly before. "Do it," Chief said. The door closed behind Mike. Being separated from Lexi and Gaz, he was once again uncertain about his destiny. In his right hand, he awkwardly held a knife. The man and woman stared at him anxiously. The man stood and approached Mike. His hands were outstretched in a "stay calm" sort of fashion.

"What's your name, son?" Mike heard the man ask. Mike was relieved that the man didn't recognize him; it would make his job easier. Mike knew that if Gaz had been sent, he would not have been able to do what was necessary.

"Hi, Mr. Reynolds. My name is Mike."

Mike watched the recognition grow on Luke's face. He knew he didn't have much time to prove himself to Chief, and he had to move fast. He lunged at Luke, the knife raised in the air. Mike had a good six inches on Luke, and when he swung his arm downward slashing at him, Luke was able to duck while side-stepping, avoiding contact. Quick as a rabbit, Luke threw himself at Mike and knocked him off-balance but Mike was not only taller, he weighed at least eighty pounds more. It was solid muscle. Mike remained on his feet and slashed at Luke again. Luke staggered backward. Leila jumped from her seat and caught him before he landed on the coffee table.

Leila's screams woke Bross and Chrystal.

"What's going on?" Bross asked groggily, trying to sit upright.

Chrystal rubbed at her eyes and shrieked as she saw Mike wielding the knife not three feet away from her. She jumped over the arm rest of the couch and crouched, making herself as small as possible.

"Get away from us!" yelled Leila. Her arms were wrapped tightly around her husband, though he tried to shove her behind him where he could protect her.

Luke took his eyes off Mike for a split second and scanned the dirty dishes on the coffee table. He grabbed a plate and smashed it on the table creating a sharp and potentially lethal shard. He held it out in front of him menacingly. "I will not hesitate to use this." Luke's voice was hard as nails. He spoke with such hatred that while Leila cringed, she didn't loosen her grip on him.

"What are you going to do, old man?" Mike took a step toward Luke and Leila.

"Where is my daughter?" Luke asked quietly.

"Who? Dagny?" Mike toyed with Luke. "None of your business. I ask the questions. Where are Chuck and Farley?"

Bross sat unnoticed on the sidelines, watching the scene. He shifted to his right, closer to Chrystal. His hand touched something poking up between the cushions—a steak knife. Bross slowly wrapped his fingers around the handle of the knife and remained watchful and still.

Leila released her grip on Luke to pick up a piece of the broken plate. Mike laughed at her. He wasn't afraid of her and her little weapon any more than he was afraid of her husband and his little weapon. He saw pure terror in her face, and he liked it. He felt his underlying violence bubbling beneath the surface.

"Where. Is. My. Daughter?" Luke's voice was steel.

Mike laughed at them. "Look at you two, all ready to fight big bad Mike. Come on; come at me. Let's make this fun."

Mike smiled a genuine, joyful smile. He saw himself in Leila's face and knew she thought he was a psychopath. He nodded at her, confirming for her what she thought about him.

"All you have to do is tell me where Chuck and Farley are and this will all be over."

"Then you'll let them go?" Bross spoke.

"Go?" Mike repeated incredulously. "No one is going anywhere. Or has that not become clear? There is no way out of here alive for them. You might want to sit there and shut up." Mike stared Bross down.

Chrystal began to whimper. Bross said, "Shh, baby," in a soft, soothing voice as his eyes darkened.

Leila spoke then. "Mike, you don't have to do this. Do you even know what you're doing? Or why?" She slowly moved to her left, away from Luke. Mike followed her with his eyes, and Bross stood up, unnoticed. When Leila had stopped, she, Luke, and Bross had formed somewhat of a triangle around Mike.

"Well, Dagny's mom, you wouldn't be calling me stupid now, would you?"

Leila responded. "I was thinking more like lost, misguided, approval-seeking, lonely, but not stupid."

Mike hated people thinking he was stupid. It enraged him. He beat people up over the slightest implication that he was stupid. This, however, was unfamiliar to him. He had never before had someone state or hint at a possibility of him being needy or having no control or being a follower. It took him a few seconds to determine how badly he had been insulted and what he was going to do about it. She didn't seem to fear him at all, and that was new to him. She had to die. He had known that from the beginning, but his original plan was to kill the man first and then the woman would be easy. This woman, however, was different. She may be a more formidable opponent than the man, standing there looking at him as though he was an invited guest.

"You'll want to watch what you say to me, old woman," Mike sneered. His upper lip was pulled back tightly against his teeth, and his eyes were narrowed into slits.

"Actually, I don't think you know where she is. You're a henchman for the aliens, but I don't think you're in their inner circle. They probably haven't told you that much." Leila paused and then continued as Mike's face heated up in anger. "Dagny is probably with Chuck and Farley. Farley is a much better boyfriend for her than Gaz ever was. I bet they're all somewhere safe together, and you will never find them."

"Shut up!" Mike took a step toward Leila.

Mike's strong reaction told the room that he did *not* know where Dagny was. Leila adjusted the shard in her hand as though readying herself for his attack. She glanced quickly at Luke. Mike saw that both were ready to pounce.

"You are not worth my time." Then Leila looked Mike directly in the eye and said, "Idiot."

Mike jumped at her. A raging scream released from deep inside his being. At the same time, Luke and Bross lunged at Mike. Leila swiftly dropped to her right onto the ground and stuck out her leg as Bross rammed him from behind. Mike sprawled on the ground face first, and before he could even begin to push himself up, Luke was straddling him, broken plate in hand held firmly against Mike's neck.

"Make a move. I dare you." Luke's tone told Mike that he was at his wit's end.

"I'll kill you!" Mike began to buck, trying to knock Luke off.

"Good bye," Luke said calmly and pressed the knife into Mike's neck. A trickle of blood appeared as the door suddenly opened.

An alien rushed into the room, knocked Luke to the ground, picked up Mike, and was gone again all in about as much time as it took to blink once.

Chapter 26

Yu was busy on the computer and operations systems making calculations, desperately trying to find a way to triangulate the precise area where Grammy, Josh, Chuck, and Farley had disappeared. Their heat signature had already faded away. It was imperative that they knew the exact position or their recovery attempt would fail. Yu marveled at Nathan's book. He hadn't known the boy well at all but wished that he had. The information and knowledge that Nathan had recorded in his book was invaluable to the continuance of the human race. Nathan probably hadn't even known how important his thoughts were when he was writing them down. Yu wished that he had had more time to get to know Nathan because he had no doubt that they could have sent the aliens on their way. *Nathan was brilliant. There are no two ways about it,* Yu thought.

Mr. Castle said, "Do you think you can do it?"

"Give me some time," Yu said. Yu's brow was creased as he worked in a heightened state of concentration. Their friends depended on him, and he wanted to put a stop to the aliens.

Yu tapped violently at his keyboard and watched whatever appeared on his screen with rapt attention. He was in the zone where his performance was at its optimum. He had to keep going. If Yu stopped, he could recover, but he would lose precious time. Every second he took in trying to figure out how to initiate a rescue operation of their friends meant that another second had passed where they could have been injured or captured or worse, dead.

Yu referred to Nathan's book again, reading and rereading the page. "Nathan's ideas were pure genius, but our technology here on Eris isn't advanced enough for us to be able to replicate most of them. Nathan suggests that wormholes to other realms or parallel universes can actually be created, but we're not equipped to put it to task. This is frustrating! We're on the brink but just can't do it!"

"We have to try! We can't leave them out there to die!" Mr. Castle cried desperately. "What do we need? I'll contact my headquarters on Earth, and they'll bring it to us."

Yu was frazzled. He flipped through some pages in the book and looked at his screen again, reviewing his calculations. He shook his head. "I can't even dissect what he's written enough to determine what we need. Why didn't you protect Nathan better?" Yu sucked in his breath. He couldn't believe what he had just said.

"Excuse me?" Mr. Castle asked. His face reddened. "I was *horrified* when I found out that Nathan was in Newfoundland that day. He never even liked to fly his ship. I often suggested he take Chuck and the rest out for a spin, but he showed no interest. How was I ever to know that he would suddenly do just that? And that he would suddenly go with those same friends in search of Grammy? I have beaten myself up over his death every waking moment since it happened. I *know* I should have protected him better, dammit! How dare you?!"

Yu had never known what shame felt like until that moment. Yu had always been matter-of-fact, calm and reasonable, and, currently to his detriment, lacking in emotion and tact. He had some serious back-pedaling to do and even more apologizing. "Castle, I am so sorry. I don't know why I said that. I certainly never questioned your parenting skills or your love for Nathan. Please forgive me." Yu had jumped up from his chair so quickly that it had toppled over. He stood before Mr. Castle imploringly. He knew he would beat himself up over that one insensitive question forever.

Sparks stayed silent but moved to pick up Yu's chair. She began reading the page that Nathan's book had been opened to. Yu sensed she was uncomfortable and wanted to leave the room, but he also knew that she wouldn't leave him unless he asked her to.

"I know you meant nothing by it, Yu. I just need some time. I'll be back shortly." Mr. Castle then left the room.

Sparks spun around and faced him. "You okay, Yu?"

Yu paused, unsure what to say. He looked up and the nose on the ceiling looked back down at him. "We need to crack this and fast. Does any of it make sense to you?"

"Not really. I know that doesn't surprise you. I just wish I had a different answer. This isn't really my forte." Sparks switched back to her own chair while Yu took his again.

"I know. Wishful thinking, I suppose. Any idea what I can do to erase Castle's memory of what I said? And erase it from my mind, too?

"Get Nathan's friends back. Get Grammy and Josh back. Keep reading Nathan's book. Something will jump out at you, but first, you need a break. You've been working non-stop, and it's beginning to affect you. I've never seen you this frustrated before." Sparks's tone was of deep concern.

"I've never felt so inadequate. I'm used to mastering everything I attempt with little effort. I'm stumped." Yu stood again. "Nathan hypothesized that portals to other planets, galaxies, and universes were everywhere. The human idea of teleportation meant that someone could move from one place to another in an instant. Nathan wrote that he believed it would be possible one day but that we aren't there yet. The portals, however, are already in existence and could be opened by way of a strong enough explosion at any entry or exit point. If Nathan was right, that is where Chuck and the others are. The mind boggles."

"I have faith in you, Yu. You *will* figure it out," Sparks said encouragingly.

"The portals are the key, I think. Nathan didn't believe that portals could be created. They had to be found. And they were precise. I liken it to walking through a doorway on a house—you must go directly through the doorway, not through the wall beside the doorway. We could go up there with all kinds of bombs and set them off and still never make it through the portal. I think you're right. I'll go for a walk and try to clear my mind. Back in thirty minutes."

Yu turned for the door when it suddenly flew open. Yu expected to see Mr. Castle rushing in with a solution or an idea, but it was Ronnie.

"Oh, hey, Ronnie," Sparks said.

"We have a situation." Ronnie seemed beside himself. His face was distorted in fear. "Where is Castle?" His blue leather shirt was misbuttoned, and the right side hung longer than the left.

"He is taking a break. What's going on?" Yu put his hand on Ronnie's shoulder to calm him.

Ronnie took a deep breath. "Earth is under attack!" His eyes were wild.

One by one, the Earth's symbols of life and freedom fell. The CN Tower in Toronto, Canada, snapped in half like a twig. The top half of its 553 meters dropped as though in slow motion into Lake Ontario. The water bounced straight up like a water fountain show at an amusement park. Escaping cars and people were crushed under the weight of the concrete and metal. Thunder roared in exception at the assault.

In New York, the Statue of Liberty had her legs kicked out from under her. Throngs of people ran in all directions trying to avoid her as she tumbled from her pedestal. Screams trailed out over the ocean.

The Eiffel Tower in Paris, France, shattered, sending beams of iron flying every which way. Some passersby were sprayed by blood as others were impaled.

The bridge connecting the Petronas Towers in Kuala Lumpur was shot out by one precise missile. Concrete, glass, steel, and charred and burning body parts showered the ground below as people darted everywhere, trying to avoid injury and death.

Hundreds of tourists were annihilated while visiting The Great Pyramid in Egypt. Two-ton stones exploded in a frenzy as three alien spaceships raced away.

In Russia, Japan, Australia, and Brazil, dozens of alien ships landed fearlessly, and the disembarking aliens raided the villages. They lashed their tongues out at every human they saw, slicing and sucking at the same time. They were so quick that a whole body was devoured almost instantly. The aliens were starving. They had failed to find the humans named Chuck, Yu, and Farley, or any of the other humans who had double-crossed them, and it was time to wage war on Earth. They were taking advantage of their attempt to draw out their enemies with the attack on Earth to fill their skeletal bodies with as much "food" as possible before they were called back to their home planet.

Each alien, for every human they ate, would have to capture a human to bring home for breeding purposes. People sprinted to escape along blood-spattered streets. Screams and cries for help fought to be heard above the din of screeching tires and horns blasting. Shop owners rushed to lock their doors in the hope of saving themselves. One merchant froze while pulling the metal gate across as he made eye contact with an alien. The alien appeared to smile a gruesome smile at him as it beheaded someone with one violent flick of its long, slithery tongue. The merchant squealed in horror as he raced to the back of his store and down the stairs to a hidden bunker he had built years prior in anticipation of such an attack.

A woman tried to keep up with her boyfriend, but her hand slipped from his grasp as she slid along the blood-covered sidewalk, trying to maintain her balance. She lost her footing and crashed to the ground as her ankle twisted. Her boyfriend saw her face contorted in pain as he leaped toward her to help. It was too late. Two aliens descended upon them and feasted.

On the edge of one of the villages, a line of people walked slowly, hypnotized, onto an alien ship. Once that ship was full, the door closed, and the ship flew away. It was out of sight in a matter of seconds. The ship that had been parked beside it opened its doors then, and the rest of the humans that had been standing single-file, motionless and expressionless, began to board the ship until it, too, was full and soared off.

Other ships maintained watch from just beyond the Earth's atmosphere. They were anticipating a counter attack but were also anxious for the appearance of Chuck and his friends. The aliens had not forgotten the battle they had lost at Gros Morne Mountain. They wanted to be ready, and they wanted revenge.

Suddenly, half of the hundred or so alien ships orbiting Earth shot off like darts and headed toward Eris. People on Earth looking up at the sky as they feared for their lives saw half the lights in the sky disappear without warning. As the alien ships on Earth filled with mind-controlled humans, the people remaining cowered in alleys, under beds, in closets, some alone, some clinging to another person. The fear was palpable. Screams and cries were heard everywhere. The large-scale attack on Earth was everyone's worst fear.

Yu was speechless. His eyes widened as he realized their situation was direr than they had known. The sound of thunder rumbled in the hall and slowed as Karona ran in. Her heavy combat boots had roared as they pounded on the tiles.

"Ronnie, what's going on?" Karona asked. "When you took off from the class, we all knew something was wrong."

"Aliens are attacking Earth," he said simply.

The alarm sounded just then. Yu had motioned to Sparks, and she had hit the button to sound the distress signal. A slow but loud *whoop* repeated over the speaker system while red lights flashed overhead on all the ceilings throughout the building. Mr. Castle came running back into the room as though beckoned by the alarm.

"Aliens are attacking Earth," said Ronnie. Yu thought it was the only thing he could say.

Mr. Castle immediately opened his communicator and contacted his forces on Earth. "What's going on?" he demanded when someone finally answered. It seemed to Yu as though it took a lifetime for someone to respond to the call. He could hear shrill screams in the background.

"Sir, we are under attack. We don't know what our loss count is, but it's happening all over the world. One saving grace is that the ships orbiting Earth seem to be leaving." The voice on the other end of the communication sounded as though it was forcing an even tone.

"Leaving to go where?" Mr. Castle asked.

"We do not know, sir. We just see the lights in the sky moving away, fast as lightning."

Mr. Castle looked at Yu. "Monitor our skies. Alien ships are leaving Earth."

Yu jumped on the controls. "All clear," he said as he settled in to monitor the situation.

Mr. Castle looked at Ronnie. "We need to get our defenses up and be ready for anything. Ronnie, prepare our fighter shuttles and have every pilot on alert."

Ronnie swallowed a huge lump in his throat. He looked at Karona and said, "You're up. You ready?"

Karona's face went white.

Ronnie stared at her and ended up asking her again if she was ready.

"Yes, sorry, yes. I thought I answered," she replied. She moved for the door where Mr. Castle stopped her.

"Be brave. Be strong."

When she swallowed hard, he hugged her tightly. She left the room with Ronnie following.

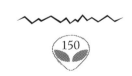

The three aliens could not find the ships they had been watching. The explosion had lit up their screen before the images turned black. There was nothing. They had watched for minutes, waiting for the reappearance of the ships that didn't happen. The inch-wide vein in Jambay's head throbbed and looked as though it, too, would explode. The door opened for Shabay to enter the cockpit. Jambay and Rebay lowered their heads, waiting for punishment in losing the ship that had surely held the humans they so badly wanted dead.

"Are they dead?" Shabay asked. His voice was pure steel.

No one spoke.

Shabay had no patience. He opened his mouth, his tongue swirling out.

"We don't know!" Besbay answered so quickly he almost tripped himself as he jumped from his chair. "Shabay, the two lights blow up and go away. They don't come back. We don't see them again." Besbay scratched his head and stared at the dark screen.

Shabay focused on Jambay and Rebay. "Yes?" he asked for confirmation.

"Y-yes," stammered Jambay.

"That's right," replied Rebay.

Shabay went to the controls and began flipping switches and moving dials while he read the readings on the screen. "There is absolutely nothing left…which is impossible. They have been pushed into another dimension. That is the only explanation."

The other three looked at each other, not knowing what to think. They began to worry that the humans had mastered creation of portals and their disappearance wasn't an accident. If the humans had that level of technology, the aliens could be doomed, and their counter-attack on the aliens at Gros Morne Mountain was a small example of their power.

"What should we do?" asked Rebay.

Shabay held down a blue button and spoke. "We need to attack now. Get thirty ships over to Eris immediately."

"Yes, sir!" was the response that came out of the speaker overhead.

Shabay released the blue button.

"Eris, sir?" asked Jambay.

"Yes. That human ship left Earth and was heading to Eris. That must be where they've been hiding." Shabay stood. "Move us into position to fight at Eris." He left the room as quickly as he had entered.

The remaining three took their positions at the controls and plotted their course for Eris.

Chapter 27

"Great. Let's get this over with." Sulinda huffed and stuck out her lower lip.

Far off in the distance, they could see two humans walking hand in hand. Both had long, dark hair, pants, and long-sleeved shirts. As day turned to night, the temperature had lowered. The trio pulled jackets from their respective bags and put them on.

"I think I should be the one to do all the speaking," Maywano said.

"I think I shall do no speaking whatsoever," Sulinda said before pressing her lips firmly together to show that she meant it.

"Maybe I can do some of the speaking once we meet them. Okay, Maywano?" Sparrow looked hopeful.

"That might work. We shall see. If I feel it could help us or would be appropriate, I shall tell you. You've got plenty of time to think about what you might want to say. Think of a pleasant experience you've had perhaps. That might be a nice way to make friends for our three-month stay."

Sparrow smiled as they continued walking toward the little town.

Maywano pulled something out of his pocket. It normally would be something he would wear around his wrist like a watch, but he wished to keep it secret that he had it. He pressed a button on it and heard the familiar *boop* sound, indicating that it still worked. He turned it off again quickly, making his own *boop* sounds in case the others had heard it. He had to be careful about who knew of its existence and ability. If it fell into the wrong hands, it could mean disaster. Maywano sighed, thinking that he may be the only living and thinking being who could make it work, and he stressed about passing on his knowledge. Troy's attitude proved to Maywano that he was not the person to whom the mechanism should be trusted. Nor did he want to give it to Sulinda. He was sure she'd take off with Troy the second it became possible.

That left Sparrow. He trusted her and knew that he and she were of like mind. She was benevolent, sweet, and had a zeal for life, albeit not the smartest or strongest link in the chain. She could easily be tricked into giving it away by anyone who simply smiled at her and asked for it.

Unless something dreadful were to happen, they planned on staying with the humans for three months. Perhaps he would befriend their leader and together they could see if the mechanism's features could be useful in the fight against the aliens.

"Maywano? Is there anything wrong? Do you need to rest?" Sparrow asked, concerned.

He looked around and realized he had stopped dancing. He was standing in one spot, which wasn't like him, and he was staring at the mechanism. He quickly shoved his hands in his pockets when he turned his head and saw Sparrow and Sulinda staring at him. He didn't think they had seen what he had held. He shook his head back and forth quickly and said, "Just needed a bit of a brain rattle. I'm fine, dears. We are nearing the people. Let us skip!!"

Maywano took off like a dart in giant leaping skips, taking him at least three feet off the ground. Sparrow laughed and followed. Sulinda ran behind them begrudgingly.

"I can't wait to see what's going to come out of my mouth when we meet them. I hope it's something clever and engages them in a lengthy, philosophical conversation. That would be delightful!"

Sparrow clapped her hands to that while she skipped along beside Maywano.

The sky slowly but steadily darkened, and the couple they had spotted earlier had disappeared. The group forged on. Maywano stopped then and pulled a bag of crushed crackers out of his pocket. The others stopped while he poured a handful for each of them. They ate silently and continued their journey when they were finished. They walked because, with the fading light, they were unable to see the uneven ground and were forced to pay attention to every step. Three hours went by before they were on the edge of the town. They saw their first human house up close. Painted on the side wall were portraits of three smiling people.

"What should we do? Should we go in?" Sparrow asked excitedly.

"I'm a bit nervous," Maywano admitted, jumping from foot to foot.

"They might be dangerous, and we're unarmed," Sulinda piped in.

Maywano nodded wide-eyed, shaking and bouncing his long braids about. "Let's keep walking until we find someone, and if they're not receptive to speaking to us, we can run away. I've noticed, we're quite fast."

They set off along the sidewalk and looked pleasant. Sulinda's scowl was less fowl. Most of the houses had no lights on inside, but at the end of the street was a three-level, fully-lit building. There were also spaceships coming and going beyond the building, perhaps close enough to them to walk to it that night. "To the building!" Maywano whispered loudly. He didn't want to wake any sleeping occupants in the nearby homes. They sped their pace, being back on level ground. Everywhere they looked, the ground had been flattened. Every painting of every smiling occupant on each house began to convince the group that they were among friendly people. Their confidence in their plan boosted. Even Sulinda was skipping.

From the looming building, a man emerged. He nodded at them and held the door open for them. Maywano nodded back and stepped through the door. The two girls followed. They squinted their eyes at the bright lights inside. Against the opposite wall, a young woman sat behind a dark, wooden desk and in a friendly voice asked, "May I help you?"

"Oh! I dare say I hope so, sweet girl. You see, we aren't from around here…"

"That's clear, sweetie! I'm excited to hear all about your trip. Was the shuttle to your liking?" She stood and held out her hand. "I'm Lesley." She wore a light pink, full-length dress, and her long, blond hair was pulled back in a high ponytail.

Maywano looked at her hand and then looked at his own. He held it out and flattened it, palm facing the ground, and then slowly turned it so his thumb was on top.

Lesley laughed in delight. "Here," she said, taking his hand in hers and shaking it. Then she shook hands with Sparrow and Sulinda.

"Can I take one of the shuttles right now?" Sulinda asked.

"Have you not just arrived? Why do you want to go back to Earth so soon?" Lesley asked, shocked.

"Not to Earth. Here, on this planet. Maybe an hour away." Sulinda was all seriousness.

Lesley's smile faltered. "Well, there is nowhere an hour away. You can walk to everything we have here on Eris, although we're building more and more every year."

Maywano gave Sulinda a stern look. She quieted.

"Fine. That's fine!" Maywano said with a big smile on his face. He held his arms out to his sides in a wide gesture of acceptance of everything. He was feeling comfortable, so he did a quick spin and was proud of how high the skirts of his robe went. He was about to spin again when he caught the eye of Sparrow who shook her head ever so slightly. Maywano stopped himself and grabbed Lesley's hand to shake it again. He had hoped she wouldn't tell him to leave for improper conduct.

Lesley squeezed his hand back and sat behind her neatly arranged desk again. "Well, welcome to Eris. What can I do to help you?"

Maywano held his arms at his sides and made the occasional gesture that looked as though he was trying to prevent his skirts from taking flight. "Dear Lesley, I think it is us who may be able to help you."

"Oh! You're with the construction team?" she asked unbelievingly and confused.

"I'm not sure what that means exactly. We know there's an alien threat, and we can help fight against it."

Lesley stared at them. The expression on her face looked as though her brain was running a mile a minute. "Prove it."

Maywano took a deep breath. "Are you the leader?"

"No, but I know who they are, and I know where they are."

"I will tell you, and then will you take me to the leader? It is imperative."

"Deal." Lesley held out her hand again.

Maywano held his out, flattened it, turned it so his thumb was on top, and clasped hers, pumping it up and down. "Yes. Okay. Deal. Deal."

Lesley said nothing when Maywano ended his story. She slowly stood and headed down the hallway to her right. Twenty steps away, she turned around and asked, "Are you coming?"

The three of them ran to her. She turned away, and they followed her down the corridor. Maywano fought between hopefulness, where he wanted to spin his skirts, and apprehension over the possibility of doing something wrong when they met the leader. He wondered what the leader was like. Was he stern? Was he happy? Did he like to juggle, and would he juggle for them? Was he a she? He wondered if she was a fan of the theory that the grass isn't always greener on the other side.

They passed several doors before stopping in front of one that had a giant brown nose painted on it. Just then, the alarm sounded. All the red lights along the ceiling began to flash.

Chapter 28

Purple fog floated toward them, bringing with it the sweet scent of cotton candy. The fog wasn't dense. They could see where they were stepping. The ground was rough with gray and black rocks and no sign of vegetation or animals. It was as though they were on a giant, bumpy, lifeless boulder that periodically breathed out a purple haze. They walked along slowly, taking care of their footing and observing the little that there was to observe.

"You okay, Chuck?" Grammy asked.

"This is insane. I feel like I'm going to wake up any second now."

Grammy squeezed his hand. "I know what you mean, dear. Being here is surreal."

"May I ask you a question, Grammy?"

"Of course. Anything." Grammy stopped walking and looked at Chuck. His face was one big question.

"Do you think we'll get off this planet? Tell me the truth."

Grammy sighed. "What do you think, Chuck? Now is not the time to despair. We have to stay positive. We've only just begun looking around, and who knows what we may find to help us?"

"I know, but..."

"It's okay to be scared. I'm scared too." Grammy smiled reassuringly. "Think of it this way. That alien ship could have blown us up, and we could be dead now. Instead, we've gone through the portal and are still alive. We can keep fighting, and as long as we're alive, we have a chance."

Chuck hugged Grammy and began walking again. He was deep in thought, considering what Grammy had just said and trying to draw conclusions. He knew that they still had a chance, but he also knew that they had no weapons, no resources, little air, and little food. He could see for miles when he looked around, but all he saw was desolation.

"At least the fog is pretty," Chuck said. He knew he had to be strong for Grammy.

"It really is! I was thinking the same thing."

"And it smells delicious! It's making me kind of hungry." Chuck laughed an almost real-sounding laugh.

"Our friends will have food waiting for us when we get back to the ship, with any luck. Of course we might get back to them sooner than expected since there appears to be absolutely nothing out here."

"That's weird, isn't it, Grammy?"

"What do you mean?" Grammy asked.

"Well, if we're on the alien planet, where are all the aliens?"

They both stopped walking and considered Chuck's observation. There were no ships on the ground and none flying in the sky, neither near nor far. If they hadn't been followed through the portal by the alien ship that had been firing at them, they could easily believe that they were positively alone on the planet. They hadn't seen or heard any sign of that alien ship at all since they had landed, and Chuck wondered why that was. Where was the ship? If it was out there somewhere, they weren't safe, and they had no defenses against it.

"Where indeed?" Grammy agreed.

They walked on, lost in their own thoughts. After an hour of the scenery changing not in the slightest, Grammy suggested they head back toward the ship and set off in another direction. They did just that, walking back and passing their ship, and continuing on for an hour. It was slow-going because of how dense the air was. They didn't get very far, but aside from the ground being jagged with rocks, it was relatively flat. They could still see for miles—miles of emptiness.

Grammy motioned with her head to turn around and go back. Chuck nodded in agreement. They were both hungry at that point, and some food might help them to think of another plan.

They arrived at the ship and entered. Meeting Farley and Josh in the cockpit, they sat down to plates of canned ham, canned corn, canned peas, and buns with no butter. Bottles of water were warm, but they had several cases which would last them for at least as long as their air would.

After they ate, Josh said, "There's been no activity whatsoever. Did you find anything?"

"Nada," Grammy replied. "We headed what I'll call 'north' and then went 'south.' You and Farley can go 'east' and 'west.' I have a couple of ideas after you've done your search, but I want to go over them in my head a little more before I share them with you guys."

Chuck and Farley nodded in acceptance. Once they were all done eating, Farley and Josh suited up and did their obligatory search, though they both felt it would be as fruitless as Chuck and Grammy's. They were right. They saw and found nothing that could help them. The entire existence of the planet seemed to provide no use at all, though they only covered a small part of it. They considered the option that perhaps only a certain area of it had been inhabited, like humans had colonized only a piece of Eris. If that were the case, they had to be prepared for the aliens to appear at some point, although they had little to prepare. If aliens did show up, the crew was at their mercy.

Josh and Farley put their suits back in the closet when they returned, and the four of them sat down to discuss their options.

"Grammy, what are your ideas?" Chuck asked.

She cleared her throat. "We can't stay here. Do we all agree with that?"

A unanimous and conviction-filled "yes" filled the cockpit.

"We can't die on this lump of rock without trying everything, and we can't leave anything unused before we die. Are you all onside with that?" she asked.

"Of course," said Chuck.

"100%," said Farley.

"I'm with you," said Josh.

"Good. Let's fire up this puppy and look for the aliens." She looked at the group and was met with furrowed brows and looks of shock and horror that turned into resignation that it was their only chance.

Farley shook his head but made no eye contact with anyone. Chuck knew Farley wasn't opposing the idea; he was just wrapping his head around it.

Josh stood and said, "When do you want to leave?" He was always ready for action and to do whatever Grammy wanted.

Chuck held his breath while he waited for Grammy to answer.

"No time like the present. Anyone need to use the bathroom before we go?" she joked.

"Actually, I do," said Chuck laughing a strained laugh. He stood and walked down the hall as Josh took the controls, starting up the engines.

Farley moved to his seat. Facing the screen, he said, "Rock and roll, baby. Rock and roll." Grammy high-fived him as she walked past and took her seat.

Chuck returned, and they buckled their seatbelts in preparation for take-off. "We'll head east then. Is that right?" he asked.

"Absolutely. Might as well take the most direct route—as far as we know—possible. We can't waste fuel, and this atmosphere is draining on our supply." Grammy looked over her shoulder at Chuck and Farley and said, "I love you guys, but I wish you weren't here."

"Likewise," said Chuck.

"Rock and roll," said Farley.

Grammy and Josh high-fived each other. The ship lifted off the ground as Josh worked the controls. "When we get there, let me do all the talking," Grammy advised. "Maybe I can get through to them somehow."

Although their ship lay on its side, the damage was not enough to penetrate its hull. The occupants were relatively uninjured—scrapes and bruises mostly. Their crash was soft because of the density of the surrounding air, and they had been able to use their weapons—at first. They had fired on the ship they had followed through the explosion into another dimension, but they did not think they had made contact. Shortly after the human ship seemed to have disappeared, their controls no longer worked. They hit the ground harder than they had originally thought, and they didn't know what to do.

Pintay rubbed the throbbing vein on his large, slimy head as he set their computer to scan all systems for functionality. "I do not know why we lost control or why all our systems seem to be shutting themselves down. I cannot stop it."

The cockpit was slowly filling up with white smoke. Red light bulbs flashed "red alert" throughout the disabled ship. Everything else was black except the three red skeletal beings standing at the control panel.

Mishay stared blankly, wordlessly. She never spoke, and Pintay had no idea why she had been on the mission other than the fact that she was given special treatment, being Chief Shabay's daughter.

Kallay looked thoughtful and said, "Maybe we can find the humans and take their ship. I really don't think we shot them down." She looked at the others.

Mishay's face remained expressionless.

Pintay shook his head but then nodded and then shook it again. "It is too dangerous to go searching for them. We do not know what condition they are in, and maybe they didn't even land."

Kallay watched as lights on their control panel went out one by one, as though counting down to their death. Only half of the lights were still lit or blinking. "We don't have a choice, as far as I can tell. Do you have a way of repairing whatever damage is shutting us down? I don't even know how to fix anything, and Mishay doesn't even know she's in the world right now."

"Does she ever?" Pintay asked. He looked at Mishay. She appeared to be not even slightly offended by the derogatory question. She smiled at Pintay instead. Pintay sighed. "I can think of no way to get us out of this dire situation either." He shook his head some more and then said, "Abandon ship. Get our suits, and let's see what's out there."

Kallay obliged and returned a couple minutes later. She looked at the controls again, and this time only a third of the lights indicated something was still operational. Smoke continued to fill the ship. Pintay knew what she was thinking without her saying a word.

"We will be fine. This ship will not catch on fire before we leave it," he said. He knew Kallay was terrified of fire, and he hurried to help her put her space suit on. He glanced at Mishay and saw that she, too, had been moving quickly to put on her suit. He saw relief in Kallay's face that Mishay also wanted off the ship.

Pintay had finished dressing in his suit and protective gear and helped the other two clamp their full-face helmets into place before Kallay ensured his was sealed properly as well. He took a last look at their computer system and watched as the last three lights blinked out for good. "Let's go," he instructed. The ship had no power. He had to manually crank the lever to open the door to the outside where the smoke was purple, not white.

The way the ship had crash-landed, the door opened to the top of the ship rather than on the side of it. Pintay climbed up first and then grabbed Mishay under her arms as Kallay hoisted her up. Pintay helped Kallay next. The three red skeletal aliens stood on their ship and surveyed the landscape, unsure of their fate. They could see nothing that would indicate in what direction they should set out. Everything was gray and rocky save for the purple dancing smoke. It smelled sweet to them and lifted their spirits ever so slightly.

Thick, white smoke followed them from the ship and reminded them that they had no time to waste. Their ship could blow up at any moment. They had no desire to be burned alive. Kallay screamed and jumped from the eight-foot height of the ship and landed expertly with a roll. She stood and brushed off the dust from the ground and looked up. "Hurry up! Let's get out of here!"

Pintay lowered Mishay to the ground and then jumped down himself. He checked his laser guns to ensure they were set at full power. Kallay did the same and asked Mishay which way to go. Mishay pointed in the direction behind them, and they began walking, guns pointed ahead.

The purple fog had dissipated again, giving them full visibility to see miles ahead. They flew low to the ground, the four of them searching the screen and windows for signs of the enemy. Josh kept a careful watch on their fuel supply and said, "For whatever reason, we aren't burning through our fuel as quickly as I thought we would. Perhaps the dense air has something to do with it, much like salt water is more buoyant than fresh water." They had flown farther than the distance they had walked but saw nothing out of what they considered to be the ordinary. Everything remained bleak and gray and the ground was still relatively flat. The flatness of the terrain offered them some relief that at least it would be harder for any enemies to hide from them. The haze stayed away in cooperation with their efforts.

"Grammy?"

"Yes, my dear?"

"What will you say to them? I mean, what could you possibly say to them? They hate us." Chuck's voice was full of doubt.

Grammy cleared her throat as she considered her response. "They didn't always hate us. We *did* used to work together, and if your theory is right and they are just as lost on this planet as we are, I don't see them having any choice but to work with us again—at least until we can figure out how to get home."

"I sure hope they appreciate logic as much as we do," Chuck said, not sounding overly sure at all.

"Let's think of it another way then, shall we?" Grammy swiveled her chair to face Chuck and Farley. "Those aliens have been eating us, yes, but they've also been capturing us. There must be a reason. I think it's them being cautious not to exhaust their food supply. It stands to reason that they might be stock-piling humans, which means they are using logic or some sort of thought process rather than letting their hunger control their actions." Grammy turned forward again to let Chuck and Farley digest what she had said.

They thought on it and five minutes later conceded that she was probably right. Chuck was still nervous about the idea and what they were attempting to do, but he knew they had to try; they were doomed on the planet anyway. Chuck never once contemplated that his last adventure with his grandmother would be one where they were both likely to die—and horribly so. He was grateful to have his best friend with him but sad that his best friend was likely to die along with him. Chuck was also grateful that his mother wasn't with them. He hated admitting that his mother would impede their efforts to overtake the aliens, if it came to that; they had a better chance at survival without having to carry her. Sheila was at her best when she had her wine and was watching soap operas. It was the simple things in life that she enjoyed, and Chuck hoped that his mother was somewhere safe with a big glass of wine in her hand.

"Farley, if we ever make it home, we should find your parents," Chuck stated.

Farley's jaw dropped. Chuck had never been close to Farley's parents since Farley had practically raised himself. He and his parents loved each other, but his mother and father were of a different breed. They never wanted to have conventional lives, waking up at 6:00 a.m. to go to work for 11-12 hours and then home to make a dinner they were too tired to eat. They weren't interested in enrolling Farley in any extra-curricular activities or sports. They didn't watch television or go to concerts or care about travelling. They were simple people who preferred a tent in the woods over a luxury penthouse apartment or a house on some sprawling piece of land with some well-manicured gardens.

Farley's parents weren't big talkers. They preferred to communicate with their bodies and with subtle looks. They didn't have any relatives with whom they were in touch, and as far as Chuck knew, Farley's grandparents had all passed away long ago. They had made their living off selling their arts and crafts. Farley's mother prided herself on how beautiful the pillows she made were. Her name was Pear, and she loved to embroider butterflies and peacocks and frogs onto multi-colored fabric pillows. The pillows were shaped into balls instead of traditional square or rectangular-shaped pillows, and they were only for wall decorations. She sewed a piece of string to the top of each ball in two spots so that it could hang from a thumb tack that she also provided. The thumb tacks were shaped into little pears of every different color, and only she would choose the perfect pear thumb tack to go with each pillow.

Lemongrass, Farley's father, prided himself on being as creative as his wife, albeit in a different manner. He was a songwriter of folk music, which was insanely popular among people in their 60s and 70s, and he made more than enough money for their family to live. While Lemongrass and Pear didn't care about money per se, they understood that they needed it in order to feed and clothe Farley and put a roof over his head. Farley didn't mind camping here and there but wasn't about to live in the woods bathing in the lake and always smelling like body odor. His parents respected his wants as a human being and did their best to keep Farley happy.

"What made you think of my parents just now, of all times?" Farley asked, stupefied.

"I was thinking about my own mom, hoping I'll get to see her again, and I realized that even though you're always at my place, you have your own parents. I was feeling quite selfish. I'm sorry about that." Chuck reached out for a fist bump, and Farley responded in kind.

"Thanks, Chuck." Farley stared off for a few seconds before continuing. "Yeah, they just sort of took off when the aliens first attacked. They didn't care to see what would happen…if we'd be able to fight them off. I really think they've been waiting for something like this to happen so they could escape to the woods permanently."

"Even though they left you, I'm sure they love you in their own weird way."

"They do. And they did ask me to go with them even though they knew what my answer would be."

"Do you wish you went with them, looking around now at where we've managed to find ourselves?" Chuck asked.

"Not a chance. Can you see me living off the land? I mean, what even are they eating—bugs? Tree roots? Moss?" Farley laughed. "I love them too, but they're way too far out there in their tree-hugging hippy ways for me. I guess I miss them. It would be nice to see them again. Sure, we'll find them if we get back home someday."

Grammy and Josh listened to the conversation without intruding on it. They stayed on their path straight ahead and kept their eyes peeled for any signs of anything out of the norm for the desolate, rocky planet.

"They brought their big tent with them this time. I guess they think they'll be staying a while longer than they did the last time they moved to live among the trees and dirt. Aliens must be a bigger threat than the ants that got into the house back in the spring." Farley laughed.

Chuck laughed with him.

"Can we go and see your mom first though?" Farley asked. "She might have real food for us."

Chuck laughed again. "Yes, of course."

"There! Do you see it?" Kallay asked, jumping into the air and pointing.

In the distance, they could see something moving in the sky but could not make it out exactly.

"Yes, something is definitely there," replied Pintay. "I wish there was something we could hide behind. I don't like being so out in the open like this." Their red space suits were definitely difficult to conceal against the grayness of everything around them.

"We need the mist again. Oh, I wish we knew what made it appear!" Kallay said desperately.

Pintay stopped walking and ran his gloved hand along the ground. "Hmm, it might just be dusty enough to cover our suits. Maybe we can blend in a bit at least."

The three lost aliens began scooping up the rock dust with their gloved hands and rubbing it into their red padded space suits. Although it helped to mask them a bit, a ship flying overhead would be able to tell that someone or something was on the planet's surface.

"If they see us and land, we must be ready to overtake them and steal their ship," Pintay said.

"I'm always ready," said Kallay. She turned to Mishay. "If they land, stay back and wait until we tell you what to do."

Mishay's eyes closed for a second in acknowledgement.

They lay flat on the ground watching the movement in the sky off in the distance. "How will we get them to stop without first shooting us?" Kallay asked.

"Good question, and I do not know." Pintay was unsure of himself, and he was not used to feeling that way. He was a decision maker at his core and rarely hesitated. He weighed the options in his head. If they allowed the ship to fly by, they may never see it again nor have the chance to take it over. However, if they allowed themselves to be seen, the humans would have a clear shot to kill them where they lay. In either scenario, they were dead.

He entertained a third option—perhaps the humans wouldn't kill them on sight. Perhaps the humans needed them too. Perhaps they could gain entry to the ship and then take it over somehow. "We need to let them catch us," he stated.

"You cannot be serious!" Kallay sat bolt upright.

Pintay also sat up. "I am absolutely serious." He walked her and Mishay through what he had been thinking.

Kallay bowed her head in resignation though she did not fully agree, and Mishay closed her eyes in acceptance of his idea.

Pintay stood. After a few moments, he held out his hand to Mishay who took it. He helped her to her feet and then offered his hand to Kallay as well. She reluctantly took it and stood beside them. He knew that even though she didn't like the idea, Kallay understood they probably did not have any other choices. She looked off in the distance and saw the approaching ship much more clearly than it had been before. Kallay raised her hands above her head and began waving them, drawing attention to their position. The others followed suit.

Chapter 29

Rod Walken's usually slicked-back, jet-black hair was disheveled at best. It hung down in his face. He wore no make-up, making him look pale and almost sickly. He looked in the mirror one last time and said, "Perfect. Let's roll."

The drone camera counted down in a robot voice, "In five, four, three…"

Rod looked directly into its lens and said, "There was an explosion in space an hour ago. It may or may not have killed Grammy, Josh, Chuck Holloway, and Farley Fillion. There is no trace of their ship. The best we can do is hope that Mr. Castle and his team will be able to locate them before it's too late. We also confirm that there have been alien attacks of the most violent and aggressive sort all over Earth. Some people have been eaten alive while others have been taken away. Countless ships have been spotted leaving Earth after loading what could only amount to hundreds upon hundreds of humans."

Rod paused for effect and ran his hand through his hair in a false effort to straighten it; he wanted to appear as though all the bad news was actually bothering him. He was really only after the ratings, and he knew how to hit his faithful audience.

"We have no death count as yet, but a preliminary count estimates the loss of thousands worldwide. It has been an absolute slaughter here on Earth, and while the attacks seem to have halted, we must stand prepared for more. Some areas were so badly destroyed that it will take years to recover and rebuild. Hundreds of homes are lost, and fires are still raging."

Rod put his hand to his ear and cocked his head as though receiving messages. "This just in! It appears all the ships that had landed on our beautiful planet have left, and the ones orbiting Earth, for the most part, have also left. My source says we are being watched by a dozen or so ships, but they are no longer firing on us. The ships that have moved away from us seem to be headed toward Eris."

Rod hung his head, shaking it back and forth ever so slightly for effect. He admired his tie while he did so. It was a black tie with blinking stars all over it, surrounding a blue and green Earth with white cloud cover here and there. He thought it may be his favorite tie next to the one he had specially made of his own image. He never wore that one out in public though. He preferred to wear it when he was home alone so he could admire it freely without the judging eyes of others watching him.

The crew watched on while the camera floated around, capturing Rod's image from all angles. He held up his tie so the camera could zoom in and broadcast it clearly. "This is our *home*. This is where we *live*. We all, every one of us, deserves to live for as long as each of us chooses to do so. We have not wronged the aliens. We have not done anything to call them here with their killing ways. We *implore* them to leave our planet and to leave us alone in peace. Aliens, if you can hear my plea, I beg of you to stop hurting us and to go home.

"I reported in the past about Luke and Leila Reynolds. Admittedly, we don't know their whereabouts. The story that they had been found dead was an attempt to lure the aliens into claiming responsibility for their deaths or their capture, but they have done no such thing. We can only hope that if the aliens did take them alive, that we still have a chance of returning them home safely. Mr. Castle and Castle Enterprises assure us they continue to use every resource they have available in the pursuit of the aliens and the pursuit of our freedom from fear and death. While we are peaceful at our core, as a species, we will defend ourselves. We will not be victim any longer. We are gathering all our forces and are preparing to fight. I do not mean to scare anyone, and yet, I mean to do just that."

Rod stood up. The camera floated higher to keep his full height in the picture as it broadcast to the world. "We need our fear to propel us into action. We need our fear to push us further than we have been pushed before. We have fought wars against one another and have been able to find peaceful resolution. We will fight this war!" Rod pumped his fist into the air defiantly and with purpose. "We will fight this war! And we will win this war!

"Reporting for Planet Talks, I am Rod Walken."

Chapter 30

Lesley knocked on the door. Maywano moved from left foot to right foot and back to left again. Sparrow ran her fingertips along the nose that had been painted on the door while Sulinda stared at her. People rushed by them in a panic, shouting at each other to "Move it!" and "Step on it!"

There had never been an alarm on Eris before for any reason. The door opened. Karona rushed through wild-eyed as she almost smashed into Lesley. She muttered an absent-minded "Sorry" and bolted down the hall. Ronnie also ran through the door and told Lesley to begin their emergency procedures.

"But…" she began.

"Earth is under attack! We need to wake everyone and be prepared in case we're next!" Ronnie turned to join the people who were dashing back toward the main lobby.

"Ronnie, wait!" Lesley's voice was shrill and stopped Ronnie in his tracks. "These people might be able to help us!"

Ronnie looked at the small group of people Lesley had been standing with and asked, "Who are you?"

"Well, my new friend, I am Maywano and these are…"

"We don't have time for this!" Ronnie said. "How is it that you think you can help us?"

Maywano's hand shook as he pulled out the device and said, "I can send the aliens away with this."

"Then why haven't you?" Ronnie asked, right to the point.

"There were too many of them for my people to fight. They outnumbered us and killed us before we even knew it was happening," Maywano said simply. "Please, are you the leader? I sense we have no time to waste."

Questioningly, Ronnie looked at Lesley, who nodded. "Come with me," Ronnie said, leading the way into the room where the brown nose stood watch on the door.

"Castle, Yu, these people got here somehow and say they can help us."

Lesley stepped up and said, "Yes, I think we need to listen to them."

Mr. Castle and Yu looked at each other, back at the group, and then at each other again. "Make it quick," said Yu.

Maywano passed the device to Yu. It was made from a goldish-colored metal. There were only two buttons on it with no indication of what each one did. "What is it? What does it do?" Yu asked.

"Well, we are from a planet in another galaxy…"

"I apologize for being blunt, but our planet, Earth, is under attack as we speak and aliens may be headed here right now. We do not have time to get to know each other, although some other time would be great. Let's get there." Yu held up the device, refocusing the attention.

"Its main ability is to track ships and relocate them." Maywano gently took the device from Yu and pressed one of the buttons. A little screen lit up that displayed letters and characters that Yu did not recognize.

"Excuse me. Relocate?" Mr. Castle asked.

"Why, yes, relocate means to take an object, person, whatever, and move it somewhere else." Maywano lifted his skirts and began to move across the room. "Like I am doing right now."

Yu and Mr. Castle looked at each other as though wondering if the strange new person was in fact an escapee from an insane asylum. Ronnie stepped in. "Okay, okay, how about we relocate to another room altogether and speak there." He held his arms out to their sides and tried to herd the newcomers toward the door.

"Please do not make us leave. We have been killed by the aliens, too, and we need safety and a new place to start. We were lucky to land here. We can help. Please." Maywano's soft eyes begged.

"Please," said Sparrow.

"Please," said Sulinda.

Sparks regarded Yu as though waiting for an indication of what he wanted her to do.

"Okay, what can it do?" Yu asked.

Mr. Castle and Yu stood beside Maywano and watched him press the button while tapping and swiping the screen every which way. The machine *beeped* and *booped* as images of space ships flashed. Yu looked questioningly at Mr. Castle, who shook his head.

"What planet are those ships from? Yours?" asked Mr. Castle.

"No, our ships aren't nearly as fancy," replied Maywano. "Most of them are from other universes." Maywano kept scrolling through the ships until he found the one flown by the aliens. "The aliens have four different types of ships, but this is their main one." Maywano did a quick spin, seemingly being careful not to let his skirts touch the humans. Yu tried to hide the fact that he thought Maywano was weird and out of his mind.

"Yes! It matches the images we've seen of the ships on Earth today!" Sparks exclaimed. "Are you saying we can make them all go away?"

"Wait just a minute," Sulinda jumped in. "What is this?" She motioned her hand at the device.

Maywano replied, "It's what I've been explaining." He looked around the room as though for confirmation that he had actually been speaking.

Sulinda rolled her eyes and with an exacerbated tone said, "I mean, where did you get it? Where has it been all this time? Could you have saved us while we've been stuck here on this dingy planet?" Sulinda asked accusingly. She walked to the nearest wall and smacked it with the palm of her hand in anger. The room went quiet save for the constant alarm.

Maywano took a deep breath. "This technology can send any ship built by those aliens right back to their home planet from anywhere in the universe. We can make them go away."

Maywano paused as the others thought about what he had said.

"So let's do it," Sparrow said. "Send those aliens away!"

Mr. Castle cleared his throat and said, "There is obviously more to it than that, or you would have gotten rid of all the aliens already." He stared at Maywano.

"Right you are, Leader."

"I am not the leader," Mr. Castle replied.

"My mistake, sir. You are the leader?" Maywano asked Yu.

"We don't have a leader. We work as a team. We discuss options and come to an agreement on what is best for everyone. Everyone who has chosen to live here on Eris has a say in how we run our community." Yu paused, waiting for questions, but Maywano and his two friends were enthralled and simply waited for Yu to go on.

"I own and operate this building, and I employ people. As owner, I make the day-to-day decisions on what kind of training I will offer and who will be permitted to partake in the training. I teach people to defend themselves and to fight. I teach discipline and confidence. I teach honor and integrity. If the use of this building must be expanded to include other purposes, such as being the headquarters for Eris in the fight against our enemy, then the town casts a vote. Everyone here plays their part to ensure our safety and survival, and everyone is of equal importance. Do you understand?" Yu asked.

"Ah yes, I see." Maywano nodded vigorously.

Sulinda sighed in a huff. "Can we get on with it?"

"We are running out of time," Sparrow agreed.

Maywano showed Yu and the others how to select the type of ship to relocate, how many ships to be involved, and how to set the destination. "Once everything is entered, you pull this button out, turn it to the left one full turn, back to the right half a turn, and another full turn to the left.

Push the button back in then, and that's that!" Maywano stepped away from the group and did two full spins with his arms up above his head.

Yu shook his head but respected the vigor of the stranger. Suddenly, a different sound could be heard from the far wall in the room. Yu dashed to his computer, followed by Mr. Castle and Sparks. There was a very intermittent blip on the screen. Yu tensed up.

"Oh no, what is it?" asked Maywano.

"While they're still hours away, they appear to be heading this way." Yu ran to Maywano and grabbed him by the shoulders. "What's the radius on that thing? Are the aliens too far away for us to use it?"

"Well, not exactly," he responded hesitantly.

"Then set it up. Make it happen. We have no idea how many there are, and we must get to work immediately!" Mr. Castle demanded.

"You see…the thing is…"

"Do it!" commanded Yu.

Maywano sighed, his shoulders and arms sinking low at his sides. "We can send them away, but some will bounce back again."

Yu was speechless as he pondered what he had just heard.

Sparks spoke up. "Excuse me? Say that again? What do you mean 'bounce back'?"

"This device is defective. It was designed to transport their ships home safely in the event of war—and for the most part it works—but sometimes ships would reappear." Maywano watched the humans. "We weren't strong enough to fight off the ships should they return, so we counted on them seeing how few of us there were left and to leave us alone as a non-threat. If they knew we had the device, it would have been the end of us."

"I do not believe this. Get out of here!" Mr. Castle yelled. "Get them *out* of here!"

Sparks lightly grabbed the gentle man by his arm and attempted to lead him out of the room. He looked panicked and said, "Wait! Please! There is more, and it *can* help us!" Sparrow and Sulinda jumped at his loud voice.

"I have given it a considerable amount of thought. What we need to do is follow them through. It's a dizzying experience, but we'll be ready for it and have the surprise element on our side. We can kill them there before we bounce back." Maywano paused. "Just think about it for a minute. Please."

"That is ludicrous," said Mr. Castle. "We would only be following them to their own territory. Unprepared or not, they would obliterate us. And we do not have any of their ships. How would we follow them through?"

Yu's initial reaction was to strangle the stranger, until his analytical mind kicked in. Then Yu's reaction became contemplative and almost exultant. Mr. Castle ran to him and said, "Yes? What is it?!"

Yu regarded Maywano and said, "We may not have any of their ships, but can we reprogram the device to tag other ships? If you can send a ship away, can you find one and bring it back?"

Chapter 31

Luke put his arms around Leila and pulled her close to him. Under normal circumstances, she would have broken down and cried, but because she was still filled with adrenaline, her hatred for Mike consumed her. She was shaking with rage. The muscles bulged in her back as she held onto Luke. She stared toward the door, waiting for it to reopen, almost willing it to reopen; she wanted to kill Mike. Leila had never hurt anything or anyone willingly in her whole life. Even spiders were spared though she was scared to death of them. If a spider was in her house, she would capture it in some sort of container and toss it outside alive, all the while screaming. Mike was a human—not a nice one, to be sure—and she wanted him dead. She wanted Gaz dead too. At that moment, she wanted anyone and everyone affiliated with Mike or Gaz to die, and she didn't feel an ounce of guilt over it.

Luke's back was to the door. He and Leila shifted around so they could both keep an eye on it. "He doesn't have Dagny. He doesn't know where she is. You got that impression too, didn't you?" she asked her husband.

"Yes. Otherwise, he would have bragged about what he had done to her or what he was planning to do to her," he replied.

Leila sighed in relief that they agreed and could focus on their next move. "I believe Dagny is either at home waiting for us or she's with her friends. From what I know of Farley, he'll do whatever he needs to keep her safe. I hope they're together."

Bross cleared his throat. "Does anyone want to explain just who that was and why we have to worry about people hurting us…as if aliens weren't enough?" Bross's tone was edgy.

Leila pulled from Luke's arms and turned to face Bross. "He's the best friend of our daughter's ex-boyfriend. He's a narcissistic psychopath. How he got here is a complete shock, but to make the story quick, he attacked us in our home. Gaz, our daughter's ex, had shown up a bit earlier that night, acting as though he was looking for Dagny. We hadn't seen or heard from her and had been worried that Gaz had actually done something bad to her. We got the jump on him and had him tied up, hoping he'd break and tell us where she was when Mike broke into our home."

Leila paused, reliving the experience.

Luke took over for her. "I actually hit him over the head with a baseball bat and was prepared to tie him up as well, but two aliens also showed up." Luke shook his head as though he still didn't believe it had happened.

Moments passed in silence.

"And then?" Chrystal asked. She had stopped crying.

Leila and Luke looked at each other and in unison replied, "We don't know."

Luke continued. "I remember seeing them coming in through our front door—and I remember thinking that I was in the realest-feeling nightmare of my life—and then it all goes blank. I have no idea what they did to us. I just know that I woke up with my wife in a small room on this ship."

"We tried to escape the room. Luke boosted me up into the air shaft. I crawled around there for a bit trying to find a way out or to even figure out where we were. It was useless; although, I did witness something terrible." She paused, took a deep breath, and continued. "A mother alien killed her own baby so the others wouldn't eat it. What kind of monsters are they that they would eat their own babies?" she asked rhetorically.

"Good! Let them eat each other!" Bross barked.

"We'll get out of this!" Luke exclaimed.

"What about you two? Do you have children? How did you end up here?" Leila asked.

Bross and Chrystal looked at each other and smiled. "You tell your story first, sweetie," Bross said.

"Are you not together?" Leila asked.

Bross shook his head. "No, we met in this room earlier today or yesterday. Who knows when it was? Time means nothing being locked in this room. I'm hoping to one day get home to my boyfriend, Sonny."

Chrystal put her arm around Bross's neck soothingly before beginning her story. "I was at home with my family when it happened. We were eating at the kitchen table when the side door of the house opened up." Chrystal stared at the far wall as though she was in a trance, reliving that day. "My husband, Henry, called out, asking who it was and saying to come on in. In Newfoundland, where my family is from, that was the norm. No one knocked. I don't think our door bell has even worked in years. Everyone knew everyone, and we were all friends save for the gossip that runs rampant in such small towns." Chrystal smiled a sad, distant smile, her eyes still fixed on the wall.

"Who was it?" Luke encouraged Chrystal to continue when it seemed she wouldn't.

Chrystal blinked a couple times and then cleared her throat. "I heard a sort of whirring sound. I can't even really describe it other than it sounded like something spinning so fast that it made that sound. Henry heard it too because he stood up to go and see what was going on, but before he was halfway there, he began walking backward. Slowly. My heart jumped out of my chest because I knew something was terribly wrong. I stood up and yelled at my boys to get upstairs." Her eyes teared up at the memory.

"I can still see the looks on their faces. Both of them looked scared, and their eyes were wide as they pushed their chairs back and started

181

to head out of the kitchen. They suddenly stopped, though, and I could see them staring toward their father. I turned to look too. I thought we were all about to die. I know I started screaming, but then just as quickly as I started, I stopped. I had no control over myself anymore, and I was petrified. Two of them came into the kitchen, and I saw what made that sound. Their tongues were spinning. They looked to be the size of baseball bats. They were spinning just like a ball player at home base winding the bat in a full circle while waiting for the pitch—except so quickly it was a total blur."

Chrystal took her arm back from comforting Bross and hugged herself. Bross then put his arms around her and returned the comfort. Luke and Leila sat enraptured by what they were hearing. All the news reports they had heard about the aliens mesmerizing their victims had seemed so unreal, and yet, there they were, hearing an account of it from one of the actual people who had been taken away. It didn't feel unreal to them anymore.

"I couldn't stop staring at those two aliens. They looked identical to me, like they were twins. My boys are twins—Jack and Jim—born four minutes apart from each other. I will die if I don't get to see them again soon. They have to be on this ship somewhere, but I haven't seen them. Not once. I haven't seen Henry either." Tears flowed freely down her face. "I was all alone until they put me in this room and I met Bross."

Bross hugged her tighter. "You needed me, and I needed you, sweetie," he said softly.

"But why? Why did they put you two together?" Leila asked.

Bross sucked his teeth and said, "Because they're stupid. Putting a gay man with a straight woman." He shook his head and laughed. "How do they think we would possibly want to be with each other intimately?"

"Excuse me?" Luke asked. Leila sensed his utter confusion.

"They expected us to have sex and procreate." Bross's expression was pure seriousness.

"We're food for them, though. What do you mean they wanted you to impregnate Chrystal?" Leila looked at her husband, hoping he was just

182

as shocked as she was, and he was—he had his eyes squeezed shut tightly and was shaking his head as if trying to un-hear what he had just heard.

"Humans are food for the aliens. Before they moved me from my other room, I overheard them talking about how they need to 'harvest' us. They're afraid they'll eat us all and run out of food. They've apparently done that before where they've eaten a whole species and were at risk of starving to death. They're learning and now realize they need us to keep having babies, and they have to control themselves to ensure they have a steady food supply. There aren't enough other types of people or aliens out in the universe for them to eat, so we are their sole focus." Chrystal paused and took a few deep breaths. "I didn't believe it until they bunked me in with Bross here."

"Wow. That is the most insane thing I have ever heard," Leila said. "And you were supposed to become pregnant and what, live in this room together for the next nine months to produce a baby? Surely they could come up with a better plan for survival than that." Leila's voice was filled with disgust.

"Hmph," Chrystal grunted. "They did."

"What do you mean?" Luke asked.

"While they held me locked up in another part of the ship, they were injecting me with something every day. I think it may have been hormones or something, but whatever it was, it's supposed to make getting pregnant super easy and somehow ensure that at least a dozen babies are conceived each time. The gestation period is cut down to only 2-3 months, and once the babies are born, they will grow into adults at an accelerated rate—less than a year, I think."

Luke rose from the couch and began to pace. The other three watched and waited for him to say something. He abruptly stopped and looked at Chrystal with his arm outstretched and mouth open as if about to speak but then began pacing again just as abruptly. That happened two more times before Leila told him to sit down again and just say what was on his mind.

"I don't even know what to say. This is the most ludicrous thing I've heard in my entire life. They can't really do that to humans can they? Is that really what this has all come to—we're food, and they're growing us so they don't run out of human food? What kind of crap is that?" Luke stood and paced two lengths of the room in silence and then sat down again. "How can we stop them? Are we powerless? It certainly seems that way. They can control us. They can manipulate us and take us from our homes. They can kill us with their lashing tongues instantly. And now you're telling me they can alter our bodies. We're incubators for their *food?* I can't even begin to get my head around this. It's insanity. It can't be possible. You must have misunderstood."

Chrystal only said, "Maybe."

The group sat in silence. With grim faces, they contemplated their futures.

"Well, then," said Bross, "let's change the subject. I heard about you on the news, Chrystal. People hadn't heard from or seen you in days, and neighbors went to your house to see what was going on."

Chrystal brightened up a bit. "Really? What else did the news say? Did it mention Raunch?"

"Yes! Your dog, right? Your dog was still there, and they gave it food and water."

Chrystal threw her arms around Bross. "Thank you! Thank you! I had always feared the worst, but this is actually some good news. Who is taking care of him now?"

"It didn't say anything more than that about the dog. Sorry."

"Don't be sorry. You've lifted my spirits even if just a bit and even if temporarily. I'm sure Henry's sister, Charis, probably has Raunch. The dog was antisocial most of the time, but he and Charis loved each other. She had a way of connecting with him that no one else—not even my boys, Jack and Jim—did."

"I'm glad I connected you to that report and remembered about your dog then," Bross said. "At least that's something good."

Leila spoke up. "What about you, Bross? What was your life like before all this?"

Bross sighed. "I am in love with a man named Sonny. We've been together for eight years, living together for three. We met at the night club that I manage. Maybe I don't manage it anymore," he said sadly. "Maybe Sonny won't wait for me. Maybe he's on this ship. I have no idea, and I don't even know how long I've been here. I don't remember anything about how I ended up here. I wish I could remember something like you do, Chrystal." Bross rubbed his temples in concentration. "Nothing. There's nothing that comes back to me at all."

"But what's the last thing you do actually remember from before you ended up here?" Luke asked.

"Sonny wanted to go skating. We live in New York City, and a new indoor theme park opened up. They have an ice rink inside, and the night we were supposed to go was hockey night. Sonny likes hockey players, so we were going to go. As part of the fee, you got to choose your favorite team's hockey uniform to wear while skating around. It was Sonny's birthday, and I wanted to make it special for him and do all the things he's wanted to do." Bross wiped a tear from his eye, cleared his throat loudly, and then sat up straight. "I know I was at home waiting for him to arrive. I'd picked up a couple of his favorite chocolate eclairs for us to eat before heading out, but I can't recall if we went out, if we ate those eclairs, if I even saw him that night or not."

Leila had a sympathetic look on her face and a sympathetic tone to match. "You poor dear. We aren't done-for yet, and anything is still possible. We have some fight left in us! All four of us do!"

"I love you, Leila."

"I love you, too, Luke."

He kissed her forehead, each of her eyelids, both cheeks, and then a tender kiss on her lips.

Bross looked at Chrystal and said, "I will be in Sonny's arms again one day."

Chrystal looked at Bross and said, "I will be in Henry's arms again one day."

They smiled at each other and hugged.

Dagny woke at the sound of the deafening alarm. She had been in such a deep sleep that she wasn't sure where she was at first. She blinked several times and wiped the crust of her dried tears from her eyes. She stood and turned on the light in the small room she had been resting in and found her black pants folded on the nightstand. She quickly pulled them on, trying not to trip herself, and then stepped into her new black combat boots. She tied the laces tightly, opened the door, and looked down the hall. Throngs of people ran in both directions, all eyes wide and projecting fear. Dagny had been nervous at the sound of the alarm, but at seeing the faces of the crowd, she filled with intense terror.

Not knowing what to do, Dagny searched the runners from her doorway for a familiar face. She didn't want to get in anyone's way and also didn't want to be inadvertently trampled. She felt helpless as she pulled her hair back from her face. She searched her pants' pockets and found her hair elastic and tied her hair back. All she needed was for it to get in her eyes and block her vision, even for a second. She knew that everyone had what was called "survival instinct" but had no idea what her own entailed. Dagny had lived a life of charm and leisure and had experienced very little conflict. When she was a child, she had been bullied by kids at school, but as a teen, she had befriended Lexi and became popular overnight. So far, her "survival instinct" had been to simply hide away and sleep. Knowing that her days of comfort were over, Dagny tried to figure out what she should do.

Dagny focused on the people—what they were wearing, what they were shouting, were any announcements being broadcast advising of what was happening or what everyone should be doing? Some were carrying guns, from simple pistols to large, complicated-looking ones like what she had seen only in movies. Everyone looked scared, but some looked determined, as though they had a destination in mind or a plan in place. Dagny still didn't know her way around Yu's dojo and figured her best bet was to try to follow those who looked like they knew where they were going. Eventually she would find someone she knew. She did a quick search in her room, opening the closet and checking the desk drawers, hoping to find a weapon she could take with her, but there was nothing. *It's just as well*, she thought. She wouldn't have known how to handle any sort of weapon and would probably have hurt herself or someone else.

Walking back to the doorway, she looked both ways down the hallway and decided to go in the direction that the people with firearms were headed. She quickly jumped out of her room and got into pace behind a group of men dressed all in black. They looked to Dagny to be part of a military team, so she thought she'd be safest to stay near them. She surprised herself by being able to maintain their speed through the hall, which spurred her on, though her fear did not dissipate. She told herself that it was okay to be scared because everyone around her looked equally scared. She also told herself she wasn't ready to sit down and die. If that was what was coming, she was ready to fight.

She had been listening to the people around her as she forged on and heard things like "aliens are on their way"…"aliens are coming"…"we're doomed" and similar bits of chilling conversation. The military-like men made the next right down a different corridor, and Dagny followed. At the end of the hall, they entered a large room, so large that it had a warehouse feel about it. The group stopped running, and Dagny stood on her tippy-toes, trying to see what was going on deeper into the room. She could see that three giant bay doors were open, and beyond that, several ships were powered up and appeared as though preparing to leave.

Dagny began to panic. "Are we being evacuated?" she asked the nearest person.

"Not exactly," the pale man answered, looking at her as though it was the dumbest question ever. "We're under attack. Who are you?"

"I'm Dagny. I'm a friend of Farley's and Sparks. The alarm woke me up, and I have no idea what's going on!" Dagny played with her long ponytail anxiously.

The pale man sighed. "Poor girl. The aliens are reportedly on their way here as we speak, and we need to be ready to defend ourselves." He looked her over. "You need a laser. Positively everyone must take part. Come with me." He grabbed her by the hand, and she let him take her wherever he was headed. Lining the wall to their right were numerous tables piled with guns and ammo, and behind the tables were people passing out the weapons after evaluating each person's skill level with using weapons.

Dagny saw Brody manning a table and pushed her way through the buzzing crown to him. "Brody!"

"Dagny! Are you okay?" he asked.

"I'm fine. I just heard what's happening. I've been asleep for a while." She looked down shamefully.

"Chin up, my girl! There's no time for pity. Here, take this one." Brody showed her how to use the simple but powerful pistol. "Just do *not* aim it at people."

Dagny was uncertain but took the weapon. She held it in her right hand uncomfortably and awkwardly until Brody adjusted it so the barrel was pointing outward and not inward toward her. "Don't be scared," Brody said. "You won't be on the front line because you haven't been trained, but you'll have to fight from here."

"Where's the front line? Just outside over there?" she asked, pointing toward the ships.

Brody looked out and sighed. "The front line will be the men and women flying those ships and fighting the aliens head-on, hopefully beyond our atmosphere. We're fueling up everything we've got and will take off once we figure the aliens are about two hours away. That should give us enough time to get out to space and position ourselves to make a stand. We should have the element of surprise on our side too."

Just then, Karona and Ronnie showed up and joined Dagny and Brody. Ronnie pressed his lips hard to Brody's lips and then jugged him tightly. Brody returned the hug before hugging Karona. "You ready?" he asked her.

"As ready as I'll ever be," Karona replied. "I can't believe I'm about to fulfill my life-long dream of being a pilot on an actual spaceship and that it'll probably mean my own death on my first time out."

"Tsk, tsk, don't even think like that. We're ready for them, and you're ready for them," Brody stated confidently.

"But my training has barely begun!"

"You were top in your class, and your demonstrations in the simulator room were flawless. You will prove to be a very agile and capable pilot; you'll see. Brody told me all about your abilities." Ronnie winked at her.

"How are you doing, Dagny? Feeling any better?" Karona asked.

Dagny noticed a difference in Karona in the short time that they had known each other. Karona seemed to be much less timid than she had been before, and she made eye contact with everyone. *That* was new. "I'm feeling much better. Sleeping for I don't even know how long was what I needed. The stress of not knowing where my parents were was killing me. I'm still beside myself, but I feel somewhat calmer and better able to deal with everything, and I know we'll find them!" The second she finished her last sentence, her gut instinct sent a wave of foreboding through her whole body. It was as though she'd had a glimpse of something terrible about to happen but without actually seeing it. Her face dropped as her eyes widened.

Karona put her hand on Dagny's shoulder. "Dagny? Are you okay? What just happened?"

"I...I'm fine," Dagny stammered. "Nothing." An image flashed through Dagny's mind. It was a photograph she had framed on her bedroom dresser of her parents holding her as a newborn baby. It settled Dagny a bit, but she couldn't shake the feeling that her parents were in danger. It was as though she somehow knew she would never see them again.

189

Just then, the door opened. Leila heard the whirring sound first and twisted around on the couch, glancing toward the entrance to the room. "No, no, no, no," she said shaking her head as she tried to climb backward over the couch, away from the doorway. "Don't look at them!" she yelled.

Luke, Chrystal, and Bross all leapt from the couch and tried to put distance between themselves and their visitors. Aliens filed into the room—two, four, five, six. A seventh alien entered the small space. Then an eighth crowded in. All had tongues swirling so quickly that the whirring sound became louder and louder.

Chrystal squatted on the ground screaming with her hands covering her ears.

Luke stood protectively in front of the love of his life and held his hands out in front of him as if to hold the aliens off. He believed he should try to reason with them and began to speak. "Look, we are obviously not a threat…"

A tongue lashed out fast as lightning, cutting Luke in half at the waist. Leila's shrieks on sight of the aliens halted as Luke's blood splashed across her face and into her throat, choking her. Blood sprayed onto the couch and across the wall in a line as two aliens jumped on his severed body, sucking up his flesh and organs as though they were liquid through a straw. In a matter of thirty seconds, there was no sign of Luke at all.

The other aliens advanced on the three humans—two per human—and began to feast. Despite the aliens being weakened from starving, they were still faster than the humans. Leila, Bross, and Chrystal did not stand a chance. Their screams filled the room and the hallway outside until they were no longer able to scream. The whirring had also stopped, and the only sounds heard were the sounds of hungry aliens slurping up the slaughtered bodies.

Chapter 32

"There!" Josh shouted, pointing at the screen. Chuck and Farley glanced at each other, unsure of their plan but committed to it. They stared at the screen until in the upper corner, they saw movement. Chuck's heart quickened in fear. He willed the screen to zoom in even though it wasn't equipped with that technology. He wanted to know exactly what they were looking at. He couldn't tell if it was the aliens or if so, how many of them there were. He couldn't see if they were with their ship. It was just a fuzzy image of something moving. He tried to be patient as they neared whatever it was, but his hands became cramped from grabbing the arm rests of his chair so tightly. He let go and shook them out, trying to relax and loosen up.

"Everyone okay?" Grammy asked. Three "yes's" responded in varying degrees of certainty. "At least we may have located them sooner rather than later. Nothing like attacking things head-on, so to speak." She chuckled, and Chuck picked up on the slight nervousness in that laugh.

Farley began jiggling his leg and tapping his foot. "So I guess we, uh, get closer and see what we're dealing with and then determine which plan to follow? Is that the plan?" he asked.

"You betcha, Farley. Hey, Farley?" Josh looked back at him.

"Yeah, Josh?"

"Remember when you used to call me 'Disease'?"

Farley swallowed hard. "Josh, I can't even tell you how sorry I am about that. I'm not that person anymore..."

Chuck piped up with his own apology but was cut off by Josh's laughter. "Work with me here. I'm just trying to distract us all from our thoughts of impending doom. I truthfully loved that nickname, and sometimes I want to wear the disguise again. It was an awful lot of fun lurking in your school hallways, listening in on all the conversations going on. I'd love to be there now," Josh said.

"I miss Nathan." Chuck's comment surprised the others, but they all agreed.

"Nathan is always in our hearts," Grammy stated.

"I miss him too, Chuck," Farley said.

"He was like the son I didn't have, though he didn't know it." Josh's eyes misted up a bit.

"Man, that guy was *smart*! I had no idea but I'm glad we saved his book. I wish we had it with us now," Chuck said.

Farley laughed. "As if any of us would even understand anything in it."

"Yeah, true!" Chuck agreed.

As their ship neared the movement they had seen in the distance, it appeared as though there were three separate life forms, but they couldn't be sure. "I'm going to do a pass or two by whatever that is until we can determine if it's safe to land." Josh adjusted the controls so they were flying faster, but he took them up higher. If whatever was on the ground wanted to fire at them, they wanted to escape unharmed.

"Back to Nathan's book for a moment. It's in the best possible hands with Yu and Castle. And don't think for a second that I feel slighted by your comment that I wouldn't understand what he had written in it." Grammy turned back and winked at Chuck and Farley.

"You *know* it would be pure gibberish to you, Grammy!" Chuck teased back.

"Well, whatever, believe what you must. Perhaps I helped him to postulate his theories," Grammy said in all seriousness. It gave Chuck pause.

Chuck and Farley looked at each other quizzically before looking back at Grammy. She sat in her chair in front of them unmoving as she waited for their response.

"Uh, Grammy?" Farley asked.

"Yes, Farley?"

"What does postulate mean?"

Grammy laughed. "It means to hypothesize, guess, propose…. A lot of what Nathan wrote in his book were his ideas about how things could work. A lot of it is simply theory, but that's only because he never had a chance to prove his theories. Rest in peace, Nathan."

"So, did you really postulate those theories with Nathan?" Chuck asked.

"No," Grammy said simply.

"Then why did you sound so serious about it??" Chuck asked.

"Because we're almost there, and I didn't want anyone to panic. See?" Grammy was pointing at the screen, and Josh began to make a wide turn around what became clear to them were three aliens on the planet's surface. To the surprise of the four humans on the circling ship, the aliens were waving at them.

Josh scanned the aliens and determined that they each had two weapons. "Our fire power outweighs theirs. We've got that going for us." Josh piloted the ship closer to the aliens. Chuck could see that the aliens wore space suits with helmets indicating that they either couldn't breathe without the protection or didn't know if they could breathe without it. If the aliens needed to keep the suits on once they boarded the human's ship, perhaps they would be weighed down and easier to subdue if it came to that. Most of the aliens they had seen or heard about were scrawny, but with the ones they were observing wearing their suits, it was hard to tell their size. One thing for certain was that their tongues were also formidable weapons—lightning fast, sharp as swords, and able to somehow suck up a whole human in less than two minutes. Chuck hoped the helmets would stay on and keep those tongues at bay.

"How do we play this?" Josh asked Grammy.

"We can't let them get close to us. We keep our weapons on them always. No one blinks. When they board—if they board but I'm sure that's why they're waving—we send them down the hall and lock them in the storage room. Chuck and Farley…go now and move everything from that room and put it in the kitchen. Move *everything*. We can't have them creating anything they can use to escape the room." Grammy sounded confident, and Chuck and Farley immediately left the cockpit to do as they were instructed.

Chuck and Farley high-fived each other as they walked through the doorway and headed down the hall, but once they were out of earshot, Chuck said in a hushed voice, "Oh man, I'm really scared."

"Rock and roll and everything but I'm trying not to crap my pants." Farley eyes were as panicked as Chuck's were.

"It's one thing to be chased by them—that's at a distance—but we're inviting them into our home now." Chuck slowed his pace as he opened the storage room door and went in. He picked up a case of canned food and walked it over to Farley. "Here, I'll pass you the stuff, and you take it to the kitchen."

"No way. Take it yourself. You carry the stuff you see, and I'll carry the stuff I see. It's faster that way," said Farley.

"I beg to differ. We'll get in each other's way. Assembly line. That's the way to go." Chuck nodded in agreement with himself.

"You're an idiot. I'm not doing all the work here, and now you're just wasting time. Let's move." Farley grabbed the bucket and mop and the eighteen-roll package of toilet paper. "Make it fast with that food." Farley speed-walked out of the room and down to the kitchen and was halfway back to storage before Chuck was halfway to the kitchen. They crossed in the hall and Farley sing-songed, "Didn't get in your way…didn't get in your way."

"Loser."

Four trips each did it, and they returned to the cockpit. They felt the ship circling as it lowered closer to the ground.

"Grammy, would you take a quick look and just make sure we didn't miss anything?" Chuck asked.

"On it," she replied as she stood and made her way down the corridor.

They were close enough to landing that they could see the red faces of the beings on the ground. "I can't even tell if they're guys or girls," Chuck said.

"Two of them kinda look like you, so I think they're girls." Farley snorted, but his eyes betrayed his terror.

"When they see me, they'll wish they looked like me," Chuck retorted. Chuck knew Farley inside and out. He went to him and wrapped his arms around him in a tight, friends-for-life, brothers always, one last time hug. "I know I'm not supposed to do this, but I don't care. I love you, Farley. You're the best friend anyone could ever have." Chuck's voice choked up.

"If we go down, we go down strong. I love you too, Chuck. Life's been good with you in it." Farley's voice also wavered.

Grammy had returned and stood watching the young men before embracing them both. She nodded with her head for Josh to join them. He put the ship in an auto-pilot holding pattern and the four of them held each other silently, each person lost in his or her own last thoughts. No one knew what was going to happen once they opened that door and permitted entrance to the aliens.

Grammy broke the silence. "Hey, let's not give up yet. I still have my negotiation skills, and I'm going to put them to full use. You're my light, Chuck, and I love you more than anything. I will do everything in my power to protect you and get us through this. Farley, you have always been like my own, and I love you so much. Josh, my partner in crime. We have been through so much together, and boy, if I was three decades younger, I'd have married you in a heartbeat! I love you, Josh."

Josh pulled a few tissues out of his pocket and passed them around. The "I love you's" went on as noses were blown.

"Rock and roll," Josh said, stretching his hand out palm down.

Grammy made eye contact with him and placed her hand on top of his. "Rock and roll."

"Rock and roll, people," said Farley, his hand covering Grammy's.

"Rock and roll, Mom and all our other people back on Earth and Eris." Chuck covered the stack of hands with both of his. "One, two, three, *break!*" Their hands went up into the air as if in victory.

Josh regained control of the ship and gently set it down approximately one mile from where the aliens waited. Four hearts raced in anticipation of death, although no one knew whose. Purple haze began to swirl about outside the ship, and the scent of cotton candy filled the cockpit. "Now!" Grammy commanded.

Sparks knocked lightly on the door before entering. Sheila sat at the desk, staring at the wall, absentmindedly lifting the glass of wine to her lips. "Hello," she said listlessly, not looking to see who had come in.

"Sheila, we don't have any news on Chuck or your mother, but we're far from giving up. Some strange people—I guess you can call them people, although they are not from Earth or Eris—have shown up here, and they say they can help us. We don't really understand how, but we're optimistic. We may be able to locate your family and bring them back here." Sparks used her most positive-sounding tone.

"What's with the alarm? And does it seem to get louder every minute?" Sheila asked, still just staring at the wall, drinking her Chardonnay. She wore a brown housecoat. Her hair looked as though it hadn't been washed or brushed in a month.

Sparks took a couple deep breaths. She didn't know how she could possibly have hoped that Sheila was unable to hear the shrill sound of the constant alarm. She secretly had wished that Sheila simply had drank so much wine that she had passed out and was deaf to her surroundings. "Ahem, ahem, ahem." She cleared her throat before blurting out, "We are under attack. The aliens have found us and are on their way here. We probably have a few hours at best before they're right on top of us. But we're like gearing up now and are going to fight our butts off!! All you need to do is stay here."

"Okay," Sheila replied.

Sparks pulled her backpack off and opened it up. She pulled out two more bottles of wine and put them in the mini fridge beside the desk. "I've gotta go and help. Just stay here and you'll be safe. All the walls and ceilings in this building are reinforced and can withstand most explosions." She also pulled out a few packages of ear plugs. "Use these. They'll block most of the noise for you."

Sheila held out her hand, and Sparks placed the tiny boxes atop it. Sheila closed her fingers around them before dropping them onto the desk. "Okay," she said again but made no move to actually take advantage of the plugs.

Sparks was slightly uncomfortable never having had to take care of anyone before. She had helped Dagny, but that only entailed giving her some tea that made her sleep. Bringing Sheila wine here and there was easy enough, but the ear plugs meant a more intimate form of help. She opened a box, and gently tucking Sheila's hair behind her ears, she slowly pushed the plugs into Sheila's ears. Sheila let her do it.

"I have to get back now, Sheila. I'll check in on you a little later." Sparks then surprised herself by leaning down and embracing Sheila. She was then even more surprised when Sheila hugged her back. They said nothing further, and Sparks backed out of the room, watching in case Sheila did say something. She paused a moment and then closed the door never to see Sheila again.

They couldn't see the aliens through the mist, but they had to assume they were approaching the ship. Josh ran down the hall and hid in the room just past the storage room. Chuck and Farley put on tough faces, grabbed their guns, and opened the main door to the ship. The ramp unfolded as it lowered to the ground. Grammy stayed perched in her seat—the position of authority. They waited as they peered out into the mist. One minute went by. Then two. Chuck and Farley stopped holding their breaths and inhaled deeply. Although still terrified, their heart rates began to slow ever so slightly. Time seemed to tick by slowly. They began to wonder if the aliens had actually been waving them down or if it had all been imagined.

"Do you see anything?" Grammy asked.

"Not a thing," whispered Chuck.

"Maybe this fog is some kind of hallucinogenic and there's nothing really out there." Farley looked back at Grammy to see if she agreed.

"Doubtful," was her response.

"Yeah, Farley, we know they followed us through the dimension-changer." Chuck looked at Farley as though he were dumb.

"Umm, it's a 'portal.' Who even says 'dimension-changer'?" Farley shook his head and resumed his lookout.

Chuck kept quiet. He didn't want to admit he had forgotten the word "portal." He, too, turned his attention to the outside. Chuck caught some movement from the corner of his eye and looked down the hall. Josh was there waving his arms and then shrugging as though to ask what was happening. Chuck shook his head and also shrugged. Nothing so far.

"Here we go," Farley said.

Chuck looked back outside and saw that the mist was dissipating. He and Farley tensed and tightened their grips on their guns, pointing them toward the opening. Moments later, standing no more than twenty feet away, were the three aliens. Chuck and Farley resisted the urge to shoot them on sight.

"Guys, we might be able to use their help. Let's talk first and resort to violence later." Grammy's voice was all steel and business. Chuck had to look back at her to see if the tiny, cane-using, sweet, little, old lady was still sitting in the captain's chair. Grammy was still there. Her back was ram-rod straight, and she seemed to have doubled in size. She exuded confidence and authority and gave off such an air of someone who was used to winning that Chuck's fear waned to the point where he actually lowered his weapon. "Weapon up, Chuck! Stay in the game!" Grammy barked.

Chuck jumped back into position and hardened his face as he stood as tall and menacing as he could. He glanced at Farley, and saw that Farley also stood erect and fierce-looking. Chuck was glad he was on Grammy's side because her tone and stature actually scared him more than the aliens did in that moment.

"Motion for them to board, but do not speak," Grammy instructed.

Chuck and Farley waved for the aliens to approach and stepped to the side, giving them room to board. The aliens looked at each other, whispered for a few moments, and walked a few steps forward.

Pintay spoke first. "Will you hurt us?" he asked.

Chuck looked back at Grammy who shook her head ever so slightly.

"Not if you don't attempt to hurt us," Chuck said. His voice was somewhat high-pitched. He mentally told himself off and vowed to speak more deeply. "Where is your ship?"

"It has been damaged and will not fly."

"Liar," Grammy said with her voice hard as nails but only loud enough so the guys heard her.

Farley turned to Grammy and bowed, enforcing that she was the leader. "We do not believe you," he said, turning back to the aliens.

"We are defenseless. We sought you out for help. We do not know where we are or how to get home." Pintay paused for a reaction and received none. "You also do not know how to return home or you would not still be here." Pintay slowly put his weapon on the ground. The other two aliens followed suit.

Farley and Chuck looked at each other. "Do you want to take this one?" Farley asked him.

"You can do the honors," Chuck responded.

"Don't mind if I do."

The aliens glanced at each other and then looked from Farley to Chuck and back to Farley, unsure what was going on.

"We know you need us. That's why we stuck around this lifeless, albeit pretty—sometimes when the purple stuff flows—rock," Farley stated.

Mishay remained silent as usual, but Kallay spoke up. "This is a trick. Why would you help us after we tried to kill you?"

"That's what makes us so nice," Chuck claimed. He saw the confusion on the faces of the aliens and elaborated. "We are a kind and considerate species. We believe that in helping you, we can fix our relationship and become friends again—you, aliens, and us, humans." Chuck imagined he was an employee of the Planetary Space Agency working in the Inter-Galactic Relations department. He had his sights set on following in Grammy's footsteps and hoped that it wouldn't upset his mother. He also hoped that all their bravado they were displaying to the aliens wasn't all for naught. He realized he had let his guard down, so he stood tall again. Chuck estimated that he and Farley were at least two feet taller than the aliens were, but he knew not to get cocky about that advantage because the aliens had their own advantages—their sword-sharp and lightning-fast tongues. The aliens were still at least ten feet away—they had been slowly moving closer to the ship during the conversation. He narrowed his eyes as he watched the aliens closely.

Pintay held up his hands in an "I surrender" manner. "We will not harm you." He motioned to his comrades, and they also put up their hands in surrender.

Grammy sat in silence, watching the communications between her family members and her enemies while keeping her thoughts hidden to all.

"And we will not harm you. But if we are to help you, you have to do what we say." Chuck waited for a response.

"What do you want?" Pintay asked. The aliens were now at the top of the ramp, one step away from crossing the threshold onto the ship.

Chuck looked back at Grammy, trying to read her facial expression, but it was blank. He said to the aliens, while still looking at Grammy, "Come aboard. We have a room that you will stay in. We will find your ship and take from it anything we can use—by 'we,' I mean all of us—and then we will leave this planet. When we get back to our realm or dimension or whatever you call it, we want to speak to your leader. That is all."

Chuck waited for a response.

"Our leader will not speak to you."

Chuck faced the aliens. "Why not?"

"You betrayed us."

Chuck became heated. "That's bull..."

"Shh." Grammy silenced her grandson.

No one spoke for a full minute.

"Never say never," Chuck finally said. "We worked side by side before, and we can do it again. We don't need to be enemies. We can help each other. This is the beginning of us repairing what's been broken." Chuck paused, waiting for Grammy to step in, but she stayed in her chair and let him run with the conversation. He felt as though he was being initiated and wanted to do well. "You shouldn't underestimate Grammy's powers of persuasion."

"So, she *is* Grammy," said Pintay.

Chuck became instantly nervous. He knew he had screwed up and said the wrong thing. He kept his mouth shut.

"And you with your blond hair...you must be Chuck." Pintay looked from Chuck to Grammy. "Chuck is your grandson." Grammy didn't flinch though the alien was attempting to unnerve her.

Chuck got his head back in the game. "You've heard of us, but sadly, we have no clue who you are. In fact, we don't know the names of any of you. What do you want?" Chuck asked the aliens.

"Why did you land?" Pintay asked.

Chuck looked at Farley, whose expression mirrored Chuck's amused face.

"Why did you wave us down?" Chuck pushed the question back.

Pintay and the others took their last steps to be fully inside the ship. Chuck nodded his head toward the button on the wall and Pintay pressed it, closing the door behind them. The aliens rested their weapons on the floor against the wall and then took off their helmets. Though Chuck tensed, he remained where he stood.

Even with his weapon now out of reach, Pintay gave the impression of unwavering confidence as he said, "Our intention was to gain your trust, gain passage onto your ship, use whatever information or ideas you have to return home, take over the ship, and kill you all. We're hungry, and we're going to devour you slowly. Or quickly, if we can't help ourselves."

Grammy laughed. It was an evil and yet delightful laugh. Everyone was speechless. Chuck had no idea what she found funny or why she was completely unfazed by what the enemy had just said. It had chilled Chuck. He had expected lies and for them to hide their true intentions, but the bluntness of Pintay's statements put fear into them.

Mishay smiled at Grammy. It was the first form of communication she had displayed since meeting the humans. Grammy smiled warmly back at her. "What is your name, dear?" Grammy asked Mishay.

Mishay did not respond but kept smiling at Grammy before passing the smile on to Chuck and then to Farley. Neither Chuck nor Farley returned the gesture. They hadn't known what to expect, but a smiling alien hadn't been on their radar.

"We haven't much seating room," Grammy said, rising from her chair, "but perhaps you'd like to form a circle on the floor, much like we used to do in days gone by." She began to pull on levers under her chair and lifted the chair off its base. "Chuck and Farley, can you help me with the other chairs so we can make room?" They were shocked, but they did as they were told, keeping their eyes on the aliens. To their surprise, Pintay also helped and unclicked the fourth chair. They rested the seats against one of the stark white walls, and Grammy motioned for the group to take a place on the cleared floor. Pintay sat directly across the floor from Grammy while Chuck and Farley took spots on either side of her. Likewise, the other two aliens flanked Pintay.

Grammy and Pintay kept their eyes on each other. She began to hum. Pintay hesitated but then also joined in. The other two aliens followed suit as Chuck and Farley sat there baffled, unable to do anything other than watch.

The humming abruptly stopped. Chuck and Farley tensed. They watched as Grammy bowed slightly without breaking eye contact. The alien named Pintay did the same.

"Yes, I am Grammy. Allow me to introduce my grandson, Chuck, and his best friend, Farley."

Pintay's tongue swirled from his mouth slowly but not to its full length and only for a moment before he reeled it back in and spoke. "I am Pintay, and this is Kallay and Mishay."

"Mishay. Offspring of Chief Shabay. You do not speak." Grammy's statements prompted another smile from Mishay. "Kallay, I have not heard of you nor have I heard of you, Pintay, but I am pleased to meet you all."

"How do you know Mishay, Grammy?" Chuck asked.

"Chief Shabay and I headed up the team that worked together to forge a future of harmony between the humans and the aliens. He often spoke of her, though we hadn't met until now. We had a lot of respect for each other, or so I thought. Then Chief betrayed us. Was it his decision to attack us?" Grammy directed her question at Pintay.

"On the contrary, *you* betrayed *us*." Pintay's eyes narrowed.

"We did no such thing." Farley defended Earth. "We don't even fight each other anymore, never mind an alien species with potentially better technology and all that. Do we even know where your planet is because I think I heard that we have no idea where you guys come from?"

"We gave you the means to replenish your planet's soil and nutrients," Grammy said. "We gave you the means to grow food again. You discarded everything. We found all the equipment we designed and built for you just floating out in space." She stared at the three aliens. When they said nothing, she began asking questions. "Did you use it? Did it not work? Did you even try to make it work?"

"No, Farley, you don't know where our planet is. Humans have never been there, and that is for our own protection. We do not trust you and would never let it be known where our home is." Kallay nodded in agreement to Pintay's words.

"And we respected that, so we didn't push to go there. It's why we worked with you near Earth to construct the equipment." Grammy went on. "I'll ask again, what happened when you used the farming equipment?"

Pintay's tongue flicked in and out of his mouth several times.

Chuck pointed his gun at Pintay and in a menacing and authoritative voice made of steel said, "Put that tongue back in your mouth and keep it there. I will shoot you on the spot if you so much as give the slightest hint that you are threatening my grandmother."

"We are being patient here," Farley added.

"It was never going to work. How could humans possibly help when they don't know what our soil is even like…what it's made of?" Pintay was becoming increasingly frustrated.

"That's right, but you didn't want us there. You brought us samples of the soil, water, air, everything we would need to replicate the environment. We did everything we could to help—our scientists alongside yours, our engineers alongside yours, our botanists alongside yours. And you abandoned it?" Grammy's frustration exceeded Pintay's. "And then you come and kill us? And eat us? We did nothing wrong. This is all on you and your kind."

Farley raised his gun and aimed at the aliens. "What do you want us to do, Grammy?"

Grammy took her eyes off Pintay's for the first time during the interaction and glanced at Chuck, then Farley. "As ambassador for Earth during dealings with the aliens, lower your guns. We are going to fix this despite Pintay's ideas of taking over our ship and then turning us into food."

Chapter 33

Troy sat outside the ship, eating, when the alarm sounded just inside. He jumped to his feet and entered the ship, racing to the cockpit. The scanners registered a fleet of ships heading in his direction—alien ships. They were coming in fast. There was no way he could outrun them. There was nowhere he could hide. Troy was in the middle of an almost empty planet named Eris where there were no trees to hide among, no deep underground bunkers, and no way of escaping.

But Troy had been a survivor. He had already lived through one alien attack. Perhaps he could live through another. He climbed aboard, closed the ship's door, and powered it up. He would have been better off in a faster, more equipped ship than the one he currently had, but the closest options were in the area inhabited by humans. He headed in that direction.

The beeping of the approaching enemy vessels sped up. They were closer and closer each second, almost exponentially so. The ships had moved so quickly that the aliens must have developed a way to super-tune their engines, almost doubling their speed. Troy's eyes were full of terror as he approached the blindingly-lit-up night sky.

Just then, another beep sounded. The radar screen revealed that three alien ships were just about on his tail. His radar registered that weapons had been locked on his ship.

Weapons had been fired.

He was done for.

Troy released his grip on the controls, placed his hands in his lap, and closed his eyes. "Good bye," he said aloud to the empty cockpit as he heard metal being torn apart by the impact of the enemy's fire power. Fire engulfed the ship moments before it shattered into pieces.

On the inhabited part of the planet, the first ship took off, leaving the deafening sound of thunder behind it. Onlookers on the ground all wore ear plugs and goggles. The other 29 ships followed suit. Karona piloted one of the last to leave while Ronnie had been in the first. Some of the other ships had been flown by her classmates and others by expert pilots. All students had been taught the skills to survive in an attack, and had practiced in the simulator room. Karona checked all her screens and radars. Something burst into flames miles behind her in the sky. She watched it while every other second checking on the scene unfolding ahead of her. Just like in the movies, three ships emerged from the smoke and flames as though they had been fired from canons. Her screen verified that they were alien ships. The aliens were already at Eris.

She screamed into her mouthpiece. "CODE RED! CODE RED! The aliens are here! I repeat—*the aliens are here!*"

Each ship was assigned a number according to its position in take-off—ships 1-30. But in case their transmissions were being monitored by the enemy, each ship number was multiplied by three to give the impression that they had three times as many ships as what they actually had. It was a tactic the humans hoped would work in their favor in leading the aliens to believe that their fleet was ninety strong. Perhaps it would frighten the aliens away or at least buy the humans some time.

"Roger that, we've got 'em on radar. There are three bogies. We do not know what they shot up, but we need to eliminate them. Ships 78, 81, 84, 87, and 90 on alert. Reverse course and take those bogies out. Over."

"Copy that," said five respondents, including Karona. The five ships performed a synchronized about-face and flew to meet the three bogies head-on. Karona accelerated and passed the other ships. When she was in range, she locked onto her first target and fired. Her missile obliterated it.

"Yes!" one of the other pilots applauded.

"Incoming!" she heard one of the other pilots shouting. She adjusted the volume downward on her headset. Something launched from one of the enemy ships lightning-fast toward her. Karona dodged and avoided impact. A second ship exploded and then the third was fired upon simultaneously by the other four pilots.

"Good work, everyone!" They all congratulated each other as they turned their ships about to rejoin the larger group. The black sky in the distance glowed and sparked like fireworks.

But fighting three ships was nothing compared to the fleet they now faced. Karona's speed had dropped, and she was no longer leading the other four ships. Then a voice sounded. "Ship 78. Are you okay?"

She snapped out of it as Ronnie addressed her. "Uh, 10-4. Goodbye to the three bogies and hello to seemingly millions of other bogies." Karona sped up.

"We're going to need everyone operational. We're counting on you, 78, and you can do this," Ronnie said encouragingly, though his voice was strained.

Karona's ship shook as a ship flying beside her was shot. Chunks of metal and debris bounced off her ride as tears streamed down her cheeks. Moments later, she was in the middle of it. It was like a giant game of hockey with spaceships flying and darting back and forth. Two ships collided and burst into flames as they fell from the sky. The alien ships were red and the human ships were silver. If the sun was shining, there would be light glinting off the silver hulls, and the red ships would appear to glow like hot, dripping lava.

On the ground, Yu and Castle worked with Maywano, steadily trying to alter the mechanics of the device. They contemplated different courses of action to take first. Find a way to make the alien ships go home without bouncing back? Program the device to send their own ships back to Earth and hopefully to safety? Focus on a way to connect the device to Grammy's ship and try to bring them back to Eris? There was no guarantee that anything they attempted would even work.

"We can't go to Earth and leave Grammy out there. We have to bring them home first!" Mr. Castle said insistently.

"Home? We could all be killed here at 'home' before we can even try to save them. For all we know, and I'm not being insensitive, they are already dead. We need to look after ourselves first. We aren't safe! There's a battle right outside our door, and they're trying to kill us!" Yu's expression betrayed shock that Mr. Castle wasn't seeing things his way. "There may be nothing to bring them home to. We need to make a decision fast!"

"Then let's send these aliens away, send us all to Earth, and then bring Grammy back. Why can't we do that?"

Yu looked at Maywano for help. He watched as Maywano did an uncomfortable spin before staring at the ceiling.

Just then a loud crash hit the roof of the building. The lights flickered briefly but held true. "Can someone turn off the alarm so we can hear ourselves? We all know we're under attack by now." Yu's frustration was getting the better of him.

Sparrow kind of danced, kind of jumped, from one foot to the other. "I'll do it, but I don't know where it is or how to do it." She hopped to the nearest wall and began running her palms along it.

Yu said, "Lesley?"

Sparrow sighed as if in relief.

"I'm on it!" Lesley ran from the room and minutes later the sounds of ships exploding and screams replaced the insistent screech of the alarm.

"This building is indestructible, is it not?" Maywano asked.

"I guess we'll see," replied Yu.

Maywano moved to a corner in the room, and Sparrow and Sulinda joined him.

It sounded as though bombs were being dropped over and over. The building held but then a window broke. Glass shattered inside the room, spraying the desk on top of which their computers sat.

"You," Mr. Castle commanded. "Come here!"

Maywano looked as though he were about to faint. He walked slowly over to Mr. Castle and Yu.

Mr. Castle said to Yu, "You make the decision right now or I will."

Lesley ran into the room. She had replaced her high heels with white running shoes. She pulled her inhaler from her purse and drew a deep breath from it before speaking. "It doesn't look good out there. I think they're too powerful for us, and I'm just letting you know that I'm making a run for it. A few of us are. If we head in the opposite direction, maybe we can find somewhere safe to hide. From above, it looks as though there's nothing on this planet but these buildings. They won't see us."

"Where's Brody?" Yu asked.

"He's coordinating the ground troops," Lesley answered.

Yu and Mr. Castle looked at each other. They both tugged on their own noses and then looked up.

"Our ground troops are useless," Yu said. He felt defeated for the first time and didn't know what to do.

"Get Brody to start up the excavator, but leave all the lights off. He can transport at least ten people at a time. Cover it with the anti-thermal tarp so no heat signatures can be detected. Take it and save as many as you can!" Mr. Castle ordered.

In a flash, Lesley was gone.

Not five minutes later, Brody attempted to contact Ronnie. "Ship 4, come in ship number 4! This is Brodster Alpha. Do you read me?" Brody held his breath as he drove the excavator into darkness. He had squeezed twelve people on board, Dagny included. Dagny sat at the back of the vehicle with her gun at the ready. "Ship number 4! Are you there?" Brody paused for a response. He looked in his side mirror at the sky behind them. Lights danced whimsically, almost beautifully. The only sound heard was the sound of crying coming from some of the passengers. There was no response from Ronnie, and Brody also began to cry. Sheila sat up front with him and put her arm around him with compassion. Though she was drunk, she gently wiped his tears away.

As Sparks ran from the building heading toward the warehouse, she came across a screaming man. He had been partially crushed by falling debris from a fallen ship—a fallen alien ship. Sparks was doing her best to free him, but the red goo that covered all the alien ships burned human skin. The man lay screaming in agony as the slime burned through his flesh. Sparks was powerless to help him. There was nothing she could use to wipe it from him. His legs were melting before her eyes.

"Kill me," he begged.

Sparks had never killed anyone before. She had never even so much as slapped someone across the face who deserved it. She looked around frantically, finding nothing that could help her or the man. She pulled her gun from her holster and stared at it. Her eyes were hollow and her grasp of the gun, limp. She sat on the ground beside the man, both helpless. The man grabbed at her, begging for help, begging to be put out of his suffering. He made eye contact with her—she looked away.

With her eyes squeezed shut, her grip loosened. The man grabbed the gun from her. She whipped her head around, and without a split second to lose, caught him putting the gun to his temple and pulling the trigger. Blood and brains splattered the ground beside him. Sparks screamed and jumped to her feet. She ran inside the building where she sank into a corner. She stayed there until an enemy missile hit that side of the building. She was crushed to death instantly under a large slab of concrete.

On an alien ship, Mike stood against one wall with Lexi beside him and Gaz on her other side. Chief Shabay faced them.

"I am disappointed in your inability to follow orders. You have not done anything you said you were going to do. I think you humans have this ritual where you ask if the soon-to-be-killed person has any last words. This is your opportunity." Shabay's eyes stared right through Mike.

"Please. You sent me in there against four of them. What kind of chance did I have?" Mike asked. Lexi had begun to cry, and Mike shot her a disgusted look as though to say it was his life on the line, not hers. Gaz stood tall beside Mike.

"Those are your last words?" Shabay asked.

"No! Please…"

Shabay looked to a hungry alien standing to his right. "Do it. I want his friends to watch him die." The alien's tongue lashed out. The room filled with shrieks. Mike, who was usually larger than life, usually unchallenged, usually in charge, crumpled as though his bones had all disappeared.

The sky above Eris was filled with so much fire, flashing lights, and ships not only pursuing each other in fight-mode but ships falling as they were hit and destroyed. Yu and Mr. Castle had to decide instantly. They both tugged on their noses and looked up. Maywano seemed to hesitate but copied them. He looked to Sparrow and Sulinda, who did the same.

"Do it," Yu instructed Maywano.

Maywano did one last spin and turning the device over in his hands one last time as though hoping the right answer would suddenly appear, pressed the button.

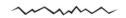

Rod Walken sat behind his desk, staring into the camera. His slicked-back hair was perfect, and his facial expression was dead serious. He hadn't primped or primed himself in the mirror for precisely two hours as he had always done. In fact, he hadn't even looked in the mirror once. Rod was scared, uncharacteristically scared.

Rod cleared his throat and began to speak. "My faithful audience, family, and friends, I fear this will be my last broadcast. The aliens are attacking our loved ones on Eris. We don't know how they did it, but they flew there so much faster than we could ever have anticipated. Our radars had either been tampered with or the aliens were somehow able to mask their true position. Perhaps they had been projecting images of their ships in some manner to make us think they were farther away than they were. We have no idea, really, and probably never will understand their technology."

Rod rose from his seat and walked around to stand in front of his desk. He had left his notes behind and began to speak from his heart. "I have no advice to anyone anymore except to say to stay close to those you love. If there is a special person out there who doesn't know what they mean to you, now is the time to tell them. I'm not saying we don't have a chance to make it through this. I'm saying we don't know. None of us knows what is going to come out of all this."

Suddenly the room went dark. All electricity had been cut off. People around the world who had been watching Rod's report had frozen out of fear when their screens had gone blank. Panic erupted everywhere.

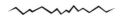

Chuck and Farley walked the three aliens down the corridor and into the empty room at the end of the hall. Grammy remained in the cockpit, putting the chairs back on their bases. She fired up the ship and over the speaker system said, "Let's go, Chuck and Farley. We're lifting off!"

Chuck locked the door so the aliens would not be able to escape the room. The moment Chuck turned away from the door and faced Farley, the ship began to vibrate, and the hull appeared to fade away. He saw the look of fear of Farley's face and said, "What the…"

Everything was black. They could see nothing. They could hear nothing. They held their breaths, waiting for something to happen when finally, someone spoke. "Where are we?"

"Chuck? Are you okay?" Grammy asked.

"Grammy? Where are we?" Chuck replied, looking up. He was confused that her voice came from above and he didn't see her on the ceiling.

Chuck looked around and saw Farley slumped to the ground. He was upright, leaning back against the wall, but his eyes were open and blank, and he was motionless. Chuck tried to take the three steps to get to his best friend, but his legs felt like rubber, and he sank to the floor. His head bounced off it. From his vantage point in the way he landed, he could see straight up the hall toward the cockpit. Something was moving slowly toward him, and he couldn't reconcile in his head what it was. As far as he knew, the aliens were locked in the room behind him. He squinted, hoping that would make the image clearer. And it did—Grammy was dragging herself toward him. He almost laughed. Grammy had looked comical to him, as drool formed in the corner of his mouth and slid out, dropping in long drops to the cold floor.

"Chuck, it's better if you don't close your eyes. The spins come next." Grammy's voice sounded slurred to Chuck. "And you don't want the spins."

Chuck blinked and tried to swallow. "The spins?" he asked as though in slow motion.

"Maywano. Maywano did this," Grammy said. "We're safe."

Chuck tried to lift his head, but it was too heavy. "We are?" It sounded like, "Weeeee aaaare?"

Grammy kept dragging herself down the hallway until she reached Chuck. Almost two minutes later, she said, "Yes, my love, my grandson, we are safe. For now."

TO BE CONTINUED

About the Author

PENNY L. SAMMS was born in Newfoundland, Canada, and grew up in Toronto, Canada, where she still resides. She worked in the corporate world for 23 years before making the life-changing decision to pursue a career in writing along with other passions. Penny fulfilled her life-long dream of publishing a book in July 2013 with her first novel, *Invasion: Earth – A Chuck, Yu, and Farley Book*. *Invasion: Eris – A Chuck, Yu, and Farley Book* is the second in the trilogy. Penny has always loved science fiction, and her favorite nightmares have always been the ones involving aliens invading, albeit they've been the most terrifying nightmares for her too.

Being a fan of other genres, Penny has also written books for children, and not wanting to leave the adults out, she was successful in obtaining permission from Wolf Blass Wines in Australia to write a wine-pairing book based on their delicious wines.

Penny looks forward to concluding the last book in the trilogy and presenting it to the world.

Printed in the United States
By Bookmasters